MISSION: ERADICATE

OBSIDIAR FLEET BOOK 6

ANTHONY JAMES

Illustration © Tom Edwards
TomEdwardsDesign.com

Follow Anthony James on Facebook at facebook.com/AnthonyJamesAuthor

CHAPTER ONE

FLEET ADMIRAL JOHN NATHAN DUGGAN was lost in thought.

Only a few short weeks ago, the human Confederation had brought about the complete destruction of the Vraxar capital ship *Ix-Gastiol*, and he knew he should still be on a high at the magnitude of the victory. As it ever was, the win came with a high price tag and there were several loose ends which gnawed at him constantly.

"Sir?"

The voice brought Duggan into the present. Two of his top scientists were seated on the opposite side of his desk. The news they brought was exciting – world-changing – and here he was, distracted by a threat which could be forty years away from Confederation Space.

"My apologies, RL Fleming. You were telling me about the breakthrough in Obsidiar refinement."

Research Lead Scotty Fleming was thickset and with the hands of a brawler, both of which seemed at odds with his position on one of the most important development teams within the Space Corps.

"Yes, sir. I won't bore you with the details – the science is contained in the finished report if you wish to look through it. You are aware that we stumbled across a way to refine tiny quantities of Obsidiar into a much more potent form."

"An unexpected consequence of our work developing the Obsidiar bombs," said RL Karla Mooney, another member of the same research team.

"I'm aware of the history," said Duggan. In fact, he knew it intimately, since he'd ordered the research in the first place. "You've discovered how to improve the process."

"Yes, sir, we have."

Mooney could scarcely contain her excitement and it started washing off onto Duggan. He leaned forward in his chair.

"Give me the details."

"We successfully transformed a fifteen-tonne block in a single go, sir."

This *was* significant and Duggan raised an eyebrow.

"What do the output tests show?"

"The Obsidiar-Teronium is vastly more efficient than the base material," said Fleming. "Perhaps twenty-thousand percent more efficient."

Duggan could hardly believe his ears, but he didn't want to get carried away just yet. "The early version of the process showed a far more modest improvement, RL Fleming."

"There's nothing about Obsidiar which conforms to the rules we're familiar with," said Mooney, her eyes gleaming. "It's as though," she paused, wondering if she should continue. "It's as though we've found a door we never even knew existed. At the same time, we've discovered how to open that door. The unrefined Obsidiar is the first rung on the next tier of our existence.

The Obsidiar-Teronium holds the potential to take us up close to the top – it has uses we haven't even thought of yet."

"The efficiency of the refinement process increases exponentially with the quantity of Obsidiar," said Fleming. "We're certain there's a cap on it, but we haven't reached the ceiling with our most recent trials."

"This is excellent work," said Duggan. "The Confederation Council will be delighted to learn of the potential civilian benefits coming from the military's extensive funding."

"Thank you, sir."

Duggan rubbed his chin in thought. "The Obsidiar power station here on Prime is undergoing final testing and is due to come online in the next few weeks. The Destiny facility contains a significant quantity of Obsidiar – is it already obsolete?"

Fleming and Mooney exchanged glances. "Refinement could easily take place in situ, sir," said Fleming. "The Obsidiar facility is modular, which means the power generators could be modified without shutting down the entire plant."

The Destiny facility was projected to generate sufficient power to meet the entire planet's needs for the next several decades and it would be politically excruciating to shut it off before its benefits could be experienced.

"It sounds like there is no problem we can't work our way around," said Duggan.

Mooney cleared her throat. "It might not be quite so straightforward."

"Meaning?"

"It's its natural form, Obsidiar is mostly quite stable, sir. However, we believe the Obsidiar-T is rather less stable."

"How much less stable?"

It was apparent that RL Mooney had drawn the short straw and she cleared her throat again. "Significantly less stable."

"Are you telling me in an exceptionally roundabout fashion that the refinement process isn't entirely good news, RL Mooney?"

"Yes, sir. We'll be able to deal with the limitations in time, but for the moment, the Obsidiar-T is not suitable for many applications."

"What might the unintended consequences be of its use?"

"Most likely it will simply produce too much power in too short a time," said Fleming. "The Obsidiar is a finite resource and we lack data on how long it will function at peak efficiency – certainly in its base form it is a viable solution for extended use. The Obsidiar-T might well burn out very quickly."

"Our research continues, sir," said Mooney.

Duggan pursed his lips. Mooney and Fleming were excellent scientists and he had no intention of haranguing them. There were few research projects which went entirely to plan, especially so when it came to cutting-cutting-edge stuff like Obsidiar refinement.

"I'm sure we'll overcome these issues," he said. "What your team has accomplished is something the Ghasts have not managed and, as far as we're aware, something the Vraxar themselves have not accomplished. We'll get there."

"Thank you, sir," said Mooney, trying to conceal her relief.

"However," continued Duggan, "there are several teams working in parallel to yours. These teams were specifically assembled to explore the military uses of Obsidiar-T and they have been investigating a number of possible uses for a refined version of the base material. What will be the knock-on effect for these other teams?"

"I wouldn't like to speculate, sir," said Fleming.

"One of these teams in particular is conducting some vital work for me. Should I put things on hold? How long until you are able to produce a stable refinement of the Obsidiar?"

Fleming grimaced. "Years, perhaps."

"We're no longer up against the clock, are we?" asked Mooney. "I thought the Vraxar were defeated."

Duggan wasn't about to confide in them. "Vraxar or no Vraxar, I am not going to take things easy."

The meeting was at an end and had been another mixed bag. Duggan climbed from his chair and politely indicated it was time for his scientists to leave him.

When the room was empty, he stood at one of his windows for a time and watched the activity on the Raksol military base. The climate on this area of Prime was far more agreeable than that of New Earth, and there was significantly less rainfall. The warmth and the brightness should have cheered him up, but they did not.

Aside from the weather, the Raksol base could have been any other military base on any other Confederation planet. The grey, brutalist cubes of the buildings depressed him more with each passing day and he wished he could tear them down and begin afresh, with a new template that respected the humanity of the Confederation's military. There was no chance it would happen on his watch. Once he was satisfied the war with the Vraxar was finished, he'd made a promise to retire.

The voice of Cerys, his personal assistant, came to him through the room's comms system. "Councillor Stahl wishes to speak with you, Fleet Admiral."

"Bring him through."

Stahl was currently on the other side of Prime. It was a long way on foot, though insufficient distance to produce a significant delay on the comms.

"Fleet Admiral Duggan," greeted Stahl, his voice affable.

Councillor Stahl had at one time been a pain in the backside. During the course of the Vraxar wars, the man had revealed a number of positive attributes and now he was no longer an outright opponent of Duggan's methods.

"What can I do for you, Councillor?"

"How did your meeting go?"

"Good and bad. The Obsidiar-Teronium shows enormous promise, except it is not yet ready for widespread use."

Stahl sounded disappointed. "Shame. Perhaps I was naïve to imagine we might learn to run before we could walk."

"My scientists advise they require another few years, Councillor."

"That long? Is there anything we can do to assist the Space Corps' efforts?"

At one time, such a question would have caused Duggan's eyebrows to fall off in surprise.

"The project is more than adequately funded. Are there any rumblings of discontent when it comes to the wider financing of our shipbuilding programme?"

"Not yet, Fleet Admiral. However, there are many on the Confederation Council who believe the war is won. If there is no further sign of Vraxar within a year or two, I expect there to be numerous voices calling for a reduction in the Space Corps' funding."

"The war isn't over," said Duggan quietly. "The Aranol exists."

"In Estral Space. They have a long way to travel if they wish to reach our little corner of the universe."

"They will come, Councillor and it would be a mistake for us to treat the intervening time as anything other than an opportunity to prepare."

Stahl was briefly quiet before he resumed. "I'm on your side, Fleet Admiral. We've had our differences, but in this I agree with you. I am only one amongst many and if this Aranol takes years before it appears, it will be an uphill battle to keep the money pouring into our shipyards and research facilities."

"The Obsidiar-T is a direct benefit of the military spending."

"It will be once it is available for civilian use."

"I'll make sure it's ready."

In the early days after his promotion to Fleet Admiral, Duggan would have been downhearted at the conversation with Stahl and the talk of funding cuts. Now, with many years in the job, he was a seasoned professional when it came to dealing with the Confederation Council. As long as he remained in office, Duggan was reasonably sure he could wring out enough money to keep the Space Corps at its peak.

"Have you learned anything new about the *Ulterior-2?*" asked Stahl. He sounded genuinely interested.

"We're certain its crew took it through the portal on *Ix-Gastiol*. When the ES *Devastator* entered the central coil in order to deploy the Falsehood bomb, its sensors captured some useful information. Using data gathered by the *ESS Crimson* and also that from the Valpian, we've been able to pinpoint the location of the Aranol and, by extension, the arrival point of the *Ulterior-2.*"

"What is your plan, Fleet Admiral?"

"To get them back. Whatever it takes."

"You have my support to take the necessary action."

Duggan didn't require the Council's support. Nevertheless, it was a gesture Stahl didn't need to make. "Thank you, Councillor."

"I'm busy, as I'm sure you are, Fleet Admiral. We will speak again soon."

With Stahl gone, Duggan came to a snap decision. "Cerys, arrange a shuttle flight from the nearest available pad."

The computer responded smoothly and politely. "Certainly, Fleet Admiral, that is done – you will depart from Landing Pad 2 in ten minutes. What is your destination?"

"Star Reach."

"That is a long distance, Fleet Admiral. Should I inform your wife?"

"No. I intend returning in time for dinner."

"Will you be accompanied?"

"Ask Lieutenant Paz to meet me at the landing pad."

"I have relayed your orders."

Duggan left his office, glad to see the back of its wood-panelled walls and artificial plants. In the corridor outside, the veneer of luxury was replaced by tiled floors, blue-painted walls and over-cooled air. He didn't pay attention to the personnel, nor to the route his feet carried him. After a few minutes, he was in the gravity-engined vehicle reserved for his personal use. The car's facia was covered with too much cheap wood and the seats were upholstered in unyielding foam and badly-stitched leather that was about as supple as the muscles in his lower back. He didn't crave opulence – so long as it was passably clean and tidy, he didn't mind.

The Raksol base wasn't a primary shipbuilding facility. Even so, it was home to a number of advanced research blocks and was also one of the manufacturing centres for the new comms units which were being urgently deployed across the Space Corps fleet. In addition, Duggan had ordered every military base to have its defences increased in the form of new ground Shimmer emplacements.

Eventually, the plan was to install numerous surface-based overcharge particle beam turrets, the power draw from which required significant upgrades to the generation facilities on each of the Confederation planets. This was one of the reasons the Destiny facility was so important – there was no short-term way for humanity to adapt to the style of mobile warfare employed by the Vraxar, hence it seemed wise to pack each world with as much offensive hardware as possible.

With everything going on, the streets were busy, as were the skies above. Lifter shuttles and construction robots floated overhead and when Duggan lowered his window, he could hear the distinctive sounds of overworked gravity engines. Activity with purpose pleased him and he felt reassured.

Landing Pad 2 was a raised square of concrete with sloped sides and surrounded by buildings which crowded in on four sides. There was a certain amount of clear area around the landing pad in order to pay lip service to the Space Corps' endless pursuit of safety for its personnel. In reality, accidents were few and far between.

There was a shuttle waiting, with its side door open. The vessel was one amongst countless others like it, being a grey cuboid box with a wedge-shaped nose. This model had a nose cannon, leading Duggan to guess that Cerys had commandeered it from a docked spaceship somewhere on the base.

His car stopped at the edge of the pad. "You are here!" it said, in a voice a little too cheerful for comfort.

There was no sign of Lieutenant Paz and Duggan twisted to look out of the rear screen.

"You are here! Get out!" the car reminded him cheerfully.

"Voice off!" said Duggan, in no mood to be ordered around by a car.

He got out of the vehicle and made his way up the ramp. His body was fully recovered from the damage it suffered during the Vraxar attack on the Tucson base, and it didn't complain too loudly at the steepness.

The shuttle's pilot was in the open doorway, waiting for his passengers. The man was dressed in the uniform of a soldier. This fact, plus the group of six other soldiers at the end of the boarding ramp, confirmed Duggan's suspicion the shuttle had come from a warship close by.

The group had evidently been primed to expect a senior officer. One saluted, whilst the rest kept a careful eye out for danger. They carried gauss rifles and sidearms, with a couple of the squad also equipped with grenade belts.

"Fleet Admiral Duggan? I'm Corporal Gardner," said the pilot. He was slender, with fading blond hair and probably due for retirement soon. "We're going to the Crater, are we?"

Crater was the informal name given to the Star Reach propulsion and research test facility. A few decades had elapsed since the last incident at the site, yet the name lingered on.

"The Crater it is, Corporal. We're waiting on one more."

"Come onboard while you wait, sir. Make yourself comfortable."

Duggan chuckled. "There's no such thing as comfort on one of these transports, Corporal. Which spaceship have you come off? The *Hammer Blow*?"

"That's the one, sir. The *Hammer* isn't due to lift off until tomorrow. Will we be joining them?"

"I don't intend keeping you long."

The interior of the shuttle was as familiar to Duggan as the contents of his sock drawer. There were metal chairs and bare walls, a viewing screen for passengers and the faint smell of rubber and sweat which he knew from experience was impossible to expunge.

Voices from outside informed him that Charissa Paz was on her way. He heard footsteps on the boarding ramp and the figure of Lieutenant Paz arrived, dressed in pale red and with her hair tied up.

"Have a seat," said Duggan. "Corporal Gardner, let's get going."

"Yes, sir," said Gardner. "You want to sit up front?"

"Not for this one."

Gardner disappeared through the cockpit door and by the time Duggan switched his attention to Lieutenant Paz, she was holding two cups of coffee which she'd obtained from the replicator in double-quick time.

"Want one?" She thrust the metal cup in Duggan's direction.

"You make it sound like an order," he said, taking the gift. "Don't tell Dr Templeton."

"Flossie? My lips are sealed, sir."

Paz sat next to Duggan and the two of them waited for the soldiers to come into the passenger bay. The group sat a respectful distance away, so as not to eavesdrop on the conversation.

The shuttle's door closed and the note of the gravity engines changed. Gardner was nothing if not efficient and the transport lifted off within a few seconds. Duggan's stomach was aware of the high acceleration for a brief moment, before the life support modules kicked in.

"Where are we going, sir?" asked Paz.

"Star Reach. I've had some mixed news on the Obsidiar-T and I'd like to see what effect it will have on the Lightspeed Catapult."

"Is the mission still on?"

"I won't leave anyone behind."

"Does Captain Blake know?"

"Only what I told him – that there might be a way and he must be patient."

"How did he take it?"

"He's learning."

"Does this news on the Obsidiar-T mean he's going to be disappointed?"

"I hope not, Lieutenant. I really hope not."

"Why didn't you use the comms to speak to Captain Decker?"

"There are things you've got to see for yourself." Duggan gave a half-smile. "And I was getting bored looking out of my window at all that concrete."

The *Hammer Blow*'s shuttle was designed for rapid deployment duties, so it came as no shock when Corporal Gardner came over the internal comms to announce their expected arrival time was only fifteen minutes.

Duggan's empty coffee cup was still warm when the shuttle landed at Star Reach.

CHAPTER TWO

THE STAR REACH testing and research facility was situated on a large island, far out in the middle of Prime's biggest ocean. This island – called Jansval – was fifty kilometres across and, in its original form, nothing more interesting than an uneven rock protruding from deep water with little in the way of flora. Before the Space Corps had chosen it as the perfect site for propulsion research, Jansval had been remarkable only for its thick layer of bird shit and the smell of fish. Now, it was clean, flat and home to several thousand assorted personnel and vast quantities of expensive military hardware.

However, Space Corps technology had failed to completely cleanse the island of its past.

"It stinks of fish," said Paz, wrinkling her nose when the shuttle door opened.

"Always has and always will, ma'am," said one of the soldiers, evidently familiar with the place.

Duggan stopped for a moment at the top of the ramp. They'd landed in the centre of Star Reach, on one of eight dedicated landing pads. The sky was a uniform light grey and it was neither warm nor cold. To the right, a lifter shuttle was taking off, with a three-hundred-metre container fixed to its gravity chains. There were two more shuttles on the other pads, and directly ahead, the buildings of the facility spread before them.

"Quite impressive," Paz conceded.

There were four huge warehouses visible from the landing pad – they were flat-sided, unadorned by windows and they rose from amongst the hundreds of smaller buildings like giants amongst children. To look at, they would have been depressingly uninteresting except for the sheer size.

"The largest is six hundred metres high and two thousand metres long," said Duggan. "They're designed to hold the largest engine modules from a Hadron battleship. They bring them in through the roofs."

"What're the latest figures when it comes to efficiency improvements?"

"Our current Gallenium engines produce eighty percent more power than the equivalent model of fifty years ago. That's an outstanding achievement when you consider the raw material hasn't changed one bit."

"Now our focus is elsewhere."

Paz was on Duggan's staff and she had a good idea of most things that were happening when it came to the Space Corps' war effort. She shielded her eyes to look at the Imposition class cruiser taking up a third of the facility's main landing strip. It was parked up less than five hundred metres from the shuttle and dwarfed every other vessel in sight.

"I was expecting more from the Obsidiar-Teronium," said Duggan, following her gaze. "The *ES Cataclysm* has already been heavily-modified to take advantage of the anticipated improvements."

"From the tone of your voice earlier, I thought the research had failed, sir?"

"Not failed, simply not what I wanted. In a few minutes we should learn exactly how far short we've come."

A standard-model gravity car emerged from between two of the smaller buildings and sped past one of the landing pads towards them. It didn't slow until the last minute, when the driver swung it sideways and brought it to a halt.

"That's our ride," said Duggan.

With Paz following, he walked down the sloped side of the landing pad. A figure climbed from the gravity car – it was a woman in her late thirties with high cheekbones and dark hair pulled back from her face.

"Captain Misty Decker," said Paz under her breath.

"One and the same," Duggan replied. He raised his voice. "Good day, Captain Decker. This is Lieutenant Paz – she's on my personal team."

"This is a surprise," said Decker. "The great Fleet Admiral Duggan, come to my facility. To what do I owe the pleasure, sir?"

"I would like to speak with you about the Lightspeed Catapult."

Decker smiled, revealing the kind of naturally perfect teeth which would have cost most people two years' salary to obtain, were dental treatment not free for citizens of the Confederation.

"Climb in, sir."

Duggan took the front seat, leaving Paz to the back. Captain Decker overrode the gravity car's safety protocols and rammed the control joystick forward. The car took off like its engine had been tinkered with to produce three times the power. Duggan was pushed into the padding of his seat.

"I'll take you to the eastern warehouse," said Decker, offering no more explanation.

"Is it far?" asked Paz through gritted teeth.

"Just up ahead, Lieutenant."

The streets on the Star Reach facility were wide and not

especially busy. It allowed Decker free rein to treat the place like her personal race track and she threw the gravity car around without apparent regard for the personal safety of herself or the other passengers. The benefit of this was efficiency and it took less than five minutes to reach their destination.

"Here we are," said Decker. She opened the door and stepped onto the pavement.

Duggan and Paz climbed from the car. They were in one of the parking lots which served the eastern warehouse. The building betrayed no new beauty from up close and the smooth wall cast a long shadow over the entire parking area. Captain Decker gestured vaguely towards a set of glass-panelled sliding doors and they headed towards them.

"The prototype is hiding deep inside," she confided.

They passed through the doors and into the lobby area, which was occupied by surly-faced armed guards, surly-faced receptionists and a few surly-faced research personnel. Not one of them dared challenge Captain Decker and she strode through, beaming at everyone.

"I tell myself that if I keep on smiling, a little bit of happiness will rub off," she said.

"Looks like they need it," said Paz.

"We're heading to Testing Area 19," Decker continued, as if she hadn't heard.

The walk took a few minutes and Duggan hardly noticed any of it. Captain Decker chatted amiably about nothing much, until she stopped in front of two metal doors upon which were the words *No Admittance for Unauthorised Personnel*.

"Here we are."

The Star Reach mainframe scanned the visitors, decided they had sufficient clearance to enter and opened the doors. The three of them stepped through into a large, cold room, lit in Space Corps blue-white. The walls were lined with screens of varying sizes and there were many consoles dotted about the floor. There were even several desks in one corner and Duggan noted people sitting at them, writing with pencils on sheets of paper. It was busy and he was impressed by the degree of purpose in the room.

"First things first," said Decker. "Let us have a look at the prototype."

There was a viewing window, which took up the whole of the opposite wall. Decker led them to it, firing questions at the researchers as she went. At the window, Duggan put his hands on the sill and stared through.

On the other side, there was a huge room which took up much of the warehouse. It was brightly lit, allowing Duggan to see the construction robots and mid-sized lifter shuttles hovering in the air. On the far side there were grey engine modules, some of them fitted with armour plates. The object he'd come to see lay directly in front of the viewing window. It was an anonymous cylinder, suspended a metre above the floor by a series of over-head gravity chains. He knew it was exactly 350 metres in length and with a 120-metre diameter. It's near-black surface glistened with a layer of ice.

The Lightspeed Catapult wasn't much to look at, but Duggan knew it held the potential to be the biggest technological leap since the first deep fission engine was created several hundred years ago. The costs were enormous both financially and in the use of the Confederation's finite Obsidiar resources. Everyone on the Star Reach facility was aware of the significance.

"There it is," said Decker.

"Some things you just have to see with your own eyes," said Duggan.

"What brings you here, sir?" asked Decker, finally getting down to business.

"I have plans for that engine. What are its projected capabilities?"

It was all in the progress reports, but Duggan liked to hear it directly.

Decker furrowed her brow. "It's undergone early testing. We've spooled it up to test the efficiency and to obtain some data on the likely output. There's a long way to go yet."

"What could it achieve in its current form? Will it go to lightspeed?"

Decker was sharp. "These plans you have – they are immediate plans."

"Yes. There is an urgent need to send a ship to Estral Space."

Captain Decker's eyes became distant and she reeled off some statistics. "A newer Galactic class could manage the journey to the known outskirts of Estral Space in thirty-six years. A Hadron in thirty. The *ES Blackbird* could manage it in twenty-two years, or fifteen if it were fitted with a second Obsidiar drive."

"There's no room in its hull for a second drive," said Duggan. "And I don't have fifteen years. How long would it take the *ES Cataclysm* to complete the journey if we fitted the Lightspeed Catapult?"

"If everything worked as intended, the catapult should generate sufficient output to complete the journey in three years."

It was disappointing. "I thought greater improvements were expected, Captain?"

"They *are* expected to be greater, sir. Much greater. This prototype contains plain old Obsidiar – it produces a far greater lightspeed multiple than a standard derived-Gallenium deep fission drive. Unfortunately, we here on Star Reach were awaiting a refined product, which is what our calculations are based upon. Standard Obsidiar is an evolution – a big evolution. The Obsidiar-Teronium is different. It has the capability to open a temporary wormhole and fling a spaceship clean through to the other side. This is something far beyond the capabilities of any of our existing power generation technology."

"Have you looked through the report on the Obsidiar refinement process?" asked Duggan.

"I had an advance copy and it's been my reading material of choice, sir."

"Does the Obsidiar-T fulfil the requirements of the Light-speed Catapult?"

"Yes, sir. It does."

"What if I ordered the production of enough Obsidiar-T to complete the prototype? Could it take the *Cataclysm* to Estral Space?"

"Yes, sir. I've already run the figures and the journey would require somewhat less than a thousandth of a second."

"What are the risks?"

"Practically everything."

"Tell me."

"Engine failure, programming failure resulting in the *Cataclysm* arriving somewhere outside of our star charts, engine destruction, spaceship destruction, crew death. Those are just the ones off the top of my head."

"We've lost the *Ulterior-2* out there, Captain Decker. Not only that, we saw the Vraxar home world."

"It'll take them a long time to get here, sir."

Duggan shook his head. "The recordings from the *ES Devastator* suggest the enemy planetship was moving. We don't know how or where they're going, nor do we have much idea of how long it'll take them. I want to know, Captain Decker. This is the last known major Vraxar asset and there's no way in hell I'm going to sit on my hands and see what they decide to do with it."

Decker was no fool. "Is the decision made?"

"Yes, Captain, it is."

"We'll require 220,000 tonnes of Obsidiar-T."

Duggan grimaced – such an amount would make a significant dent in the Confederation's remaining stocks. On the other hand, the potential gains – gathering data on the Aranol as well as locating the missing *Ulterior-2* – were enough to take the gamble.

"You'll have what you need. How long after receipt can you have the ES *Cataclysm* ready for flight?"

This time, the answer was a pleasant surprise. "Seven days. Perhaps six."

"I'm going to send our best people on this one, Captain Decker." He didn't spell out exactly what he meant, though Decker caught on easily enough.

"There's a chance it'll work and a chance it'll fail, sir." She smiled sadly. "If I put it like that, I can almost convince myself that it's a fifty-fifty."

"Isn't it?" asked Paz.

"Not even close, Lieutenant."

"Get the Lightspeed Catapult ready, Captain Decker. We'll speak again soon."

"Yes, sir."

Duggan had seen enough. Some amongst his staff might have thought his visit to Star Reach a waste of his valuable time. For Duggan, he needed this proximity in order to make his choice. After all, he was soon going to order a number of men and women into the unknown. They deserved his absolute attention.

"We're leaving," he said.

"Do you know the way, sir? I've got a lot to do." said Decker, not even slightly abashed.

"I'm sure we can find our own way out," said Duggan.

He left the room, bringing Paz with him. He hadn't been paying attention to the route on the way in, yet his feet knew the way out. The surly-faced guards and receptionists were still in the lobby and the souped-up gravity car was still parked in the lot. Duggan had no qualms about taking the vehicle and drove it towards the waiting shuttle at a speed only slightly reduced from that demonstrated by Captain Decker. Paz kept her mouth closed.

He took them directly past the *ES Cataclysm*, simply on the basis that he wanted a closer look at the warship. It had a few additional modifications that were designed to run off a refined Obsidiar power source. Testing was so far limited and there wouldn't be anything like enough time to finish the trials.

Duggan turned away from the cruiser and steered the gravity car to the landing pad.

"There's the shuttle," he said, stopping the car at the bottom of the ramp.

Five minutes later, they were onboard once again and the transport took off from the Star Reach facility. During the short flight, Duggan occupied his mind with the logistics of what he planned. In theory, the Aranol could be anywhere by now, yet he felt the urgency of the situation. The enemy were still out there and it was imperative the Confederation discover their intentions. Not only that, he owed the crew of the *Ulterior-2*, he owed Captain Blake and he owed Lieutenant McKinney. Duggan always paid his debts.

The shuttle landed and he returned to his office.

CHAPTER THREE

FOR CAPTAIN CHARLIE BLAKE, the weeks since the destruction of *Ix-Gastiol* had not been filled with delight. He was finding it difficult to get over the loss of his crew and, though Fleet Admiral Duggan had offered him extended leave, Blake preferred to make himself available for the numerous analytical, strategic planning and research teams who were very interested in learning his opinions on both *Ix-Gastiol* and the Aranol. As a consequence, he found himself in meeting after meeting, which ultimately failed to provide the necessary distraction.

There was one promise he was able to keep, that being a night of drinking with some of the soldiers from his last mission. Alcohol was forbidden on the Raksol base, though there were plenty of places in the vicinity which would gladly serve a man or woman with enough spirits to get paralytic.

"This stuff tastes like cow's piss," said R1T Jordan Mills, sniffing his empty glass.

"Didn't stop you finishing it," said Sergeant Johnny Li.

"And it won't stop me ordering another!"

"I think it's Garcia's round, isn't it?"

"Nah, I got the last one," lied Garcia.

"I'll get them," said Blake, with an exaggerated shake of his head. He was onto his fourth beer and it wasn't having the desired effect. He felt stone cold sober.

Blake took himself to the bar and ordered another round of drinks. While he waited, he cast his eyes around the room. The bar was a small building, dimly lit, with prefab concrete walls, a wooden floor and toilets which likely hadn't been cleaned since they were fitted. It was quiet tonight and, given the state of the interior, probably quiet every night. It wasn't the sort of place Blake would usually spend time in, but he didn't mind. The choice of venue had been Garcia's.

There were plenty of soldiers here, so it took two trays to carry the drinks. Once Blake was seated again, Sergeant Demarco asked the question she'd clearly been waiting for an opportunity to ask.

"The war isn't over, is it, sir? Everyone's cheering the Confederation's victory – maybe it's a bit premature?"

"I don't think anyone knows what our situation is, Sergeant."

"You have your own thoughts, don't you?" Demarco was easy enough to talk to and Blake felt the urge to speak.

"It's not over. The Aranol will come and it will start again."

"What if they take forty years? That should give us plenty of time."

Lieutenant McKinney had been mostly quiet up until now. "People forget, Sergeant. The funding stops and the fleet gets older. The Vraxar? They don't stop. They'll build and they'll build. The Aranol was big enough to fit a hundred thousand of their warships inside and still have room to spare. If it comes, there isn't enough time in the world for us to match them."

A lot of McKinney's words were supposition, but Blake didn't correct him. McKinney had been out of sorts since the loss of the *Ulterior-2* and it wasn't simply down to the lack of combat duty.

"Maybe Captain Blake has a plan to go and rescue your girl-friend," said Huey Roldan, finishing his old drink and picking up a new one.

"Yeah, maybe," said McKinney. The jokes were meant to cheer him up.

"Is there anything, sir?" asked Demarco, realising that McKinney wasn't going to press Blake on the matter.

"Not that I know of, Sergeant. Did we come here to talk about the Corps?"

"It's all I know."

Blake laughed. "Me too. What about you, Lieutenant?"

It was McKinney's turn to grin. "I haven't got a clue what a normal life is."

"Fine, we'll talk about the Corps," said Blake. "Not that I have anything to tell you."

"I reckon Fleet Admiral Duggan is a planner," said Sergeant Li. "He'll have something on the go, mark my words."

"If he does, I'd be interested to hear what it is," said Blake. "The alternative is that everyone in the Confederation sits waiting for the Vraxar to come, only this time they'll be riding on a spaceship that's as big as a moon and, as Lieutenant McKinney said, likely filled with the ships they used to finish off the Estral."

"Thousands of spaceships?" asked Roldan.

"That's what the intel guys reckon."

"How'd they figure that one out?" asked Li.

"Your job is to shoot aliens, Sergeant. Their job is to derive concrete numbers from the unknown."

"Yeah. I'll stick with the shooting."

"It'd be nice if we could find another wormhole or some-thing," said Roldan. "That way we could go and have a look for ourselves. Maybe even find out what happened to the *Ulterior-2*."

24

"There's no way it's still intact," said Li. "Uh, sorry Lieutenant."

Blake didn't usually look for hope where there was none. On this occasion, he wasn't so sure. "I trusted my crew, Sergeant, and they took the battleship through the portal. They wouldn't have done it if they were sure they were going to die."

"What if they gathered up lots of data on the Aranol and sent it via the comms? It'd take a year to reach us, wouldn't it?" asked Li.

"Two or three months," said Corporal Bannerman from the adjacent table. "Probably less, given the *Ulterior-2* had those new super-duper comms fitted."

"Is there anyone not listening in to our conversation?" asked Demarco, giving Bannerman a wink.

"I am definitely listening in," said Vega.

"Me too," said Garcia.

"Since *Ix-Gastiol* had a way to open a portal to Estral Space, you'd think we'd have a way to do it as well," said Sergeant Li.

"Yeah, I'd happily volunteer to go looking for the *Ulterior-2*," said Garcia.

"You've still got a thousand Vraxar to shoot," Blake reminded him.

"I got that number down to 984, sir. Before we left *Ix-Gastiol*."

"You'd better bring a spare rifle with you, soldier. Anyway, I'm not aware of any new tech coming onstream that will permit us to cross into Estral Space in fewer than fifteen or twenty years." Blake felt something vibrating in his pocket and he fumbled out his communicator cylinder. The device told him who was waiting and he blinked in surprise.

The communicator had a clip-on earpiece which he removed and pressed into his ear. "Blake."

The conversation wasn't a long one and Blake was only

required to speak a few affirmatives and then the channel was closed by the caller. He looked up to find numerous expectant faces watching him carefully. The squad hadn't survived this long without a well-developed sixth sense.

"We've been called in," said Blake.

"Who, sir?" asked McKinney.

"All of us. There's a mission. We're going into Estral Space."

"Ha ha ha," said Sergeant Li.

"No joke," said Blake. "They've got a warship ready for us, fitted with something called a Lightspeed Catapult and it's going to take us to the place we saw through the portal in *Ix-Gastiol*'s coil."

"Well, shit," said Demarco.

"Does that mean now?" asked Garcia. "I was just about to get the drinks in."

"Good idea," said McKinney. "Let's have a drink for Munoz."

Garcia couldn't object and he soon returned with many tiny glasses filled with the same spirit Mills had been drinking earlier. Blake took a sniff and was indeed put in mind of acrid cow's piss.

"To Rudy," said McKinney, knocking back his drink.

The soldiers drank to their dead squadmate and Blake discovered the taste of the spirit was much more pleasant than its smell. He gave thanks to R1T Munoz for his service and then ushered the squad from the drinking hole and into the empty streets outside. The warm air washed over Blake and he suddenly felt giddy – not from the alcohol, but from his excitement at the coming mission.

They piled into the twenty-seat base transport they'd commandeered for the evening, and Blake gave the order for it to take them to Raksol. It headed off at once, carrying them through the kind of mismatched buildings which sprung up in the vicinity of every Space Corps military base. Blake stared out of the window, his eyes seeing without his brain registering the sights.

"I need to take a piss," said Dexter Webb.

"Too late for that," said McCoy, entirely devoid of sympathy.

A shape appeared in the darkening sky. It began as a speck, far above, dull where the stars were bright. The spaceship grew bigger and Blake watched it, fascinated.

"Look!" said Clifton.

The soldiers had seen more than their fair share of spaceships over the years, though it didn't stop them taking an interest. They leaned across to see out of the transport's left-side windows.

"Any idea what it is?" asked Joy Guzman. "It's coming in fast."

"Imposition class cruiser," said Blake. "It's similar to a Galactic but the proportions aren't quite the same."

Even as he spoke the words, he realised there was something different about this particular vessel. It was still too far for him to see what it was. The transport vehicle entered a street of taller, flat-fronted buildings and the cruiser was lost from sight.

"That's not ours, is it?" asked Whitlock.

"Nah, they'll load us onto a Crimson class and take us to a rendezvous point somewhere," said Li, equally uncertain.

"Did Fleet Admiral Duggan tell you, sir?" asked McKinney.

"We're assigned to the *ES Cataclysm*, Lieutenant. It's an Imposition class."

McKinney raised an eyebrow. "Coincidence?"

"I think not."

"We could be on our way in less than two hours."

Blake nodded. "I'd best ask for some meds before we leave. It's a court-martial offense to fly a fleet warship under the effects of alcohol."

Building was not permitted within two kilometres of a military base and the transport entered an area of rocky, broken ground which the Space Corps hadn't seen fit to level. The road was wide and perfectly flat, with many other vehicles travelling in both directions along its twenty lanes. The cruiser was no longer visible amongst the sprawl of the Raksol base.

A female voice came through the vehicle's speakers. "I have provided this transport with details of your new destination, ladies and gentlemen. You will board the ES *Cataclysm* immediately and await orders."

The voice went quiet.

"Who was that?" asked Clifton.

"That was Cerys," said Blake. "It's a computer node which deals with Admiral Duggan's business."

The transport continued into the outskirts of the base, its engines humming softly. It sailed through the first security checkpoint, which was a low building flanked by two Gunther medium tanks and a pair of minigun turrets.

"Didn't even stop," said Li. "That's what happens when you got clearance."

The Raksol base was spread over many square kilometres and it took several minutes before the transport entered the landing strip. There were a couple of construction trenches in the distance, where the Corps was assembling two new Galactics. The Raksol base wasn't at the forefront when it came to construction, but every trench was put to use during the war.

"There's the *Cataclysm*," said McKinney.

Night fell quickly on this part of Prime and the sky was now almost entirely black. The base lights were on to allow a continuous shift, and they illuminated the sleek shape of the cruiser. Blake kept himself up to date with each new warship and he vaguely recalled reading about a number of classified design alterations to the *Cataclysm*. Usually, each spacecraft was assigned to a battle group or sector during the construction phase. The details for the *Cataclysm* had been left blank. It had intrigued him at the time, but he didn't have the energy or the clearance to pursue the answers to every single mystery in the Space Corps.

"No rear particle beam domes," Blake said to himself. "Strange."

"Is that a Havoc cannon on top?" asked McKinney.

"You're right, Lieutenant. I can see two up there – they seem smaller than the ones fitted to the *Ulterior-2*. Maybe the *Cataclysm*'s hull couldn't take the stresses."

"There's a particle beam front centre," said McKinney, squinting ahead.

"A single overcharge beam," confirmed Blake.

"Perhaps it's designed for reconnaissance only, sir."

"Somehow, I don't think so."

When the transport came closer, Blake was granted a better angle at which to view the cruiser. Its shape was identifiably Imposition class, albeit with a few evolutionary changes to make it bulkier and more like the shape of the *Ulterior-2*. At 2500 metres long and 600 at its highest point, it was otherwise standard, except for the presence of the two upper Havoc cannons.

And then the transport carried them across the front of the spaceship and Blake saw the circular hole in the armour. It opened at the nose and went deeper into the cruiser. It was absolutely, utterly dark within and Blake was sure he saw ice glittering on the external plating nearby.

"Incendiaries?" asked McKinney. "Like the Ghosts have?"

"That's got to be the Lightspeed Catapult."

"Doesn't look like much," said Garcia. "I mean, it's probably great – it just doesn't look all that great."

"Maybe you should stop trying to be positive, Garcia," said Whitlock. "I'm not sure it suits you."

"The man's gotta learn," said Roldan. "Leave him be while he takes his first steps."

The transport came to a halt under the cruiser's overhanging nose section and deep within the vessel's long shadow.

"Please board the *ES Cataclysm*," said Cerys.

"That means us," said Blake.

The squad jumped down from the transport's two exit doors and onto the reinforced landing strip. The *Cataclysm*'s front boarding ramp was already lowered and there were soldiers guarding the entrance. There was a figure amongst them, significantly taller and broader than any of the men.

"What the hell?" said Li, quietly enough that his voice wouldn't carry.

Blake walked swiftly towards the gathering and his eyes located the familiar face of Duggan.

"Good evening, sir."

Duggan left the boarding ramp and came over.

"Captain Blake. I apologise for the short notice. I wasn't expecting to sign off the *Cataclysm* until tomorrow, so I didn't cancel your night off. Things took a positive turn and Star Reach installed the Lightspeed Catapult earlier than planned."

"What are our orders, sir?"

"The *Cataclysm*'s navigational computer is programmed with the necessary information regarding your destination. Once you activate it, you should find yourself in Estral Space. From there, you have two missions – the primary one is to learn whatever you can about the Aranol. Where is it and where is it going? The secondary mission is to rescue our personnel from the *Ulterior-2*." Duggan growled angrily. "I hate to lose the Hadron. After what it's gone through it feels like part of the family. Never mind – I've learned to accept it's not coming back."

"Find the Aranol, find the *Ulterior-2*, come home," repeated Blake.

"Easily spoken. There is information I need to provide you with before your departure," said Duggan. "In addition, there is someone I'd like you to meet."

The huge figure of the Ghast, which had been standing two paces to one side, stepped closer. Blake looked into the alien's pale grey eyes and saw something human in them. The Ghast grinned, revealing the whitest teeth Blake had ever seen.

"I am Ran-Lor," said the Ghast, his harsh voice replicated and smoothed by the translation module pinned to the thick grey cloth of his uniform.

"Pleased to meet you," said Blake. He'd met a few Ghasts before and still couldn't get over their striking similarity to humans, even whilst they retained much that was distinctly alien.

"Ran-Lor is coming with you," said Duggan, letting Blake know something he'd just that moment guessed. "There are others with him."

"I am pleased to have our allies with us," Blake replied truthfully, nodding to Ran-Lor.

"Let us get on with our preparations," said Duggan. "I'd like you to be on your way in less than an hour."

Duggan didn't usually hang around and he strode up the steep boarding ramp of the ES *Cataclysm*. Blake followed, wondering what the hell he was in the middle of this time. One thing was certain – he had no fear and he felt the knots of excitement in his stomach. He was going to find his crew and he was going to fight the Vraxar.

CHAPTER FOUR

THE INTERIOR of the *Cataclysm* was standard. It was cool and spartan, with smooth-walled corridors cut through several billion tonnes of charged Gallenium. Duggan led the way, talking as he went. Blake kept up, aware of Ran-Lor's hulking presence behind him. Meanwhile, the squad were on their way to the troops' quarters.

"Ran-Lor and his team are trained in combat and also trained in other things. Estral things. He will report to you, or, in combat situations, to Lieutenant McKinney."

Most people in the Confederation were aware that the Ghasts had broken away from the Estral a long time ago. They were effectively one and the same.

"Are we planning to study the remains of the Estral civilisation, sir?"

"The Ghasts are aware of our mission, Captain. However, I like to think they might be useful – they have a more in-depth knowledge of the Estral language and technology. We don't know what you're going to find."

"You've been there, sir."

"And I was damned glad to have some Ghosts along with me."

"Shouldn't we bring a few more soldiers with us? If we're planning for the unforeseen."

Duggan paused mid-stride and then continued. "I'd like that. Unfortunately, the teams responsible for the life support modules have suggested the Lightspeed Catapult is pushing the capabilities of the hardware. I have been advised to limit the number of people onboard. Don't forget, it's not only your crew we're looking for. There was a shuttle full of injured soldiers whom Lieutenant McKinney ordered back to the *Ulterior-2* and we don't know if they are alive or dead."

"Precisely how many people are the life support modules predicted to sustain, sir?"

"Two hundred."

"We'll have more than two hundred on the return journey, assuming all of the injured lived."

"The margins are tight. I'm unwilling to send the *Cataclysm* with fewer people than we currently have onboard. There are other precautions you will be required to take prior to activating the catapult – your new crew will fill you in on the details."

"I'm not going to like it."

"Probably not. It's one risk out of many risks, Captain Blake. I won't pull punches – there's a chance the Lightspeed Catapult will fail, killing everyone onboard. Also, the calculations involved in covering a distance so great are exceptionally complicated. The *Cataclysm* has eight clusters of sixteen Obsidiar cores to manage the task, but I must warn you - the navigational system might deposit you a long way from where we intend. If that happens, you might become temporarily lost."

"Temporarily?"

"You may need to complete the journey using the deep

fission engines. If things go completely wrong, it will be a long trip."

"Could we use the Lightspeed Catapult again?"

"I would strongly advise you keep it for the return journey and nothing else. Aside from the fact it's powered by an unstable substance with a high burnout chance, the catapult also has many untested technologies – some of the components are one-offs."

Blake was beginning to understand the obstacles.

"What about the rest of the *ES Cataclysm*? I saw Havoc cannons and only one particle beam turret."

"They are second-generation Havocs," said Duggan. "Designed to be fitted to smaller vessels, without compromising the strength of the projectile's impact."

"Sounds good."

"The *Cataclysm* was originally intended as a test bed for both these new Havoc cannons and a new particle beam type."

Blake pricked up his ears.

"I wasn't aware we had any significant advancements due in that field, sir."

Duggan laughed. "I'm allowed a few secrets."

"What are the capabilities of the new particle beam?"

"It was developed with the idea that the Obsidiar-Teronium would be a stable, usable power source. The new particle beam combines the power of a full overcharge with the faster firing rate of a lower-intensity model. A much faster firing rate, as it happens."

"An overcharge repeater?"

"Don't get too excited. The weapon has an incredible power draw and it's tied in to the Obsidiar-T. I was in two minds about whether or not to have the turret disabled. In the end, I decided it should remain active on the basis that it's better to have a poor option than to have no option at all. If you are required to use the beam, I would advise you to be judicious."

"I won't piss about."

"I know you won't. Just remember that every use of the Obsidiar-T increases the likelihood of its failure."

"Are we relying on it for our energy shield?"

"The ES *Cataclysm* is equipped with a single standard-Obsidiar core, dedicated to the energy shield."

"It's a capable warship."

"We aren't building anything that isn't these days."

They reached the bridge and the blast door rose into the ceiling. The bridge itself was straight out of the Space Corps' design manual, with console stations for weapons, comms, engines and a front-centre console for the captain's use. There was seating for twelve, though only five seats were occupied, one of them being a second Ghast.

Duggan strode off across the floor, pointing out the crew as he went. "Lieutenant Becky Conway – weapons. Lieutenant Trudy Flynn – comms. Lieutenant Alfred Dunbar – engines." He stopped next to the final human on the bridge. "Captain Misty Decker, currently acting as *Lieutenant* Misty Decker. No one knows the Lightspeed Catapult better. Lieutenant Decker will provide guidance and advice."

Decker smiled. "I've heard a lot about you, Captain Blake."

"All of it scandalous, I'm sure," said Blake, following Duggan towards the final occupant on the bridge. The second Ghast sat at a spare console and the symbols on his screen suggested he wasn't connected to the Space Corps network. The alien stood, all eight feet of him.

"I am Hiven-Tar," he said.

"Hiven-Tar and Ran-Lor have been assigned places on the bridge," said Duggan. "They will not interfere with the running of the ES *Cataclysm*. Speak to them if you need to."

Blake nodded politely, wondering if the Ghasts were simply here in order to strengthen the alliance, or if there was more to it.

He was sure Duggan wouldn't do anything to place the mission in jeopardy, so he put the matter from his mind.

"What if we find the Aranol and there's an...opportunity, sir?"

Duggan smiled sadly. "I was saving that for last. The *ES Cataclysm* is carrying bomb number 000050, which has been given the name Sorrow."

"It is reassuring to know we have something."

"I couldn't send you on this mission without an ace to hide up your sleeve. Now, is there anything else you'd like to know?" asked Duggan.

Blake had plenty of other questions, but he could see which answer he was expected to give. "I think I have what I need, sir."

"Good – it's taken a lot of effort to get the *Cataclysm* ready so quickly. We should also count ourselves lucky the Obsidiar-T research project came up with something to allow us to finish the Lightspeed Catapult. Even so, it's weeks since we defeated *Ix-Gastiol*. Our best efforts might well be in vain."

"I won't allow myself to think that way, sir."

"Bring our people back, Captain Blake."

Duggan didn't say anything else. He left the bridge and began the short journey towards the forward exit ramp.

Blake took his seat and found his console was powered up and online. He couldn't help but notice the small metal case filled with auto-injecting syringes which someone had left in front of the tactical screen. He picked them up, studied the label and put them down. The presence of the needles, ominously labelled with the words *Life Critical*, reminded Blake he'd consumed too many beers to be flying a warship capable of wrecking the entire planet if he messed something up. There was an emergency medical kit located behind a panel in his console. He pulled out a detox pill and crunched it with his teeth. It tasted like the terminal of a battery and he shuddered.

"Everything okay, sir?" asked Flynn.

"Hunky-dory. Lieutenant Flynn, seal the ship as soon as you're able."

Flynn was slim, in her late-twenties, with a local accent and dyed purple hair. "Will do, sir. They're holding everything on the base until we depart."

"Lieutenant Dunbar – engine status please."

Dunbar's voice was harsh enough that he could have been half-Ghast, were such a thing known to exist. "Everything is set for lift-off, sir. No alarms and no concerns."

"Lieutenant Conway? Weapons?"

"We could punch a hole through the ten moons of Ramesius, sir."

Conway's response only served to reinforce Blake's immediate impression that she was on the more eccentric end of the spectrum. Perhaps it was a common trait amongst weapons officers, given that his usual officer - Lieutenant Dixie Hawkins – was also particularly individual.

"Lieutenant Decker, is there anything I need to be aware of?"

"We shouldn't attempt to use the catapult until we're ten minutes lightspeed from Prime, sir."

Blake twisted in his seat. "That's a long way."

"We don't want to be too close if something goes wrong." Decker flashed him a grin. If it was meant to be reassuring, it failed in its intention.

It took Duggan a few minutes to exit the ES *Cataclysm*, during which Blake ran through his pre-flight checks. Whichever teams had prepared the warship, they'd gone over it with a fine toothcomb and there wasn't an amber light even on the most minor of subsystems.

"I've sealed the ship," said Flynn. "Fleet Admiral Duggan has boarded a ground vehicle along with the soldiers assigned to guard him. They should be far enough for us to take off in a minute or two."

Blake was fairly sure Duggan wouldn't be especially bothered if the ES *Cataclysm* lifted off a hundred metres behind him, but it seemed best to wait a few extra seconds in case the resulting turbulence flipped the transport. That wouldn't look good on his record, nor do much for his personal relationship with Duggan.

"They have left the landing strip," said Flynn.

"Activating the autopilot," said Blake. "Prepare for a rapid departure."

As he issued the command to the *Cataclysm*'s main AI, Blake felt the detox pill kick in, neutralising the effects of the beers he'd finished in the bar.

"The wonders of modern medicine," he muttered.

Under the autopilot's control, the cruiser rose vertically into the skies. Higher and faster it climbed, trailing a series of sonic booms. The external sensors showed the ground receding steadily, until the whole of Prime was visible on the main screen. Half of the planet was in darkness and the line of night advanced from east to west, vanquishing the sun's warmth and bringing darkness.

"Lieutenant Dunbar, pick a destination ten minutes high lightspeed away from here. Any direction you choose."

"We shouldn't activate the catapult close to anything solid," said Decker.

"Very well, ensure we're far from anything we might break," said Blake.

"Very far away."

Blake experienced a brief irritation. "Does this Lightspeed Catapult do anything other than explode and kill everyone, Lieutenant Decker? Is there even a tiny chance it might do what we require?"

"Of course there's a chance, sir."

"Lieutenant Dunbar, take us somewhere suitable."

A few seconds later, the *ES Cataclysm*'s deep fission engines spooled up and cast the warship into lightspeed. The transition was smooth – nearly undetectable – and Blake took advantage of the short flight to get a cup of water from the replicator to wash the taste of the detox pill from his mouth.

In the few seconds it took him to drink it, Blake watched the two Ghasts. They stared intently at their consoles, as though entirely unconcerned at the coming risks. Blake smiled inwardly as he remembered Nil-Tras from the Ghast battleship Sciontrar. Nil-Tras hadn't been bothered by anything and that attitude was common amongst the alien species.

Blake took his seat once more. "Full area scan once we exit lightspeed," he said. "Shields and stealth active." He wasn't expecting trouble, but there was no harm in being prepared.

Right on schedule, the *Cataclysm* entered local space, far from any known celestial bodies. Dunbar activated the warship's defences and Flynn completed her scans efficiently.

"No hostiles," she reported.

"Send a courtesy message to Raksol, advising them we're in position to activate the Lightspeed Catapult."

"On it."

Blake spun in his chair, to find Lieutenant Decker staring at him. "Anything I need to know?" he asked.

Decker nodded, her expression serious. "I have to fire the catapult from my console, sir. It takes a short time to wind up, during which there might be some noise and vibration. There's a possibility it will interfere with the shields and the stealth."

"After that?"

"We arrive safely in Estral Space."

"If the catapult works the first time, does that mean there's a greater chance it'll work for the return?"

"If anything, the chance will be diminished."

Blake picked up the pack of auto-injectors. "What are these for?"

"To combat the feeling of unadulterated crapness we're anticipated to experience when the catapult launches."

"We really are at the forefront, aren't we?"

"Oh absolutely. Even if the Obsidiar-T were entirely reliable and stable, the Lightspeed Catapult wasn't expected to be ready for a manned flight for at least eighteen months."

"Oddly enough it doesn't bother me," said Blake. "What about you, Lieutenant Decker?"

"I'm excited. I've spent the last five years on the team responsible for the research into this tech. Who'd have thought I'd be given the chance to test it out?"

The others of the crew were pretending to be busy. Blake was sure they'd each have their own story, though the telling would need to wait until after the event.

"When do we stick ourselves with these needles, Lieutenant Decker?"

"Any time from now, sir. With your permission I'll start bringing the Lightspeed Catapult online."

"Wait." Blake pulled out one of the needles. It was a hollow metal tube, with an activation button on top. He curled his lip, familiar with this model of injector. "Lieutenant Flynn, use the internal comms and advise our passengers to use their syringes."

"Yes, sir."

Blake pushed the end of the injector against his thigh.

"Stop!" said Decker.

"What's wrong?"

"The drugs only work when they're injected directly into the neck or the heart."

"You're shitting me?"

"Yes I am. They work fine in the thigh as well."

Blake couldn't stop himself from laughing. The laughter quickly changed to a wince of pain when the injector rammed its long, fat needle deep into his flesh and forced a large quantity of ice-cold fluid into his veins.

"Dammit," he swore. He had no idea what was in the needle, but it felt like a sack of rats was pushing its way through his body.

One-by-one, the rest of the crew injected themselves. Ran-Lor and Hiven-Tar followed suit, without apparently giving the matter too much thought.

As soon as he'd received confirmation that everyone on the *Cataclysm* had used their injectors, Blake gave his permission for Decker to bring the Lightspeed Catapult online.

"Noise and vibration," he repeated.

"A little of each," said Decker. "I have the coordinates we're aiming for – Lieutenant Dunbar won't be in control of this one."

"Once this is done, we'll be ready to go?"

"As ready as we'll ever be."

Blake accessed the monitoring systems for the catapult and watched as a series of gauges climbed rapidly. The needles reached the end of their travel, whereupon the scale on the gauges was recalculated by the warship's processing clusters. Blake was aware of the Obsidiar refinement project, but he wasn't up to speed with the results.

"This is impressive," he said. "The catapult is already generating as much power as the backup Obsidiar core."

"We're just getting started," said Decker.

A few seconds later, the Obsidiar-T's total output surpassed that of the *Cataclysm*'s Gallenium engines and showed no sign of slowing.

Then, the noise came. It started as a background whine, coming from the nose of the ship. Blake detected a gentle vibration through his chair, like the Space Corps had suddenly decided to stump up for a massage function on the seating.

The whining increased in volume until it was as annoying as the bridge alarm. It levelled off and climbed no higher.

"Are we ready?" asked Blake.

"No - this is only the warmup stage," shouted Decker.

The gauges on Blake's screen held steady. The Lightspeed Catapult's output was astounding and he wondered how much higher it would go.

"Time to heat things up!"

The needles jumped and the gauge scale recalculated twice more. The whining became a shriek, accompanied by a bass rumble so low it was felt, not heard. Blake's vision blurred and he blinked to clear his eyes. He realised it wasn't his eyes at fault – nothing on the bridge was entirely in focus, as though it was a split second ahead in time. He turned his head and everything lagged.

By now, the noise was so loud it was painful to hear. For some reason, Blake found it didn't bother him and he wondered if the drugs were having an effect on his perception of pain.

"Lieutenant Decker?" he asked.

"Nearly!" she shouted.

The needles stabilised and held in position. A red light appeared on the Lightspeed Catapult's monitoring system. There was a code assigned to it which Blake didn't recognize. A second red alert light appeared.

"Do we need to abort?" he yelled at Decker. Failure at this early stage was unthinkable.

Decker's response was lost in the howling of the catapult. From the concentration on her face, Blake could see she had no intention of pulling back from the brink.

The blurring became more pronounced and Blake's entire body felt numb, like his skin belonged to someone else and been badly grafted onto him. He tried to understand the readings from the status screen and found the letters had turned into smears of green and blue.

Blake should have been scared. There was a part of him which wanted to be terrified and to hide from what was happening. Instead, he felt exhilarated at the privilege of being the first to experience this new technology which could bring humanity further and faster than ever before.

Suddenly, the noise and the vibration faded into the background. The blurring on his vision remained and Blake was certain he was dislocated in time from everything else. He looked over his shoulder and noticed that most of the crew were in complete focus, sharply outlined against the indistinct background of the bridge. For some reason, Lieutenant Flynn's form was different and her movements were slower as if she were out of phase with the rest of the crew. He looked back at his console, just as a third red alert appeared on the catapult's status display.

"Launching," said Decker, her voice as clear as if they were all in a quiet room together.

The *ES Cataclysm* shook violently and the whining shriek intruded once again. Blake felt his vision dim. There was no pain, but he knew his body was suffering. He became convinced his seat harness would snap and he gripped the arms of his chair tightly.

The noise ended, the shuddering stopped and the *ES Cataclysm* vanished.

CHAPTER FIVE

BLAKE HAD no idea how long he'd been unconscious for, or even if he'd been unconscious at all. He cracked an eye open and light streamed in. He grunted and tried to pull himself together. His body didn't feel quite right and he was sure the drugs were masking the worst of it. Movement was an effort, so he tried speaking.

"Anyone there?"

"I am here," said a Ghost voice. It might have been Ran-Lor.

With a grimace, Blake sat upright. He had plenty to do and couldn't allow his physical limitations to prevent him from checking the status of his ship. His vision cleared and, with relief, he found everything had returned to its usual focus.

He squinted at his console. The Lightspeed Catapult was offline and unavailable. He tried to access its status screen and found the entire control system unresponsive. Blake had no idea if this was expected behaviour, though it certainly didn't look right.

The hulking figure of a Ghost appeared next to his seat.

"Would you like assistance?" asked Ran-Lor. "Your crew have yet to rouse themselves."

"I resent that accusation," mumbled Lieutenant Decker.

"Have you been trained in the use of this ship?" Blake asked the Ghast.

"Your Fleet Admiral John Duggan has allowed us to install our interfaces onto those two stations. We may be able to help."

Hiven-Tar was awake as well and showed no outward signs of physical suffering. It wasn't surprising – the Ghasts were known to have the constitution of an ox.

In the end, Blake didn't want to risk letting the Ghasts loose on his warship, especially since he had no idea how well-trained they were. At first, he thought his decision was vindicated when Lieutenant Dunbar, who appeared to be peacefully asleep, snapped awake, vomited onto the floor and weakly reported himself ready for duty.

"Lieutenant Dunbar, activate our shields and stealth modules."

Dunbar wasn't quite as ready as he thought and he uttered something incoherent. Time was a luxury they didn't have, so Blake accessed the warship's stealth modules himself and tried to activate them.

"Offline," he said. "Let's try the energy shield."

The energy shield didn't respond either. The *Cataclysm*'s Gallenium engines were generating, as was the backup Obsidiar core, so the failure had a different source.

"Lieutenant Dunbar, sort yourself out and tell me what's wrong with our defences."

"Yes, sir."

Blake thumped the arm of his chair. "Come on everyone! Let's get this together!" he urged.

"Yes, sir," said Lieutenant Conway.

"Lieutenant Flynn? I need sensors, as well as an idea of

where the hell we've ended up. That's assuming we've gone anywhere."

"The Lightspeed Catapult launched successfully," said Decker.

"Where are we?"

"I have no idea."

Decker had once commanded a Galactic heavy cruiser and by all accounts the reports were glowing. Blake could only imagine what life must have been like working under Captain Misty Decker. *Interesting* was the most charitable word he could come up with.

"Lieutenant Flynn?" asked Blake, louder this time.

"I think something's wrong," said Decker.

The memory of Flynn's blurred appearance during the final moments before the catapult launch jumped into Blake's head. He swore and struggled from his seat, his head thumping.

Flynn was upright in her seat, with her purple hair thrown back and her eyes closed. Blake shook her gently, trying to rouse her. Something was wrong. Blake dashed to his seat and opened an internal channel to Lieutenant McKinney.

"We need a medic on the bridge at once," said Blake. "Do you have any casualties?"

McKinney was a practical man and before he responded to the question, he shouted an order for Grover to get himself to the bridge.

"No casualties to report down here, sir. A few thick heads."

"We're not so lucky on the bridge. To update you – the catapult fired, but we don't know where we are yet. I'll keep you updated."

"Yes, sir."

Blake closed the channel and tried once again to wake Lieutenant Flynn. Decker came over and pressed her fingers onto Flynn's neck.

"Dead," she whispered.

"Back to your station, please."

He felt trapped – one of his crew was out of action and he couldn't wait around for Medic Grover to reach the bridge.

"Ran-Lor, you asked if we needed help. Are you familiar with comms?"

"I can access your warship's sensor and comms array from my terminal."

"Do it, please. I need information."

Ran-Lor must have served for a decade on a Ghast battleship given the speed with which he responded.

"The local scans are clear, Captain Charles Blake. Here is the external sensor feed."

The main bulkhead screen came to life.

"Stars and vacuum," said Blake.

"We are [Translation imprecise: in the middle of nowhere]."

"Can you pinpoint our position relative to the intended destination?"

Ran-Lor made a rumbling sound in his chest while he checked his terminal. "I'm gathering data from the position of the visible stars."

"How long will that take?"

"It is done."

"Where are we?"

Ran-Lor raised his head and it was difficult to be sure what his expression indicated. "Estral Space. We are in Estral Space."

"I knew it would work," said Decker, keeping any hint of celebration from her voice.

"That was not what you said earlier," said Hiven-Tar in puzzlement. "You believed there was a high possibility of our deaths."

The Ghasts were unfamiliar with the human ability to make

words jump through hoops – lying and exaggeration were diffi-cult for the aliens and they struggled with the concepts.

"I hedged my bets," shrugged Decker.

"I see," said the Ghast. He scratched his thick, black hair and then laughed. "I have read about such things and now I am expe-riencing them first hand."

Blake wasn't paying much attention to the conversation. He stood at Ran-Lor's shoulder and studied the charts of the local stars. In truth, it didn't make anything clearer.

"How far are we from our intended destination? The naviga-tional experts on Prime told me they'd got a pretty good idea of where the Aranol was from the ES *Devastator*'s sensor data."

Ran-Lor poked at a screen with his thick fingertip. "We are not far off."

"How long will that take us on the fission engines?"

"If this were a Ghast Oblivion, it would take approximately four hours."

Although the Ghasts were allies, they didn't spill out all their technical data to the Space Corps. Therefore, there was an element of estimation when it came to working out the capabili-ties of the Ghast ships. The latest Oblivions were known to be *pretty damned fast*, though it was unlikely they were twenty years ahead of the ES *Cataclysm* when it came to deep fission propulsion.

"Lieutenant Dunbar, how long?"

"I'm just checking the updated star chart. Here we go - five hours, sir."

"I'll settle for that. Now, please tell me what is wrong with our defences."

"The shield and stealth modules are showing no alerts," Dunbar replied. "They just won't activate."

"Lieutenant Decker, did you say there was a chance the Lightspeed Catapult would interfere with these other systems?"

"I did say that. As I mentioned, our testing has been limited and we haven't been able to work out every possible interaction with existing hardware. The possibility of the catapult shutting down energy shields and stealth was thought to be a theoretical and remote outcome."

Blake drummed his fingers against the edge of the engine console in thought. The *ES Cataclysm* wasn't close to anything of interest, therefore it was unlikely any hostile spacecraft would stumble across the cruiser while it was at a disadvantage. The major problem was one of time.

"We missed the target by a long way, even given the distance we travelled."

"I should be able to fix that for the next time," said Decker. "I can already see where the calculations went wrong and I believe I can reduce or eliminate the variation."

"That would be appreciated." Blake moved onto the next problem. "Ran-Lor, can you attempt contact with the *ES Ulterior-2*? We should be able to see them on the comms, right? Even without a point of reference from Confederation Space."

The Ghast wasn't thrown by the question. "If they have their comms active, I will be able to connect with them."

"Please try."

Ran-Lor tried a few things on his console, the efficiency of his movement impressing Blake. "There is nothing. I am not able to establish a connection with the *Ulterior-2*."

Blake's heart sank. "Are they offline? Dead? Out of range?"

"I do not have that information."

It wasn't the answer Blake was looking for. The rational part of his mind told him the *Ulterior-2* had been destroyed by the Aranol, however Blake had long ago accepted that not everything came down to logic. There was a different part of him which insisted the *Ulterior-2* was out there somewhere and its crew were still alive. He gave himself no other choice than to believe.

"Keep searching for the *Ulterior-2*. If something happened to them, they may be sending a low speed or low strength signal."

"I do not think they are here, but I will do as you ask."

Blake returned to his seat. The *Cataclysm* was drifting gently through local space after its transit, so he pushed the control bars forward until it was at maximum velocity. It gave him a sense that he was doing something.

The squad medic, Armand Grover, arrived, lugging his medbox. He was a man of few words. Without speaking, he crouched down and attached two wires to Flynn's forehead.

"I'm sorry, sir. She's dead."

Hearing the words drove home the finality and Blake could only nod. "Please arrange for the body to be taken to the medical bay, Medic Grover. Can you tell us the cause of death?"

"Internal trauma. The body will bruise up in an hour or so."

Blake didn't need it explaining to him further – internal trauma was a risk dating back to the early days of lightspeed travel, resulting from the inability of the life support modules to keep the individual protected from harsh, instant acceleration. On this occasion, he was certain it was a side-effect of the Lightspeed Catapult. He caught Decker's eyes and the sadness in her face was unmistakeable. None of this was her fault and he said so.

For the next few minutes, the crew continued with their duties. Meanwhile, Blake become progressively more agitated at the lack of updates.

"Status reports, please."

"I can't reach the *Ulterior-2*," said Ran-Lor. "The local star map is nearly populated from the sensor feeds – the data you humans have from this area of space is ancient and incomplete."

"We haven't been this way in a long while."

"The energy shield has just this second activated," said Dunbar. "I have no idea how that happened. And there go the stealth modules." He rubbed his chin. "I wish I could claim the credit."

"Find the cause, Lieutenant. This is a side effect of the Lightspeed Catapult. If we need to use it again, I'd prefer it if we weren't defenceless when we arrive at the other end."

"It'll take some time to check through the audit logs, sir."

"You've got five hours to find us some answers, Lieutenant Dunbar. We're going to the target location at fastest speed. Do it now."

Dunbar didn't miss a beat. "The coordinates are set, we'll exit local space in eight seconds."

The *ES Cataclysm* launched away from this featureless area of Estral Space, heading directly for the intended target of the Lightspeed Catapult. This unwanted addition to the journey was in some ways welcome, in that it allowed the crew a chance to recover from the original transit. It was far more than a simple physical recovery they required, though Blake privately admitted that he felt like he'd been squeezed through a wringer. What the interval allowed was an opportunity to regroup after the death of Lieutenant Trudy Flynn, an officer Blake didn't know well, but who showed great promise during the very short time he worked with her.

For much of the flight, Lieutenant Dunbar kept his head down and searched for answers as to why they'd lost shields and stealth. Elsewhere on the bridge, Lieutenant Decker checked out the red alerts on the Lightspeed Catapult and tried to work out the reason Flynn alone had died.

Dunbar didn't come up with anything concrete, whilst Decker had a few things to say.

"We came close to overloading the Obsidiar-Teronium," she said. "This stuff is far less stable than the initial reports suggested."

"Will it take us back when our mission is complete?"

She chewed her lip. "Honest answer? I wouldn't like to guess. I've managed to clear one alert, but these other two relate to the detonators we use to kick-start the catapult."

"Detonators?" asked Blake.

"Only in the loosest sense." She aimed a finger unerringly at an output graph. "If you believe this, everything is great. Amazing."

"I take it looks are deceiving?"

Decker was worried and it showed. "This stuff is so new we didn't even get to finish the monitoring tools. This graph could be telling us a load of crap. At best, it could be giving only a partial story of the catapult's status."

"Can we do anything to limit the chance of fatalities on the return flight?"

"I'll keep looking." She swore, the first sign of a real crack in her composure. "We needed far more time to get this ready."

"Time we didn't have. If the catapult fails, can you fix it?"

"Highly unlikely."

"In that case, we can't worry about it. Let's deal with the things we can control and if this heap of junk blows up on the way home, we'll be thankful we got this far."

Decker was about to object to his use of the words *heap of junk* when she saw he was trying to lighten the mood. She gave him a wink which meant everything and nothing.

There was something to celebrate. When he spoke with Lieutenant Conway, Blake found that the repeating particle beam turret was still connected to the Obsidiar-Teronium power source. The Lightspeed Catapult might well fail the next time they activated it, but the *Cataclysm* would still be able to blow the crap out of more or less any other spaceship in the meantime.

Except the Aranol, thought Blake sourly. *And until the Obsidiar-T decides it's had enough and burns out.*

The five hours passed and when Lieutenant Dunbar gave the ten-minute warning, Blake returned to his seat.

"We've targeted an area a little way out from where we saw the Aranol," he said. "Even so, I want us to be ready for anything, meaning full alert upon arrival."

The crew weren't battle-hardened, but they were exceptionally well trained and each knew what was expected. Ran-Lor and Hiven-Tar were so competent that Blake was sure the Ghasts had sent some of their finest officers.

At exactly the predicted time, the ES *Cataclysm*'s fission drive grumbled faintly and the warship's processing cores switched the cruiser onto gravity engines, sending it into its destination solar system.

On the bridge, the crew worked hard. It soon became apparent that something entirely unexpected was taking place.

CHAPTER SIX

"NOTHING IN CLOSE PROXIMITY," said Ran-Lor, after reading through the sensor data.

Blake nodded in acknowledgement. He had the ES *Cataclysm* at half speed, with its energy shields and stealth modules active. As it happened, this part of Estral Space was close to where Fleet Admiral Duggan had taken the ESS *Crimson* many years previously, and the Space Corps had extensive records of the local solar systems. However, the star charts weren't in any way essential to the task of locating an object with a six-thousand-kilometre diameter.

Aware that the Aranol might be on the blind side of a planet or moon, Blake ordered a series of short-range lightspeed transits through the solar system, until the *Cataclysm*'s AI informed him the likelihood of missing such a large object had fallen below one tenth of one percent.

"The Aranol has gone elsewhere," Blake said. "Keep checking for the *Ulterior-2*."

"I am checking," said Ran-Lor. "Should I begin detailed surface scans of the planets in this system?"

The Aranol wasn't here, but that didn't mean there wasn't anything at all of interest. It was possible the *Ulterior-2* had crashed somewhere nearby. Even if it were reduced to burning wreckage, Blake wanted to know exactly what had befallen his crew.

"We have eight planets and a medium-large sun," he said. "A couple of gas giants, two stone spheres clad in ice and the rest varying from very hot to cool. If the Hadron crashed into any of them, there'll be a visible sign of it. Please begin the scans, starting from the closest planet to our position."

The nearest planet was a million kilometres away and it was the fourth from the sun. It was a solid ball of grey rock with a large diameter and a surface covered in peaks and canyons. It was the type of scanning job they threw at new recruits to weed out the ones who couldn't handle the pressure.

Conway cleared her throat. "The Aranol is our primary mission, sir."

"I know that, Lieutenant. It isn't here and until I can think of a way to track it down, we might as well start searching for our missing people."

"If the Aranol is gone, what exactly does that mean for the Confederation?" asked Conway.

"It could mean absolutely nothing, Lieutenant. The Aranol may be simply moving amongst the ruins of the Estral Empire, picking up the remains of the Vraxar fleet. It could be an hour's lightspeed from here, for all we know."

"You are unconvinced," said Ran-Lor.

"You're damn right I'm unconvinced! The Vraxar will keep moving until they've killed every living creature in the universe."

"Such a feat is beyond them," Ran-Lor replied. "They might defeat your Confederation and they might defeat the Ghasts. The universe is large and they will eventually encounter one of the many advanced civilisations with the technology and the determination to stop them."

"Like the Estral?"

"The Estral were strong. Do you really think there are not other species out there, even mightier than the Estral?"

"I would prefer it if humanity were given the opportunity to become one of these mighty species you mention. The Ghasts too, if that's what your race desires."

"We will expand and grow at our own pace, Captain Charles Blake. If anyone tries to dictate otherwise, we Ghasts will destroy them."

It was no idle boast as the Confederation had once found to its cost. The Ghasts fought hard and they were a formidable, relentless opponent.

Blake fell silent, thinking. If the Aranol was gone, there might be no way to trace the Vraxar. It was possible they'd left behind a positron trail from their entry into lightspeed. Such a trail would fade over time and if the enemy ship had departed a long time ago, it would be impossible to pick up again.

"I have completed my scan of the visible side of the fourth planet," said Ran-Lor. "There is no wreckage."

"I'll bring us around so you can scan the remainder," Blake replied.

"Your *Ulterior-2* isn't on this planet."

"What makes you so sure?"

Ran-Lor spoke words. His language module hesitated. [Translation unclear. Concept unclear.]

"Is this the Ghast equivalent of a *hunch*?" asked Blake.

"Guesswork based on feeling," rumbled Hiven-Tar, as if the idea were incredibly novel.

"No, Captain Blake, this is not exactly a hunch," said Ran-Lor.

"What is it, then?"

"A knowledge of certainties," the Ghast replied. "The *Ulterior-2* is not on the fourth planet."

Blake wasn't quite ready to alter his search plans based on the alien's mystifying implication that it knew things it couldn't possibly know. On the other hand, he wasn't ready to dismiss the Ghost's claims just for the sake of it. There were people in the Space Corps' Projections Team who could divine probabilities from the tiniest amount of evidence. It could be that a few members of the Ghast species were similar.

"Does this mean the *Ulterior-2* is not destroyed?"

"I do not know."

"I have a reading from the third planet," said Hiven-Tar.

Blake jumped to his feet. "What have you got?"

"As I said - a reading."

Pages of Ghast script covered the screens of Hiven-Tar's console. The Ghast pointed helpfully at a few lines of symbols, which Blake was entirely unable to read. He took a spacesuit visor from the bridge locker and placed it over his head. The HUD automatically translated the symbols into words and numbers he could understand.

"How did you find that?" asked Blake.

Hiven-Tar had somehow intercepted an irregular outbound transmission and tracked it to its source. In the process, he'd identified dozens – hundreds – more, travelling through space in many different directions.

"The transmitter is using a similar method to that employed in Ghast installations," said Ran-Lor.

It took Blake a few minutes to unravel the method used by Hiven-Tar. The transmissions themselves were tiny, encrypted packets, probably little more than handshake requests for the receptor. They were also banded exceptionally tightly, to prevent random interception.

"Where's the transmitter?"

"On the surface of the third planet."

"Can you show me it?"

"We are seventy million kilometres away and the transmitter is small. I do not believe this warship's sensors will be able to provide a detailed visual from this range."

"Do you think you have located some kind of comms hub?"

"Yes."

"A comms hub should be easy enough to locate from here."

"The power source and control units will be shielded deep beneath the surface."

Hiven-Tar appeared to know a great deal about the comms hub he'd discovered and Blake took a moment to realise why. When he came up with the answer, it seemed obvious.

"This is an Estral installation."

"Yes."

"An active Estral installation."

"Automated comms routing hubs are not unusual," said Ran-Lor.

"I thought the Estral were defeated," said Dunbar. "How come they've got a working facility?"

Hiven-Tar gave a barking laugh. "The Estral may have lost the war, but there is no way the Vraxar could have made them extinct. We are not talking about a species living on a dozen worlds! The Estral were spread across thousands of worlds, with their technologies deployed on thousands more! To wipe them out them entirely would be an impossible task!"

It was an interesting idea and Blake found himself drawn to it. The Estral had once tried to destroy the Confederation, yet he couldn't help but have sympathy with any species which fought the Vraxar.

"Do you think the Estral will ever recover?" he asked.

"Not soon," said Ran-Lor. "It will happen eventually if they are given time."

"You don't sound concerned. I thought you were mortal enemies?" said Blake.

"Perhaps one day there will be a rapprochement."

It was a fascinating subject, though something to be pursued another day. It was definitely in the Confederation's interest to be aware of any shifts in the Ghast attitude towards their parent race. Not that there was currently any easy way for the two sides to meet.

"A comms hub will be equipped with a sensor array," Blake mused.

"Not necessarily," said Decker. "A routing station wouldn't require any scanning capabilities."

"That is true," said Ran-Lor. "However, it is possible a routing station would have relayed information gained from another source."

"Monitoring stations or satellites," said Blake.

"Which may well contain information relating to the Aranol's presence in this solar system," said Decker.

"It is difficult to disguise the presence of a monitoring station," said Hiven-Tar. "It is likely the Vraxar neutralised any Estral monitoring stations in the vicinity."

"We don't know where the Aranol has gone to," said Blake. "Any possible leads will be contained in the audit logs of the Estral routing station."

"Are we going to take a look?" asked Dunbar.

"Yes, we are. Take us in with an SRT to an altitude of forty thousand klicks, Lieutenant. I'll get the computer to spit out a name for this place."

The *Cataclysm*'s databanks assigned a name to the third planet.

"Folsgar it is," said Blake.

The short-range transit was completed in a few seconds and Blake established a stationary orbit directly over the Estral station. He didn't like to dwell on the subject for too long, but he was painfully aware that without Lieutenant Flynn's death, the Ghasts might not have been so involved in the search and they might have missed this place entirely.

"Show me what we've got."

Ran-Lor brought the image up on the bulkhead screen. Folsgar was only moderately cold and with an atmosphere not too far from being able to support life. Had chance left this planet only a few million kilometres closer to its sun, it may well have spawned its own forms of life millions of years ago.

The visible part of the Estral transmitter was a metal rod, a single metre in diameter, which protruded forty metres above the surface. It was in a high-sided rocky valley which would limit its broadcasting angle, whilst significantly reducing the chance anything in space would detect the antenna. It bore the hallmarks of a facility created by a species on the run.

"This space here is suitable for landing a shuttle," said Hiven-Tar, tapping the screen. "I believe there are signs of fracturing on the rock from where they landed a craft too heavy for the ground." He indicated another area nearby. "This is the entrance."

The *Cataclysm* was near enough to produce an image of razor-sharp clarity, but the entrance looked like nothing more than an imperfection in the ground.

"They hid it well," said Blake.

"They had no choice," replied Hiven-Tar.

"How did they build this facility?" asked Conway. "There are no signs of excavation."

"Geological remodelling when the construction was complete," said Ran-Lor. "Or perhaps they tunnelled in from a more suitable location a thousand kilometres away."

The casual answer was a reminder of exactly how advanced

the Estral had once been. There were few obstacles they couldn't overcome.

"How the hell did they lose to the Vraxar?" said Dunbar.

"We've seen only a fraction of what the enemy have to offer," said Blake. "We've destroyed everything in Confederation Space, but it's certain the majority of the Vraxar forces were left here to mop up the Estral."

"Forty years' travel away," said Conway.

Decker had the clearance to find out the truth. "We've learned of at least three ways the Vraxar can cross such a distance, Lieutenant. They'll try it again."

"Ran-Lor, will you be able to operate the equipment in the facility below?" asked Blake.

"More than likely. I would suggest Hiven-Tar and Raxil-Ven are more capable."

"Very well, make arrangements."

Blake opened a channel to McKinney.

"Get suited up and ready for deployment, Lieutenant."

"Yes, sir. What's our objective?"

"There's an Estral relay station on the surface of a planet. There's no sign of the Aranol or the *Ulterior-2* and it's possible the base below us has a record of their departure."

"Are we expecting hostiles?"

Blake glanced towards Ran-Lor. The Ghast simply shrugged.

"We don't know. The relay station may be fully automated, or its crew might have died thirty years ago. Equally, it might be full of Estral troops with itchy trigger fingers."

"We'll be ready, sir. I don't think Corporal Bannerman knows how to operate an Estral comms station."

"He won't have to. You'll have some Ghasts with you."

"That's fine with me, sir. We've been getting along great so far."

"I'm sure you have. There are only two shuttles on the *Cataclysm*. Let me know when you're in the first."

That was the extent of the organisation. It was the sort of mission Blake would have enjoyed were there not so much at stake - he felt he worked better when he was required to plan instinctively.

Hiven-Tar exited the bridge and Blake paced nervously. It was McKinney and the others who were taking the risks this time, but Blake couldn't help but feel directly involved. He checked the bridge clock and discovered only five minutes had elapsed since he'd given the order for deployment.

After an interminable wait, McKinney reported in. "We're in Shuttle One and awaiting orders, sir."

"I'm opening the bay doors, Lieutenant. The little information we know is downloaded into your visors. Don't hang around."

"I won't, sir."

"The shuttle is exiting our bay," said Ran-Lor, a couple of minutes later.

The *Cataclysm* was carrying two of the Space Corps' newest, most-heavily armed shuttles and the first of them dropped into the highest reaches of Folsgar's atmosphere and sped away towards the surface.

CHAPTER SEVEN

SHUTTLE ONE MIGHT HAVE BEEN new, but it wasn't luxurious. Lieutenant Eric McKinney sat in a seat which looked as though it had been ripped clean out of a gravity-engined taxi and there was a sticky brown substance on the floor which Sergeant Li peered at suspiciously. Li was an excellent soldier, yet he could be incredibly fastidious where dirt and grime were concerned.

Aside from the low-rent interior, the shuttle hummed smoothly towards Folsgar. It was equipped with front and rear chainguns and thick armour plating, neither of which McKinney wished to test in the near future.

The third seat was occupied by Raxil-Ven. There were another three of the aliens sitting out back and McKinney could hear them trading good-natured insults with the squad. The Ghasts didn't seem bothered by anything, a trait which the men did their unsuccessful best to exploit.

"What do you expect to find in this Estral facility?" asked McKinney.

Raxil-Ven turned his head. The Ghost was dressed in a sandy-yellow spacesuit which appeared to be constructed of a material that was part metal and part cloth. A Ghost-sized helmet was on the floor next to his seat. The helmet was a solid-looking metal object with a flat, clear faceplate and information panels packed inside. It was peculiarly archaic in appearance, yet McKinney couldn't help but think it probably contained a lot more computational power than the Space Corps' equivalent.

"I believe this relay station is likely to be automated."

"Does that mean there'll be no maintenance crew?"

"I would not like to speculate. It is a possibility."

"If there are Estral will they be hostile to humans and Ghosts alike?"

Raxil-Ven gave a wide grin. "They are unlikely to recognize us as Ghosts."

"What the lieutenant is asking is will they shoot or will they talk?" said Li.

"I imagine they might do one or the other."

"Has anyone ever taught you Ghosts how to give a straight answer?" asked Li. "I charge by the hour if you want lessons."

"You are a very funny man, Sergeant Li. I like you."

"I'm glad to hear it."

McKinney brought the shuttle lower and kept it under manual control. It was significantly faster than any other transport he'd piloted and its autopilot nagged him continuously to hand over control. He ignored its complaints and guided the craft into the far end of the valley in which the Estral facility was situated.

"Eight klicks to go," reported Li.

The valley was wide and there was no danger of an impact against its sides. The *ES Cataclysm*'s sensors had picked up no sign of defences, but McKinney preferred to come in low regardless. A short while later, the navigational computer highlighted an area ahead.

"That's the place," said McKinney. Grudgingly, he activated the autopilot, so he could get on with the preparations to deploy. He poked his head through the open doorway into the passenger bay beyond. It was brighter here and he squinted. "Grab your things. We'll land in less than two minutes."

The passenger bay held seating for fifty, and the shuttle came equipped with internal gravity clamps to allow it to carry heavy loads, such as artillery. There was a repeater already fixed to the end of the bay and its multiple barrels swayed slightly with the movement of the shuttle.

The bay wasn't close to full. McKinney's usual squad were reduced to fourteen, plus there were four Ghasts. The human soldiers pulled their suit visors down, whilst the Ghasts fitted their helmets into place with hisses of tightening seals.

Most of the human squad carried plasma repeaters in addition to their gauss rifles. Two of the Ghasts had their own – much larger - repeaters, whilst the remaining two carried long tubes with protruding triggers. These guns had been the cause of much curiosity in the squad, since they were nearly the same size as a plasma launcher. It turned out they were a wide-bore version of a gauss rifle. They looked cumbersome, but the Ghasts carried them with ease.

"Landing, landing," said the androgynous voice of the shuttle's autopilot.

The squad gathered near the flank exit door. A red light glowed to one side and McKinney tapped his foot as he waited for it to turn green.

The shuttle's autopilot set the craft down so neatly that McKinney was startled when the light changed. He stepped forward and activated the door. The side of the shuttle swung outwards without a sound until it was resting on the ground.

The voice of Ran-Lor on the *Cataclysm*'s bridge came through McKinney's earpiece.

"There are no threats detected in the vicinity. You are free to deploy."

"Out!" said McKinney.

He was first onto the ramp. It was daytime on Folsgar and the light from its sun illuminated the rocks and turned them into an over-bright yellow. The sensor in McKinney's visor adjusted, cutting out the glare and protecting his eyes.

The side wall of the valley climbed steeply away for three or four kilometres. It was bare rock, covered in wind-blown dust and with many loose boulders, some of them balanced precariously. The rocks cast gnarled and unpleasant shadows which seemed to shimmer in the steady breeze.

"Minus twenty outside," said Sergeant Demarco. "Don't take your coats off."

McKinney reached the end of the ramp and took his first step onto the surface of Folsgar. There was no ice and little in the way of wind. It was the sort of remote, peaceful place a man craving solitude might come to live out his final days.

He turned his head until his saw the antenna. The map overlay in his HUD traced a red line to their destination nearby.

"Three hundred metres over there," he said on the squad open channel. "Let's move."

With the ES *Cataclysm* watching overhead, McKinney felt more reassured than he might have otherwise. Nevertheless, he kept his gauss rifle ready and scanned the ground ahead and to the sides. The antenna was nothing out of the ordinary – just a thick metal pole, dull and near-black. His suit HUD suggested it may contain a quantity of Obsidiar, with the rest being an unknown substance. The entrance was fifty metres to the right of the antenna. The doorway was ingeniously incorporated into a natural outcrop in the stone and it took McKinney a few seconds to distinguish the outline of the door itself from the surroundings.

The dust crunched softly underfoot as the squad made their way cautiously towards the entrance. McKinney stopped at the door – it was three metres high and two wide, making it big enough for an Estral to walk through without knocking its head.

"Are you going to use the number cruncher, Lieutenant?" asked Sergeant Li.

Li's words reminded McKinney of the weight he was carrying. This was a different model to the one he'd lugged through the middle of *Ix-Gastiol* and it wasn't any lighter. If anything, it felt as though it weighed twenty pounds more.

"There's an access panel," whispered Garcia, as if he feared there were someone listening in.

The panel for the door held no surprises. It was a smooth, square piece of transparent material. Symbols glowed softly, which McKinney's HUD gamely tried to interpret.

He repeated the literal translation. "Shut and code required for shut to de-shut."

"De-shut?" asked Li. "Who the hell programs this stuff?"

The Estral and Ghast tongues had several hundred years in which to diverge, so in reality it was something of a feat to get anything even partway intelligible from the language modules.

"Can one of you Ghasts get this open before I start triggering alarms by smashing through the security protocols with this ISOP?" asked McKinney.

"It is easy," said Raxil-Ven.

The Ghast was two paces back and he stepped past McKinney. The alien made a couple of intricate sweeping gestures with his fingers.

"There."

The door opened to reveal a blue-lit airlock room that was

large enough to accommodate fifty Estral. It was quiet and empty, except for a panel set against one wall.

"Inside," said McKinney, walking across the threshold.

The was no ambient warmth inside the airlock and McKinney wondered if that meant the place was deserted. He hoped so – it was one thing shooting the Vraxar, but he had no desire to start putting holes in every other living species out there, even if they had a history of hostility towards the Confederation. He approached the panel, with Raxil-Ven alongside him.

"Go on," encouraged the Ghost. "Like I showed you."

"The outer airlock door is open," said McKinney. "I'm not sure I want to depressurize the interior."

"It will be safest to kill anything that might be inside," warned Hiven-Tar. "In this instance it doesn't matter - the outer door will close when the inner one opens."

McKinney reached out a hand and did his best to copy the hand movement to open the door. The symbols changed to a new formation which his HUD translation informed him was the word No! He tried again and then for a third time.

"Like this," said Raxil-Ven.

The Ghost performed the gesture with exaggerated slowness and to McKinney's eyes it was exactly the same as he'd tried himself. The outer airlock closed and a second door in the opposite wall opened. McKinney gritted his teeth.

"A lift," said Sergeant Li. "Big enough to squeeze in a dozen Ghosts and their rations."

There was room for the entire squad inside the lift, though McKinney didn't intend sending them all down at the same time in case there was something unexpected at the bottom. He looked inside - it was cylindrical and when he tapped the side wall, it sounded thick and solid.

"Garcia, Roldan, Raxil-Ven, you're coming with me. The rest of you wait here until I tell you otherwise."

The chosen group followed McKinney into the lift.

"Here's your big chance, Lieutenant," said Huey Roldan. "Take us to the bottom."

"How does it work?" asked McKinney.

"The same as the doors," said the Ghost.

McKinney was starting to believe the alien was playing tricks on him. He performed the sweeping motion with his hand three times before he struck the panel in frustration.

"Our children can do this at an early age," said Raxil-Ven. He activated the panel and the lift door closed.

There was a sensation of movement and McKinney lifted his rifle to his shoulder. The other men did the same, whilst the Ghost stood impassively.

The lift stopped after twenty seconds, which told McKinney they'd descended a long way. The door opened, revealing a passageway through the rock. More blue light came from spheres embedded at regular intervals in the floor, walls and ceiling. Whatever the Estral had used to cut the rock, it left the surface polished and with a faint reflective sheen.

"It's still minus twenty," said Roldan. "And the atmosphere is the same as on the surface."

"Ain't nothing living down here, Lieutenant," said Garcia.

McKinney wasn't ready to be convinced just yet. "Not unless it's in a suit." He looked at Raxil-Ven. "Does any of this look familiar to you? Can you tell us anything?"

He saw the Ghost narrowing his eyes through the helmet faceplate. "Proceed with caution."

"What do you know?"

"I know nothing you don't, human. You asked my advice and I said we should proceed with caution."

McKinney stepped out of the lift. The passage was about twenty metres long and it ended at a T-junction. He listened – the suit picked up a slight movement in the air, but there was otherwise no sound at all. He touched the walls to see if he could feel a vibration from the facility's power source. There was nothing.

With quick strides, McKinney reached the T-junction and peered both ways. To the left, the corridor opened into a room, whilst to the right it ended at another T-junction.

"Is there anything there, Lieutenant?" asked Garcia.

"There's a room along here. It's got some kind of console in it."

"Can we use it?" asked Roldan.

"How the hell should I know?" asked McKinney testily. "Something doesn't feel right."

"I agree," said Raxil-Ven.

"I'm attempting contact with the *Cataclysm*," said McKinney, wondering if he was allowing himself to become spooked. He tried the channel to the warship and, as he'd feared, there was only a quiet background hum.

"You'd think the comms would work great inside a damned comms hub," said Roldan.

"Let's get on with it. Raxil-Ven, go up and fetch the others."

"Yes."

The Ghost backed into the lift. A moment later, the door closed, leaving McKinney suddenly and acutely aware of his isolation.

"Come on," he said, waving Garcia and Roldan towards him.

"Are we going to explore?" asked Garcia anxiously. He sounded like he'd had enough and they'd only just arrived.

"We have to." McKinney pointed to the left with the end of his rifle. "Let's check out this room."

They approached the room as quietly as they could manage. At the doorway, McKinney stuck his head around the corner to see what was about.

"Empty."

Roldan expelled his breath loudly. "Maybe we got lucky with this one, Lieutenant."

"The next time we get lucky, I'll pay everyone in the squad's bar tab for an entire evening." With that promise, McKinney entered the room for a better look.

It was a square space, twelve metres to each side and with a high, domed ceiling. Across from them, there was another door, this one closed. In the centre of the floor, was a complicated, circular console, with five angular metal seats around it. The console was online and powered up, and McKinney recognized a few features which he associated with comms, though doubtless Corporal Bannerman would have a better idea. A thick pillar rose from the middle of the console and vanished into the ceiling.

"Is that the antenna we saw above?" asked Roldan.

"It's in the wrong place, soldier. Maybe this facility has a number of sub-surface antennae. I guess I don't really know how this stuff works."

The sound of footsteps made the men turn and the rest of the squad came into the room with rather less caution than that exhibited by McKinney earlier.

"We left McCoy, Whitlock and Nian-Lin topside," said Sergeant Li. "In case the *Cataclysm* needs to get a message to us."

"Good thinking, Sergeant. Our comms are dead in here."

"Figures, doesn't it?"

McKinney ordered the squad to secure the area.

"Should I take a look along that way?" asked Demarco, indicating the second T-junction.

"Look, but don't go any further."

"Roger."

Demarco chose Vega and the two of them hurried away. McKinney beckoned Corporal Bannerman and Hiven-Tar over.

"I take it this is a comms console. Can we obtain the data we need from it?"

"I don't know, sir," said Bannerman. "It'll take me a few minutes to familiarise myself with the Estral hardware."

The Ghost was more forthcoming. "This is a conduit for the signal. There will be a booster room directly below, acting as an amplifier. This console will not hold a record of either outbound or inbound signals."

"What are we looking for, then?"

"Something similar to this, except bigger. It will likely be on the level below us."

The Ghost spoke with confidence and sometimes that was all McKinney needed.

"There's no point in hanging around here if it isn't what we want."

Hiven-Tar nodded. "We should search for a lift to take us deeper into the station."

Something was bugging McKinney and he realised what it was. "There are chairs around this middle console," he said. "Why would they need chairs if the facility was automated?"

"I don't have an answer," said Hiven-Tar. "Other than to suggest the need for vigilance."

Sergeant Demarco and Vega entered the room with no particular appearance of urgency.

"Well?" asked McKinney.

"More corridors, sir," said Demarco. "No sign of life. This place must be deserted."

"We aren't making that assumption just yet, Sergeant. Stay alert."

McKinney approached the single exit from the room and signalled for Garcia and Mills to cover the door. With his rifle in his right hand, McKinney used his left to trace a pattern over the access panel, bracing himself for some piss-taking from the soldiers. The door took him by surprise and opened to reveal a passage leading away through the rock. A waft of slightly warmer air came through the opening, which his visor HUD analysed and informed him contained a higher oxygen content than the part of the relay station they'd explored so far.

"This place wasn't automated," he said. "Not a chance of it."

With that, he gathered up the squad in readiness.

CHAPTER EIGHT

THE PASSAGE LED DIRECTLY into a similar room, with the same type of console and another conduit going between floor and ceiling. Once again, it was silent.

"One exit, same as the last room," said Li.

McKinney checked the map his HUD computer was in the process of plotting for him. There wasn't enough evidence for certainty, but it appeared as though these conduits were linked in such a way that they formed a circle around the central antenna on the surface.

"Look at this, Lieutenant," said Guzman.

It took a second or two for McKinney to recognize the object she was holding in her hand.

"A cup."

"It's got some frozen stuff inside it as well. Grey goop like the Ghasts eat." She knocked the cup on the side of the console and it clunked.

"Put it down, soldier."

"This is a replicator," said Tren-Fir, standing in front of a slot in the wall. There was no apparent way to activate the device and the Ghost didn't try.

Any lingering doubts about the nature of this facility were gone - there had once been Estral here.

"Where are they?" said McKinney. "There's no sign of a fight."

"Do you think everyone's dead, Lieutenant?" asked Clifton.

"It would make things easier."

McKinney repeated the process of carefully opening the exit door. As expected, there was another corridor and his HUD computer slotted in another piece of the map it was building. The layout of the Estral base wasn't elaborate and it likely didn't need to be.

There was no further evidence of life in the third room and the only difference was the presence of two exits instead of just one. The additional exit had no door and was simply a passage which led directly towards the centre of this outer ring of conduit rooms.

"This way," said McKinney, indicating the passage. He felt uneasy. It wasn't that he was scared of combat and he'd been in plenty of alien facilities before, there was just something eerie about this comms station. The place had a story to tell – a tiny story in the context of an enormous war between Estral and Vraxar, but a story which was nonetheless significant to those who'd played a part.

"Anyone else getting the creeps from this place?" asked Mills.

"Normally I'd feel obliged to say *no* just to piss you off," said Garcia. He didn't elaborate and his meaning was clear. None of them liked being here.

"Are those lifts I can see at the end?" asked Demarco.

"Lifts are what we want," McKinney replied. He, too, could see what he hoped were more lifts. "The sooner we get out of here, the better I'll like it."

They came to an antechamber which was large enough to fit everyone inside. McKinney was wary about bunching up and he left Roldan and Vega in the conduit room to keep watch. There were symbols etched into a set of double doors in the opposite wall. McKinney's language modules tried to make sense of them, but could only offer a garbled interpretation which made no sense.

"Access Lifts – Lower Levels," said Hiven-Tar.

McKinney took a deep breath. "Garcia, Mills, with me. Let's take a look at what's below."

The lift took a short while to open, suggesting it was originally at the lower level. The squad kept watch in case there was something unexpected waiting for them inside. It was empty.

"In."

The three of them entered the lift and McKinney activated it. Garcia began saying something and then thought better of it. The lift descended in silence and when the doors opened, it was clear they'd found what they were looking for.

"Shit, look at this," said Mills under his breath.

McKinney looked to the left and right. There was no movement and no sound. It should have been a relief, but it only served to increase his apprehension.

The command area of the Estral comms hub was a massive, circular chamber. The lift had opened onto one side of the space and, when he looked upwards, McKinney saw the ceiling was eighty metres above and domed. The opposite wall was ninety metres away and the stone was polished in the same way as everywhere else in the facility. There were at least a dozen consoles arranged evenly in a ring around a huge, central structure of dull alloy.

"What the hell is that?" asked Garcia.

"The power source and main transmitter," said McKinney, not sure why he was so certain.

The transmitter was a cylinder with a diameter in excess of twenty metres. There were screens installed at regular intervals, a few feet from the floor.

"Goes up and through the ceiling," said Mills.

"We're directly under the surface antenna, according to my HUD map."

None of them moved from the illusory sanctuary of the lift and they stared into the room for a short time. It was bright, cold and unwelcoming.

"Garcia, think you can operate this lift?"

"Easy."

"Go on and bring the squad down here."

McKinney gave Mills a nudge and the two of them stepped into the room, keeping a careful watch for anything that might constitute a threat. The lift doors remained open behind them.

"What are you waiting for, Garcia?"

"You didn't find it easy, Lieutenant," said Garcia, swiping at the lift panel in obvious frustration. "Maybe these things work better if you've got fat fingers like a Ghast. Me? I'm an artist, with artist's fingers."

"Yeah, whatever," said Mills.

It didn't take long for McKinney to lose his patience. "Come on, out." He swapped places with Garcia and then had second thoughts about leaving the pair of them alone in the room. "Change of plan, we'll all go up. I don't want you two shooting the place up by mistake."

With the three of them in the lift once more, McKinney attempted the panel. His belief that he was getting the hang of it faltered and it took him several tries. Eventually, the lift doors closed and the two men heard it moving through the shaft.

"Don't quote me on this, Lieutenant, but I reckon we're going down, not up," said Garcia.

Mills thought the same. "I didn't want to say anything."

McKinney closed his eyes, telling himself it was only a lift. "We don't need this crap."

This time the journey took a full minute to complete.

"We're going to be ten klicks under the surface by the time this thing stops," said Garcia.

Mills stamped once on the floor. "It's slowing."

The lift came to a halt and there was a short pause before the doors opened. This time, the exit room was square and only a few metres across. McKinney looked out and saw corridors going left and right as well as a third one ahead. The lights flickered sporadically, as though someone was flicking the switch randomly. It was unpleasantly disconcerting.

"Maybe the power is failing," said Mills.

"Yeah. What does that sign say on the wall over there?" asked Garcia. "My HUD translates it as *Person Space*."

"Living quarters," said McKinney. "There are doorways ahead."

"Are we going to take a look?" The tone of Mills' voice indicated his preferred choice in the matter.

McKinney's feet carried him out of the lift. He didn't know why he felt the compulsion to look – certainly the correct choice was to try and get the lift working again. For some reason, he felt a connection with this place. It was a forgotten outpost in an endless war and he was filled with an urge to capture a record of events here.

"Lieutenant?" said Garcia. "Maybe we should get back."

"One minute, soldier. I'm just going to look in one of these rooms."

McKinney crossed the antechamber and entered the corridor opposite. The others followed him reluctantly, their footsteps the only sound. The flickering of the lights interfered with McKinney's perception of distance and he found it took longer than expected to reach the closest two doorways. They were on opposite sides of the passage, with their doors open. Between this point and a T-junction ahead, there were another three sets of doorways.

With his rifle raised, McKinney put his head into the room. It took only this glance to tell him what he needed to know.

"Bodies," he said. "Four of them and they didn't die happy."

With three quick steps, he crossed the passage and looked into the opposite room. Like the first room, there were three metal-framed double bunks, fitted with paper-thin mattresses. There was a large viewscreen in one wall and a table with three metal cups and a tray. The furnishings could have been lifted directly from any barracks in any Space Corps installation.

There were five more bodies on the floor. The Estral were dressed in drab grey cloth uniforms and their eyes were open, staring. Ice had formed a glistening veneer on their skin and they were frozen in poses which indicated they'd been caught unawares. There was a single pistol on the floor, close to the far wall.

"What killed these poor bastards?" asked Garcia.

"I don't know, soldier."

"Not a mark on them."

McKinney shook his head sadly. "I thought we might find answers. All we've got are more corpses." He backed out of the room, his desire to explore further gone. "Let's try the lift again."

They hadn't travelled more than a few paces, when the noise came to them. It was a shuffling, scraping thump, somewhere around one of the corners at the T-junction. The men stopped in their tracks and turned slowly, silently in the direction the sound had come from.

"What the hell was that?" breathed Garcia.

"I don't think I want to find out," said Mills. He lowered the barrel of his plasma repeater into the firing position.

"We're going back to the lift," said McKinney. He wasn't a

coward, but he had no appetite to face whatever it was made the noise. "Keep it quiet."

The three of them walked steadily backwards in the direction of the lift, occasionally checking over their shoulders in case they tripped. The thumping came again – it sounded like a sack of dead bodies being dragged a single, long pace before they were dropped to the floor. Whatever made the sound, it was big, heavy and coming closer.

McKinney glanced behind – the lift wasn't far and its steadily-glowing interior beckoned through the wild flickering of the personnel quarter's lights. It was tempting to turn and sprint towards it, but the sound of running feet would definitely alert whatever it was coming, assuming it didn't already know about the soldiers.

"A little faster," said McKinney.

Garcia and Mills required no encouragement and they kept pace. The sound came for a third time and then a fourth. The interval was much shorter than before.

"It knows we're here," said Garcia, fingering one of the grenades in the belt across his chest.

"We can shoot it, whatever it is," said Mills.

They entered the lift, just as the sound came again. It was difficult to be sure exactly how far away it was and McKinney tried hard to believe it wasn't too close to the T-junction corner.

"Get this lift moving, Lieutenant."

The lift was big, but the doors opened wide. It was difficult to remain entirely hidden and McKinney was intensely aware that one side of his body was visible when he attempted to operate the access panel. His first try failed, as did his second.

"It's coming," said Mills.

McKinney kept trying. "Can you see it? Shoot if there's movement."

"I can't see it, Lieutenant. The sound is right around that corner."

The scraping seemed to echo off the walls and the thinness of the atmosphere added a strange muffling effect. McKinney swiped the panel again.

"Got it!" he said, watching the doors pull closed.

The last thing McKinney saw through the gap was a huge shape drag itself into sight, sixty metres away. It was pitch-black, yet with a glistening sheen on its flesh. Its overall shape was unclear, but it left McKinney with the certainty that it was colossal and incredibly deadly. Whatever the hell it was, he had no idea how it had got down here or what it was doing.

The lift ascended and the three men inside remained silent, each with an unspoken certainty of how close their deaths had been.

"We've gotta get what we came for and get out of this place, Lieutenant," said Mills.

"I hear you, soldier."

To McKinney's infinite relief, the lift doors opened on the uppermost level and the three soldiers found the rest of the squad waiting expectantly.

"Any luck?" asked Sergeant Li. Then, "What's wrong?"

"There're two levels below us," said McKinney. "We found the bottom by accident and there's something down there. I think it killed the crew of this station."

"Are we going to shoot it?"

"Not a chance. We're all of us getting in this lift and we're going to the middle level. We found what we're looking for."

The squad filed into the lift, a few of them picking up on the latent fear in McKinney, Mills and Garcia.

"That bad, huh?" asked Roldan.

"Yeah."

McKinney wasn't going to take any chances. He pointed one

finger directly at Hiven-Tar's chest. "You can operate this damned lift. Take us to the middle floor and nowhere else."

The Ghost drew his fingers over the panel and the lift door closed. The sensation of falling reached McKinney's stomach and then the lift doors opened, this time at the main operating room for the comms hub.

The squad hurried out and McKinney gave them a warning.

"No one uses this lift except Hiven-Tar or one of the other Ghosts. Do you understand?"

The men did understand. It was unheard of for McKinney to be scared of anything and they had no desire to see what it was for themselves.

"We need to move fast," he continued. "Whatever it was, it got to the lower levels somehow and there might be a way for it to reach us here."

"There ain't no doors in this room, Lieutenant," said Guzman.

It was true – the only access was through the lift shaft and that was the worry. McKinney crouched close to the floor of the lift and listened, half-expecting to hear the scrape-thump from below. There was nothing, though it didn't make him feel any better.

He pushed himself upright and surveyed the scene in the room. Hiven-Tar and his Ghosts were already gathered around one of the consoles, with Corporal Bannerman listening in to their conversation. McKinney strode over to find out what they were planning.

CHAPTER NINE

"DO you think you can access the logs?" asked McKinney.

"Yes, given sufficient time," said Raxil-Ven. The Ghast was sitting on a metal chair, tapping out a series of commands on one of the many keypads.

"How much time?"

"I don't know. Minutes or hours."

McKinney would have preferred a more precise answer. He didn't want to pressure the Ghast, especially since he had no idea how much effort was involved in accessing a comms hub log.

"Raxil-Ven is one of the team responsible for the hardware design and programming of our latest comms hardware," said Hiven-Tar.

"That's reassuring, but we still don't have much time," said McKinney, repeating the obvious.

"You are concerned by what you have seen on the level below," said the Ghast.

"I'm concerned by everything at the moment."

Hiven-Tar took a seat near to Raxil-Ven and continued speaking to McKinney. "Ghast and Estral technology stems from the same original seed. There is divergence, yet I can see the similarities." The Ghost smiled. "If a way of doing something is good, then it will always be good."

"I won't argue that."

Minutes went by and McKinney made three more visits to the lift. On each occasion, there was no sound to be heard and, while he didn't exactly relax, he began to think the creature beneath them had no way to get up the shaft.

"Have a look at this," said Raxil-Ven.

The Ghost had found a map of the installation in the Estral databanks. He brought it onto one of the display screens in order for McKinney to see it. The surface antenna was the tip of what was an impressively-large iceberg. In addition to the areas they'd already discovered, there were several more interconnected parts of the facility, as well as two further levels below the living quarters, which were themselves eight thousand metres below the main transmission room. The map didn't make it clear what equipment was installed in these other sections.

"This is a large base for a species in hiding to build," said McKinney.

"It is fifteen years old, according to the records. Perhaps the Estral are not so utterly defeated as our respective intelligence teams would have us believe. This hub has the capability to route comms for two hundred worlds or more and it has the capacity for expansion. It is far more than a simple relay station and that surface antenna must be incredibly advanced."

McKinney's head swum. "Even Fleet Admiral Duggan believes the Estral are neutralised."

"The presence of this base suggests otherwise, whilst at the same time proving nothing."

"Maybe the Vraxar are regretting a war on two fronts."

"It is not unknown for one side to believe its opponents are defeated, only for contrary facts to emerge."

"What's this here?" asked McKinney, tracing a line on the map with his finger.

"One of the original construction passages, I believe." Hiven-Tar decreased the zoom level on the map and more of it became visible. "Here are two more such passages."

"Other ways inside."

"Perhaps. Each of these tunnels have been sealed in three places." The Ghast paused before it spoke again. "What do you think you saw, Lieutenant? Vraxar?"

"It wasn't any kind of Vraxar I've seen before."

"We should finish here quickly."

"Amen to that."

After another few minutes, the squad were distinctly edgy. McKinney had a word with them, hoping to keep them distracted. He knew what the problem was – when it came to combat, it was the *anticipation* which was the hardest part to handle. Once the fighting started, these soldiers were trained to respond - they'd shoot straight and without hesitation. Now, they had the threat hanging over them, without a chance to do anything about it.

Raxil-Ven came up with the goods.

"I have unlocked the audit data trail," he announced.

McKinney was there in a flash. "Can you unravel it?"

"Some of it will require analysis on your warship. However, what I can tell you is that this facility is receiving a stream of data from a deep space monitoring station far beyond the outer reaches of this solar system."

"What did the monitoring station see?"

"An unusually large object appeared between the first and second planets. It remained there for a period of several weeks."

"The Aranol."

"This object vanished several hours ago."

"Then it's lost to us?" McKinney swore.

The Ghast shook his head. "Perhaps not. The Estral moni-toring station harvested a huge quantity of data, including an exact record of a series of decaying particles left behind when the Aranol vanished."

"The Space Corps has some kind of predictive modelling software. It tells us where a spaceship has gone to by the fission cloud it leaves behind after a transit through lightspeed."

"The Estral monitoring station was equipped with a similar facility. Our forebears' technology remains in advance of ours."

"Will this data fit into the memory array on our visors?" asked McKinney. The weight of the number cruncher on his back reminded him of its presence. "Maybe we can download it into this?"

Raxil-Ven rapped on the side of his suit helmet with his knuckles. "There is ample storage in here to contain many hours of the stream data."

"How long will it take to extract from this transmitter?"

"It is ongoing. There is more, Lieutenant Eric McKinney."

"What kind of more?"

"This station is routing a considerable amount of other traffic. The data is encrypted and undoubtedly military in nature, yet it would be a useful source of information for our leaders were we to recover a quantity of it. Assuming our decryption hardware has sufficient brute force to break open the files."

"Are you able to bring some of this data with you?"

"Of course. I will extract as much as I can until the array in my helmet is filled."

"How much longer?"

The Ghast stood. "It is done."

"Is there anything else we require from here? I don't think we'll be coming back."

"I would prefer to spend several more days documenting the

technological capabilities of this comms station. However, in light of our circumstances, it would not be wise."

It was all McKinney needed to hear. He used the open channel to round up the squad and urged them towards the lift. A few of the soldiers had been poking around, but there wasn't far for them to go and they came running. They crowded into the lift and Hiven-Tar stood guard near to the control panel.

"Do not touch," he said.

It was shock to realise that Hiven-Tar was concerned about the creature below. It was the first time McKinney had seen anything close to fear in one of the Ghasts and he didn't like it. He was about to order the lift to the upper level, when Ricky Vega got in first with a question.

"Can you hear that?"

It was as though Vega's words had the power to freeze everyone in place. The squad remained utterly still, listening. McKinney heard it – there was a pattering sound coming from somewhere beneath the lift. The sound was rapid and metallic, like a swarm of steel-legged spiders running up a pipe.

"Take us up!" said McKinney. "Now!"

An object scraped against the underside of the lift. McKinney stamped hard, to remind himself how thick the alloy was. His foot produced a thud which should have been reassuring. Something struck the lift from below with incredible force and the floor buckled. The entire car shook, but its gravity winch held it in place.

"Shit," said Clifton, jumping away from the warped section of the floor.

Hiven-Tar got the lift moving and, for a few seconds, the squad could hear the pattering sounds resume in pursuit. The noises faded rapidly away until the visor sensors could no longer detect them.

While the lift climbed, McKinney did his best to remember

from the map how much distance there was between the transmission room floor and the upper level of this lift shaft. It was two or three thousand metres, he guessed.

At the top, the lift stopped and the door opened.

"Get out!" McKinney ordered. The lift was half-empty before the words had left his mouth. "To the exit lift! Clifton, not you. Or you, Hiven-Tar."

The Ghost hadn't gone far, whilst Clifton was only a few paces away. The soldier stopped mid-stride. "Lieutenant?"

"How many charges are you carrying?"

"Enough to blow the eyebrows off every single Vraxar that ever existed."

"Put them in the lift. On a timer."

"Yes, sir, Lieutenant, sir!"

"Do it quickly. No pissing about."

Clifton dropped his pack, pulled out a charge the size of two fists and set the timer on it. He dropped it onto the floor and casually side-footed it into the lift. The device ended up against the far wall, its countdown timer visible. Clifton scooped up his pack.

"Is that going to be enough?" asked McKinney. He knew what the answer was as soon as he asked the question.

"Yes, sir, it will. I am sure you're aware that each charge can be set to create either a minimal, shaped blast, or I can turn it all the way up to a full ten. In this case I have..."

McKinney cut off the lecture. "Fine. Hiven-Tar, send the lift down."

The Ghost leaned inside, activated the lift and jumped back quickly before the doors closed on him.

"Move," said McKinney, waving them ahead.

Clifton wasn't finished. "Letting off that single charge within the confined spaces of a lift shaft will create a channelled effect on the blast, which may well..."

"I get the idea."

"...be sufficient to incinerate us if we don't run a hell of a lot faster."

With his message delivered, Clifton turned on the speed and pulled out a three-pace lead over McKinney and Hiven-Tar. The Ghasts weren't known for their outright pace, but this one gave no impression he was keen to die in the immediate future.

"Couldn't you have used something smaller?" shouted McKinney, following Clifton into the closest of the upper conduit rooms.

"You asked me to use the entire pack, Lieutenant!" said Clifton accusingly. "I only used one charge."

The charge exploded when they were halfway across the second conduit room. The explosion rumbled and created a shockwave which McKinney felt through his feet. His vision blurred for a second, making him wonder if his eyeballs were vibrating in their sockets. Instinctively, he looked behind, expecting to see the rushing ball of flame which usually accompanied one of Clifton's efforts. For once, there was none, though he saw a cloud of dust and smoke billowing in the previous room.

The squad didn't slow down, even when the tremors died away. McKinney stopped once to listen for sounds of pursuit, but the relay station was quiet once more. He reached the surface lift last and found everyone else inside waiting for him. There was more than one derogatory comment about the standard of fitness amongst the Space Corps' officers, which McKinney chose to overlook. He jumped into the lift and Hiven-Tar activated the panel.

They reached the surface airlock room. Clifton and Whitlock were lounging against one wall and did their best to look alert when the lift doors opened.

"Any news from the ES *Cataclysm*?" asked McKinney.

"Nothing significant. Did you find anything, Lieutenant?"

"We got what we need and now we're getting out of here."

Clifton and Whitlock picked up on the mood, but saved their questions. The squad hurried out of the installation. The shuttle was waiting exactly where they'd left it and McKinney couldn't remember being so relieved at the thought of getting onboard. The group piled inside and McKinney reached the cockpit just behind Sergeant Li.

Once the external door was closed and he was sure everyone was onboard, McKinney fed power into the shuttle's engines and pulled hard back on the control stick. The vessel lifted directly away from the surface. McKinney didn't let up and waited until they were several kilometres above the surface before he activated the autopilot. Only then did he allow himself to wind down.

"What was that all about?" asked Sergeant Li.

"We disturbed something and I haven't got any idea what it was. What about you, Hiven-Tar?"

The Ghost shrugged. "Some things are better left unguessed."

The choice of words left McKinney with a feeling that the alien had ideas which it wasn't going to reveal. He told himself he'd ask about it later if the opportunity arose. For the moment, he was content to remain ignorant. This part of the mission had been a success and that was what counted.

A few minutes later, Shuttle One docked with the *ES Cataclysm*.

CHAPTER TEN

CAPTAIN CHARLIE BLAKE studied the data obtained from the relay station with great interest and mounting trepidation. The Estral monitoring station had recorded detailed observations on the movement of the Vraxar in this solar system. There wasn't only a visual stream, there were also reams of other data to accompany it. This data contained all manner of information, some of which was seemingly irrelevant. The most important fact was that the relay station had received and then re-transmitted the movements not only of the Aranol, but also several hundred additional Vraxar spaceships.

"They had sufficient vessels in this solar system to flood the Confederation and destroy everything," said Blake.

"Perhaps we should be grateful for the ongoing resistance of the Estral," said Decker. From the expression on her face it was clear she knew the history. Humanity's past conflict with the Estral didn't make her words any less true.

"There must be a dozen intel teams in the Space Corps who would kill for this information," said Blake.

The monitoring station hadn't quite caught a perfect view of the Aranol. The Vraxar planetship was half-concealed by the second planet and the background light from the sun made the spaceship appear as a pitch-black semi-circle, like a moon coming out from behind its planet.

"I am trying to enhance the image," said Hiven-Tar. "There may be clues about the enemy capabilities."

"Please focus your efforts on the activities of these other spaceships," Blake replied. "Have you finished a count?"

"The Estral monitoring station observed 857 Vraxar space-ships," said Hiven-Tar promptly. "The largest was approximately twenty-three thousand metres in length. I also confirmed the presence of exactly twenty Neutralisers."

"I hoped I wouldn't run into any more of those bastards," said Blake with feeling.

He sat and replayed several of the sensor streams, building up a picture of recent events. The feed from the Estral monitoring station went back several weeks, which was the furthest extent the Ghasts had chosen to download into their suit helmets. The Estral method of recording time was unfamiliar, but the Ghasts were able to make something of it. The upshot was, the feed didn't go back quite far enough to capture the moment the *Ulterior-2* was thought to have traversed the portal within *Ix-Gastiol*'s central coil.

"No sign of the Hadron," Blake said.

"The Aranol does nothing for many days," said Ran-Lor.

"Waiting."

The majority of the action took place over a few short hours. The monitoring station was tuned to read the fission clouds of inbound spaceships and, in groups of seven or eight, the Vraxar ships arrived in this solar system. They made no hostile moves, so were evidently unaware they were being watched, and they were clearly unaware of the relay station. As soon as the enemy warships exited lightspeed, they headed directly for the Aranol.

"As far as I can see, they all docked," said Blake.

"I concur," said Hiven-Tar.

"And then, eight minutes after the final Vraxar spaceship docked, the Aranol vanished into lightspeed." Blake swore loudly. "We missed them by five hours."

"What exactly were we planning to do?" asked Decker.

"I don't know, Lieutenant."

"I'm still working on the predictive modelling," said Dunbar. "The Vraxar left behind a signature type I've never seen before. It's making it difficult to be sure I'm entering the correct parameters into the software."

"The monitoring station got the raw data, we need to turn it into something useful," said Blake. "In the meantime, let's keep up the search for the *Ulterior-2*."

When McKinney first reported the success of the mission to Folsgar, Blake had been uplifted with the thought they had obtained solid information they could put to good use in the search for the *Ulterior-2* and the pursuit of the Aranol.

"I should have known nothing would come that easily," he said under his breath.

If it came to it, he didn't have a clue what he was going to do if he ever did come face-to-face with the Aranol, beyond the vague plan of dropping the Sorrow bomb somewhere close by and then running into lightspeed with his fingers crossed. When it came to ultra-high explosives, there was no need for subtlety, but he worried that a lack of finesse would show up in the final outcome.

For the next hour, Blake piloted the ES *Cataclysm* on a computer-generated course that allowed them to scan as much of the solar system's planets as possible, in the hope they'd find a clue about the *Ulterior-2*'s location.

Lieutenant Dunbar spent the time struggling with the predictive modelling software and secretly, Blake was grateful that he wasn't yet required to make the choice between chasing the Aranol, or searching for the missing Hadron.

Lieutenant Decker was not idle. Although the death of Trudy Flynn was in no way attributable to anything other than an unfortunate accident, Decker had taken it hard, even if she tried to hide it. She spent every spare minute trying to find out exactly what had caused Flynn to remain in a different phase when the Lightspeed Catapult had fired. It was important work – if the mission to recover the *Ulterior-2* was successful, there would be a lot more people coming on the return leg of the journey.

Decker came to speak with Blake. He looked sideways, juggling his focus between her and the ongoing search.

"Have you learned anything?" he asked.

"Bits and pieces. The return might be rough."

Blake caught the meaning. "You think we got lucky to only lose Lieutenant Flynn?"

"Yes, sir. In a nutshell, the catapult switches everyone to a zero-time condition, which effectively means that for the infinitesimally tiny moment during which we travel through the wormhole, our physical bodies are immune to any harm whatsoever. Then, the catapult switches us back to normal time. With Lieutenant Flynn, there was either a software error or a hardware fault and she was exposed to some of the effects of the launch into the wormhole. Next time it could be far worse."

"Can you mitigate?"

"Given time I should be able to find out exactly what went wrong and prevent it from happening again. I've got one or two things in mind. It's difficult without my team."

"You've become too accustomed to having backup," he replied, not unkindly.

"It's been years since I last captained a warship." She laughed. "I'm not sure if I miss it."

"We're relying on you to get us home, Lieutenant."

"I know. I'm giving it everything I've got."

"How is the work going on the accuracy?"

Her face brightened at the question. "I think I've got it nailed. Sometimes you need the data from a live test in order to highlight faults in the theory. Next time we should end up on the nose."

"There *will* be a next time," Blake said. "One way or another, we'll make it home."

Decker nodded and tried to smile. "Absolutely."

Thirty minutes later, Lieutenant Dunbar worked out how to extract the information they needed from the fission prediction software. Not only that, he had two extra pieces of highly-significant data.

"The Aranol took off in this direction, sir," he said. "You should have the star chart overlay on your screen."

"Got it," said Blake. A red line marked the course along which the Vraxar travelled and it ended in another solar system, this one five hours' high lightspeed travel away. The *Cataclysm*'s data banks held almost no details about what they would find there.

Dunbar felt obliged to explain the reason for the delay in obtaining the results. "The Aranol's propulsion systems are different to ours, sir."

"As you'd expect, given the size of the thing," said Conway.

"It took me a while to analyse the energy readings. The details were familiar but at first I didn't realise exactly what I was looking at."

"Get on with it please, Lieutenant."

"The Aranol left behind a similar particle to that emitted by our Lightspeed Catapult. Except not quite so concentrated."

"What have you concluded?"

"The enemy ship's propulsion system is based on similar principles to that of our catapult."

"Do you mean to say they've also worked out how to refine Obsidiar?"

"No, sir, definitely not. I think they have modified the base material so that it generates a greater output than standard Obsidiar. There is nothing *refined* about the end product."

Blake considered the words. It more or less added up – the centre of *Ix-Gastiol* had been filled with bands of what he'd initially thought were depleted Obsidiar. Yet those bands had possessed the ability to create a portal across unimaginable distances and to maintain that portal. The power requirements for such a feat were immense. Where Obsidiar had originally been considered a source of unrivalled power, now it was beginning to seem limited.

"The more power you can generate, the more you need and the faster you invent new things that demand ever-increasing quantities of it," he said.

"That sums it up, sir. I can't imagine how much raw Obsidiar would be required to keep something like the Aranol going."

"Everything they've managed to plunder, no doubt."

"There's more," said Dunbar. "Once I figured out what they were using for propulsion, I was able to extrapolate the data and come up with a couple of theories. Firstly – I predict that the journey which will take five hours in the *ES Cataclysm* will take them only one."

"The *Cataclysm* isn't exactly a slow ship."

"It gets worse. If I'm right, they used only the smallest fraction of their available engine output on that lightspeed jump. They have a lot in the tank."

"How much?"

Dunbar's reaction showed he'd been put on the spot and he

was reluctant to shoulder the responsibility of what he was about to say.

"Best case, it'll take them a year to reach Confederation Space. If they ever decide to do so."

"What's the worst case?"

"Less than a week."

"Damnit!"

"They are tied up with the Estral," said Ran-Lor. "It could be they lack motivation to travel further afield."

"They'll come, whether sooner or later."

"A likely event is not a certain event."

The Ghast's words were true, though not especially helpful. To Blake, it felt as if he were always up against the constraints of time. Every negative possibility was due *soon,* and each victory over the Vraxar only produced a new set of negative possibilities, each one requiring instant action to counter or overcome. It was extremely irritating.

Then, Dunbar dangled the carrot.

"The *ES Ulterior-2* followed the Aranol, sir."

The words caught Blake unawares. "What?"

"At least I'm pretty sure it's the *Ulterior-2*, sir. They must have been watching from way out with their stealth modules activated. The Estral monitoring station didn't know it had found a spaceship, but it harvested enough data for me to work out that one of our spaceships was on the outskirts of this solar system, and keeping its engine readings heavily suppressed. Those readings vanished a short time after the Aranol entered lightspeed."

"That's got to be them," said Blake, not quite able to believe it.

"There are no other Space Corps vessels out here, sir."

"Lieutenant Dunbar, that is excellent work. I think I should kiss you."

"No, sir. That will absolutely not be necessary."

It was an outstanding application of skill to find the *Ulterior-2* at such a distance, particularly when its stealth modules were active. The discovery revealed just how advanced the Estral's monitoring stations were and it also showed how talented Lieutenant Dunbar was when it came to data analysis.

"We've got our first proof that the *Ulterior-2* is operational," said Blake. "They must be alive."

"They remain unreachable on the comms," said Ran-Lor. "I have tried again to make contact."

"There could be many reasons for that," Blake replied, only really able to think of one or two. "We're going after them."

"I've entered the details into our navigation system," said Dunbar. "I will activate on your word, sir."

"Five hours, you say?"

"Four hours, fifty-six minutes."

"If the Aranol completes the journey in a single hour, and if they are already more than six hours ahead, they will be ten hours ahead of us in total when we arrive." Blake leaned on the edge of his console to think. "Is ten hours enough for them to complete their business and then move elsewhere? If so, we may well lose them for good."

"I can't recommend a second activation of the Lightspeed Catapult, sir," said Lieutenant Decker.

"I was only half-considering it," Blake admitted.

"It's not yet a reliable method of travel."

"Agreed."

Use of the Lightspeed Catapult would be a huge gamble, and, in the circumstances, Blake conceded it would be an inexcusable risk. He gave the order to enter lightspeed and Lieutenant Dunbar obliged. The *ES Cataclysm's* engines spooled up and fired the warship at maximum velocity along the course taken by the Aranol a few hours previously.

Blake endured the journey and spent much of it in thought.

He felt as though he and his crew were interlopers into a war the Confederation were not part of. It was highly significant news to find the Estral and Vraxar were, to all impressions, still locked in the middle of a ferocious conflict that the Space Corps believed was concluded a long time ago. When it came to gathering reliable intelligence across such distances, it was no wonder there was a margin for error. While it could be the case that the Estral were, in fact, close to final defeat, Blake didn't think it likely. If so, the Aranol would have followed *Ix-Gorghal* and *Ix-Gastiol* into Confederation Space.

"If we manage to wipe out the Aranol using the Sorrow bomb, what happens after?" he wondered. "Will we end up trading the Vraxar for the Estral?"

"We're buying time, sir," said Decker. "It's the most valuable resource - even more so than Obsidiar."

He knew she was speaking the truth, even if the implications were chilling. It meant that humanity had entered an era in which conflict was continuous and unavoidable. It was a time in which the Confederation would be required to fight tooth and nail for every added second of existence in a universe filled with species which seemed to think it was not only their right, but a necessity, to murder every other living creature they encountered.

Blake asked himself if he was becoming too cynical. With sadness, he knew his eyes were now wide open to the realities of the present and the future.

CHAPTER ELEVEN

IT WASN'T LONG after the *ES Cataclysm*'s arrival that Captain Blake realised things were about to get complicated. As per his instruction, they'd exited lightspeed on the fringes of the solar system, so as to observe the enemy positions without being detected. Therefore, the *Cataclysm* – with its stealth modules active - flew at a distance somewhat in excess of three billion miles from the local sun, which the spaceship's computer named Vaean.

"Even an object as large as the Aranol may be difficult to identify from here," said Hiven-Tar.

"We're not rushing in," Blake replied. "Not yet, anyway."

"There are twelve planets in this system and in excess of forty significant moons," continued the Ghast. "There is a thirty percent chance the Aranol may not be directly observable from here."

"Once you've completed a super-fars sweep, we can execute a short-range transit to the far side of Vaean."

If there was one thing the Ghasts didn't do, it was complain. Hiven-Tar and Ran-Lor used the sensors to gather information from the surrounding space and then began analysing it for any anomalies which might indicate the presence of an enemy warship.

"The fifth planet was once inhabited," said Ran-Lor. "Now it is not."

Blake crossed over to look at the sensor feed. The fifth planet was larger than average and, at first glance, appeared to be just another cold rock.

"See this area," said the Ghast, zooming in the sensors. They were too far away to get anything more than a rudimental image, but Blake realised what he was looking at.

"Cities made of metal," he said.

"Now melted and their occupants certainly dead," said Hiven-Tar.

A large area of the planet's visible side had been levelled by terraforming machinery. This flat area was covered in undulating fields of metal – endless kilometres of it, some of it burning hot from retained heat.

"There are temperatures of several hundred degrees in places," said Ran-Lor. "I cannot imagine anyone has survived, unless they are far beneath the surface."

"Deaths without meaning. Countless lives gone," said Blake sadly. "Why build here, in a place so bleak?"

"We Ghasts have similar cities to this – we are not so different from our forebears. Some planets will not sustain life except that which is sealed against the vacuum outside."

"There must have been something valuable for the Estral to establish an operation on such an inhospitable world."

"In the midst of a war there may be no opportunity to completely terraform a planet into something beautiful, Captain Charles Blake. The Estral have done what was necessary in order to survive."

"Except the Vraxar found them."

"They did. The sensor visual image is not clear, but an analysis of the readings shows a mixture of alloy and carbon on the planet's surface, consistent with the use of incendiaries."

"The Vraxar have enough Estral in their armies," said Blake.

"Yes – this has become a pogrom. The Vraxar have no need to finish their war with the Estral, yet they have chosen to continue."

Blake's mind whirled with everything he'd learned, both from his personal experience with the Vraxar and the reports from elsewhere. The enemy said so many different, conflicting things, there was hardly any sense amongst it. They claimed other species as their children, yet did everything they could to exterminate those who resisted them, or those they no longer required to fill their ranks. Nothing about the Vraxar fitted.

"This is madness," he said.

"That is obvious to any observer," said Hiven-Tar.

"You don't understand," said Blake. "An entire species cannot be collectively driven by madness."

The Ghost blinked his grey eyes. "They are controlled by an individual who is mad."

"It's the only explanation for everything. The telepathic Vraxar which Lieutenant McKinney met on *Ix-Gastiol* told him they once had noble aims. Perhaps it was right, but now those aims have become corrupted until they are unrecognizable from what they once were!"

"The Aranol," said Ran-Lor.

"Perhaps the name encompasses more than just the planet ship. What if it refers to the being which guides the Vraxar?"

"The death of this leader will stop our enemy."

Blake felt suddenly exhausted, as though his burst of inspiration had drained him of energy. "The death of their leader will only come with the defeat of the Aranol."

The discovery of the recently-destroyed cities suggested to Blake that the conflict between the two alien species must still rage in parts of the Vaean system. That meant the Aranol could be close enough to direct the ships in the Vraxar fleet.

"The enemy have a presence here," said Blake. "Find them."

"I have located wreckage," said Hiven-Tar. "Between the fourth and the fifth planets."

"What kind of wreckage?"

"I cannot tell you for certain. There is much of it – there has been an extensive conflict in this solar system. The emissions readings are faint from so far, but I believe we have missed the most intensive part of the fighting by only an hour or two."

Blake had a look at the sensor data and found that Hiven-Tar had understated the quantity of debris. Pieces of hot alloy and Gallenium drifted in a wide band for several thousand kilometres and some of it was on a collision course with the sixth planet.

"There must have been a hundred or more ships involved," said Blake. "This was a major confrontation between two powerful fleets."

"If the Aranol came there can have been only one outcome."

"Find those bastards!" snarled Blake with sudden anger. "Let's see how their shields hold against our bomb."

"We will concentrate our search on the fourth and fifth planets," said Ran-Lor.

Blake caught something in the words. "What have you discovered?"

"Our sensor feed registered the presence of a [Translation unclear: *ghost*.]"

Comms operators hid behind the word *ghost* when they found an anomaly which they weren't yet ready to admit was a spaceship. The best officers always knew.

"You're sure," stated Blake.

"There is a spaceship in orbit around the fourth planet," the Ghast confirmed.

"The computer has named the place Jonli if that's any use," said Dunbar.

"A hundred trillion planets, a hundred trillion names," said Lieutenant Conway. "And I can remember fewer than thirty of them."

Blake wasn't listening and he spoke to Ran-Lor again. "Is there just the one spaceship? I assume it wasn't the Aranol?"

"It wasn't the Aranol," said the Ghast. "This was closer in size to an Oblivion."

"Sir, there are inbound fission signatures on the far side of Jonli," said Dunbar.

"How many?"

"I can't give you a definitive answer - there are several over-lapping particle clusters. I'd guess we have somewhere between five and twelve craft incoming."

"Estral? Vraxar?"

"I don't know."

It was starting to get hot in this area of Estral Space and Blake wasn't sure how to take advantage of it. He kept his eyes on the sensor feed of Jonli, trying to divine something useful from the image. The planet – a red sphere of dust and rock with a single, equally-arid moon - gave away nothing.

"Could the Aranol be hidden behind Jonli?" he asked.

"The planet is large enough to conceal it," said Hiven-Tar. "As are all of the planets, assuming the positioning was correct."

"Is it likely?"

The Ghast wasn't sure how to respond. "If the Aranol were behind a planet, there is a greater chance we would see its edges than for it to be completely obscured."

"Except for the first and eleventh planets, which are behind the sun," added Ran-Lor.

"I want to see what the hell is going on," growled Blake. Deep down, he wanted to get involved. At the beginning of this war, when he was a less experienced captain, he'd have ordered the SRT by now. As it was, he'd learned the benefits of caution. He caught Ran-Lor watching him.

"No battle is won on tip-toe, Captain Charles Blake."

The words hit home and Blake nodded. There was something happening around Jonli and if the Aranol was on the far side of the planet, hidden from view, there might be a chance to use the Obsidiar bomb on it before the Vraxar realised what was going on. Of course, only a fool would SRT straight into the middle of a dogfight.

"Lieutenant Dunbar, we are going to execute a short-range transit. I would like to arrive as close to the surface of Jonli's moon as possible. Keep us out of sight of those newly-arrived spaceships."

"That'll involve a bit of guesswork, sir."

"Do your best. We only need a second or two in order to activate the stealth modules."

"I have chosen a target, sir."

Blake was interrupted before he could give the order to activate the SRT.

"There are signs of conflict close to Jonli," said Ran-Lor. "We are too far away to provide specifics."

At that moment, something detonated off the planet's surface, covering much of the visible side in the Vraxar's dark energy. Blake watched the grainy image, wondering if the enemy had chosen to destroy the entire planet. Gradually, the darkness faded, revealing a glassy sheen to the area touched by the weapon.

"Sir?" asked Dunbar. "What are your orders?"

"Activate the SRT."

"Yes, sir."

The ES *Cataclysm*'s fission engines created an opening into lightspeed and the cruiser raced across nearly three billion miles in much less than one second.

"Activate stealth modules and shields!" said Blake.

"Both are online, sir."

"Confirm our position."

"We are six hundred kilometres above the surface of Jonli's moon," said Hiven-Tar. The Ghast gave a familiar grin. "A good shot."

It was a little too close for comfort, but Blake wasn't about to complain. He took hold of the control bars and waited for the sensor report.

"There are no enemy craft visible to our sensors," said Ran-Lor. "It is likely they detected our fission cloud and will be aware there is an unknown vessel in the vicinity."

"We'd best not hang around for them to come looking," said Blake.

He checked his console to orient himself. The *Cataclysm* was entirely hidden from Jonli by the planet's moon. Unfortunately, there was still a chance the Aranol could be somewhere, also hidden. The stealth modules were a reassurance, but they'd failed before and Blake didn't want to stumble into trouble.

"Let's do this carefully and see what's going on," he said.

The control bars were comforting to hold and he pushed them along their perfectly-machined alloy slots. They had the perfect amount of resistance and the cruiser accelerated across the moon's surface. The underside sensor feeds showed exactly what he expected – wind-blown red dust, jagged peaks and canyons guarding untold secrets in their endless depths.

A half-orbit was enough to bring the edge of Jonli into view. The parts struck by the Vraxar dark energy weapon had fused into a red-grey glass, which continued to spit and froth.

"Why did they fire at the planet?" asked Blake.

"Sub-surface defensive emplacements," said Hiven-Tar. "There are signs of alloy amongst the fused rock."

"What the hell is going on here?" said Blake.

He brought the ES *Cataclysm* out from the protective cover of the moon. Jonli was half a million kilometres away and he increased the warship's speed until it was at maximum.

"There are two Vraxar warships visible on the cusp of the planet," said Hiven-Tar. "I have fed the details into the tactical system."

Two red circles denoting the enemy spacecraft appeared on one of Blake's screens, along with details on their distance and vector. Both of the craft were larger than the *Cataclysm* and they were at an altitude of one hundred thousand kilometres.

"Let me see."

"On the screen," said Ran-Lor.

The Ghost brought up an image of the Vraxar spaceships. From this distance, the two of them were visible on the same screen. Suddenly, one of them was ripped apart by an enormous explosion of mixed whites and blues. One moment the spaceship was there, the next it was no more than torn pieces of metal, spinning along a thousand separate trajectories.

"What on earth was that?" asked Dunbar in shock.

"A surface-launched missile," said Conway.

"Not just one, surely?" asked Blake.

"I picked up only a single source for the blast, sir."

Blake shook his head. "The payload must have been incredible."

The second Vraxar ship went the same way as the first. This time the central section of the spacecraft remained mostly intact and it rotated wildly, out of control. It was struck again and this time the job was finished.

With sweat beading on his forehead, Blake aimed the *Cataclysm* towards the recent engagement, hoping the stealth modules would fool the Estral ground emplacements as well as any Vraxar ships which might be over the horizon. At two hundred thousand kilometres from Jonli, he altered course to bring them into a high orbit of the planet in order to get a top-down view of the scene.

"There are five more Vraxar warships at an average distance of three hundred thousand kilometres from us," said Ran-Lor. "They are bombarding the surface."

There were four cruiser-sized vessels and a battleship. The largest craft was eight thousand metres long and Blake recognized the type from the engagement on the Tucson base. Missiles streamed from its launch tubes, destined for targets on the surface which the *Cataclysm*'s sensors couldn't yet see.

"There must be something down there they don't want to completely destroy," said Conway with a flash of inspiration.

Blake nodded. "Else they'd have used those incendiaries again."

The five Vraxar ships were allowed to launch their missiles for ten or fifteen seconds, before another of the huge ground-launched missiles exploded, this time against the battleship. The blast expanded into a sphere nearly twenty kilometres across and it engulfed the Vraxar ship.

"What the hell?" said Conway. "Did I just see that?"

"See what?" asked Blake. "Speak clearly, damnit!"

It wasn't Conway who answered. "That missile bypassed their shield, sir," said Lieutenant Decker. "Like it wasn't there."

"You're shitting me?"

The enormous blast sphere which enveloped the battleship receded enough for Blake to see that the spaceship wasn't completely destroyed. Plasma writhed across its hull, keeping the metal ablaze and creating a thick haze of filthy, shimmering smoke. The vessel was badly damaged and there was an uneven crater three thousand metres across, which was rimmed in white.

"How the hell did it survive that?" asked Conway.

"Its armour must be hundreds of metres thick," said Blake in wonder. "That's why they sent it – to absorb the hits from the surface missile station."

"The battleship is operational," said Conway. "It's still firing."

The Vraxar missile onslaught continued, more sporadically than before. Through the smoke, Blake caught sight of numerous smaller explosions and he wondered if the Estral had brought other air defences to bear. Then he realised what these blasts were.

"The battleship is so hot, some of its missiles are exploding in their tubes."

"The wise move would be for that vessel to withdraw," said Hiven-Tar angrily. "Their captain should be ashamed of his incompetence."

"I've suspected for a while their warships are controlled from elsewhere," said Blake. "The Vraxar pursue their military aims until one side or the other is defeated."

"Mutual destruction suits nobody," said Ran-Lor.

"It suits nobody *living*," Blake corrected him. "Or anybody with understandable motives."

A second missile hit the Vraxar battleship. The warhead passed cleanly through its energy shield and tore the craft into two pieces, which Blake's tactical showed him would eventually crash into the surface of Jonli. The largest of the two pieces burned as though the flames were consuming the metal itself. Like a meteor, it dropped towards the ground.

"Impact in ten minutes," said Ran-Lor. "It will make a crater of some magnitude. The second section will impact in twelve minutes."

"Find out what it is the Estral are firing," ordered Blake. "I want everything recorded and stored in our databanks. A missile that can pass through an energy shield is a potential game changer."

Even with the ES *Cataclysm* travelling at full speed, the surface of the planet rotated beneath with a frustrating slowness. They finished crossing over the area of fused rock and the sensors showed dense clouds of dust, which swirled furiously in tornados a hundred kilometres high. During the brief moments in which the surface was visible, the warship's sensors detected missile craters, still glowing with plasma heat.

"I have located two more Vraxar spaceships," said Ran-Lor. "We have line of sight on six."

"Where's the Aranol?" Blake muttered.

"Unless it is sheltering on the far side of the sun, I believe it is elsewhere," said Hiven-Tar.

"The Vraxar have an interest in this place, so why isn't it here?" asked Blake. He slapped his forehead in anger that he hadn't guessed sooner. "The Aranol does not wish to be struck by a barrage of Estral missiles which can fly straight through its shields."

"So it chose to send its warships here instead," said Dunbar.

"With the implication that the Aranol is somewhere close by," said Decker.

Blake hadn't thought of it that way, though Decker's words made perfect sense. The Vraxar were here for something and they wanted it badly enough that it prevented them from simply destroying the entire planet.

"They want the Estral missile tech," he said. "They want missiles which can bypass energy shields."

"There is a facility on the surface," said Hiven-Tar. "I have put it onto the bulkhead screen."

And there it was. The Estral weapons station was almost completely hidden beneath a sea of plasma as the orbiting spaceships continued their attack. The *Cataclysm*'s sensors identified four black pyramids, each more than a thousand metres high and arranged in a square about a central complex. This main building was a low, flat structure, exactly fifteen hundred metres along each side. The pyramids maintained an energy shield protecting the entire facility from the missile onslaught.

"There are two ground launchers within the shield," said Ran-Lor. "Other than that, the Estral have no active defences."

The *Cataclysm*'s battle computer detected a launch and an Estral missile burst away from the surface. It passed through the facility's energy shield and, three seconds later, destroyed one of the Vraxar cruisers. Blake rubbed his eyes.

"Thirty-three thousand klicks per second," he said. Speaking the words didn't make it any easier to comprehend.

"It was still accelerating," said Lieutenant Conway. "It struck the Vraxar ship at slightly more than fifty thousand klicks per second."

Blake's jaw hung open. The Shimmer missiles were the pinnacle of Space Corps ballistic technology and the latest models topped out at 4500 kilometres per second, which was slightly quicker than the latest Ghast Shatterer missiles. Here were the Estral, knocking Vraxar spaceships out of the sky with missiles which not only travelled much, much faster than anything else, they also carried an enormous payload and could fly straight through energy shields. It was unthinkable.

"We can't allow the Vraxar to steal any of those missiles," said Blake.

At that moment, Lieutenant Dunbar announced something which reminded Blake that not every decision was his to make.

"There's another inbound fission signature, sir. Bigger than the last one and coming in right on top of us."

Blake swore. "Battle stations! What are we facing, Lieutenant?"

"More Vraxar, sir. They've sent reinforcements."

The crew scrambled to prepare and another seven Vraxar warships appeared in the vicinity of Jonli.

CHAPTER TWELVE

CAPTAIN BLAKE WAS a firm believer in the principle that if one were facing two powerful and hostile foes, it was best to let them slug it out between themselves before stepping in to the fight. There was a total of twelve Vraxar spaceships within sensor sight, six of which were larger than the *ES Cataclysm*. They positioned themselves about the skies of Jonli and eleven of them unleashed a storm of missile and beam weapons at the Estral energy shield.

The final ship didn't fire. This one was four thousand metres long and from its shape, Blake recognized it as a cargo vessel, similar to the one which had carried the remains of the *ES Determinant*, what seemed like years ago when the Vraxar first came to Atlantis.

Higher above flew the *ES Cataclysm*, with its crew anxiously watching as events unfolded.

"Can you determine how long their journey was by analysing the fission cloud, Lieutenant Dunbar?" asked Blake.

"I can give you a rough estimate now or a detailed one after five or ten minutes of modelling."

"I only require a rough estimate."

"Between thirty and sixty minutes."

"Meaning the Aranol could reach here in a few minutes," mused Blake.

"I guess so, sir."

Blake had the faintest stirrings of an idea, which he couldn't act on yet. Instead, he concentrated on the Vraxar assault on the Estral base. "They aren't holding back," he said.

"What if the Estral shield simply fails?" asked Lieutenant Conway. "The facility will be destroyed and there'll be nothing left to steal."

"The data arrays will be deep underground," said Hiven-Tar. "The Vraxar don't care how much damage they do to the surface."

The Estral fired one of their huge missiles and a Vraxar cruiser was ripped into pieces. A few of the smaller fragments came within a hundred metres of the *ES Cataclysm* and Blake wiped his forehead with his sleeve.

"They can't launch their missiles very quickly," said Conway. "In fact, the irregular intervals make me believe there's a manual element to the loading procedure. Either that or they're having difficulties we're unaware of."

"This must be an experimental facility," said Blake. "We've seen what the Vraxar did to the rest of the planet, as well as to those cities on the fifth planet out. I bet the Estral had plenty of other defences in place until a few hours ago."

"Those pyramids contain a considerable quantity of Obsidiar," said Lieutenant Dunbar. "The energy they provide has a recognizable signature and it's flooding into the shield."

"Can it hold?"

"It *is* holding, sir. Those pyramids are huge and they can probably keep this up for as long as it takes."

"The Vraxar have met their match," said Blake, not for a moment believing it.

The Estral fired again, and this missile tore four thousand metres away from the front section of the largest Vraxar battleship. Positrons scattered away from its engines, but it didn't stop firing, nor attempt to break off. Another missile arrived, thirty seconds after the first and this one was sufficient to finish off the battleship, reducing the mighty vessel to burning wreckage. Dunbar did a quick scan of the largest remaining section and concluded it was completely out of action.

"Another few minutes of this and the Vraxar will need reinforcing again," laughed Conway.

There was something uniquely satisfying about watching the Vraxar get picked off, but Blake couldn't bring himself to smile. They'd been drawn into a side-mission he didn't really want. He knew it was vital to stop the Estral missile tech falling into the hands of the Vraxar, however in reality he wanted to find the *Ulterior-2* and then get after the Aranol. There was the added problem of keeping the ES *Cataclysm* in the midst of the enemy fleet. When their current distraction ended, they stood a far greater chance of detecting the presence of the Space Corps cruiser.

"The Estral have stopped firing," said Conway. "This is the longest interval between launches."

They waited and watched expectantly. No further missiles emerged from the surface launchers.

"What's wrong?" muttered Blake. "This isn't a good time for them to break down."

"It could be anything, sir," said Conway. "If you asked me to lay a bet on it, I'd say they've simply run out of ammunition. Or they're unable to get their existing stocks to the magazine."

It wasn't good news – Blake wanted to see this episode concluded, to give him an opportunity to act. Minutes passed and the Vraxar didn't let up in their attack. Equally, the Estral shields didn't show any sign they would be depleted any time soon. From what Blake knew of the Vraxar, they'd end up losing patience and then blow up the entire planet.

Something else happened.

"The first section of the destroyed Vraxar battleship will impact in sixty seconds," said Ran-Lor. "It's coming down within three hundred kilometres of the facility."

The tumbling wreckage hadn't been high in Blake's mind – he assumed it would land elsewhere on Jonli, yet here it was about to land in the vicinity of the Estral base.

"What's that going to do to the surface shield?" he asked.

"In theory, it's just another impact for it to absorb, sir," said Dunbar.

"In practise?"

"If the Estral shield doesn't penetrate deep enough underground, the shockwave might do them some damage."

The first piece of wreckage struck the surface. It weighed approximately sixteen billion tonnes and, though it wasn't travelling at high velocity, it was nevertheless a grievous event for the planet. The *ES Cataclysm*'s sensors followed the object until the moment it landed. The collision produced a crater with a diameter of several hundred kilometres and a depth of eighty. The shockwave radiated outwards, carrying the surface grit in a red, stinging torrent. Vast fissures snaked away from the epicentre and it looked as though they were engaged in a game of chase with the storm of dust.

"There is significant seismic activity within a thousand kilometres of the impact," said Hiven-Tar.

"You don't say?" said Conway.

"Yes, I do say," said the Ghast in puzzlement.

"Keep your eyes on the Estral base," Blake warned.

The rocky ground upon which the base was established

shook violently, such that the movement was easily seen on the sensor feed. The shocks showed no sign of abating and Blake asked himself if this was terminal for Jonli.

"The second section will impact in ten seconds," announced Hiven-Tar.

The other half of the battleship thundered into the ground at a slower speed than the first. It landed on the edge of the first crater, closer to the Estral missile base. A second series of overlapping shockwaves joined the first, rippling through the ground and making it undulate.

"Look," said Ran-Lor. "I will focus the sensor."

The bulkhead image changed to show a zoomed-in image of the western third of the base. The shockwave struck the invisible perimeter of the shield, forcing thick slabs of rock high upwards, where the shield held them suspended in the air. The seismic waves didn't stop and they pushed progressively greater quantities of stone against the shield.

"How deep does that shield go?" wondered Blake. "That's the question."

The answer was *not deep enough*. The western side of the base was soon covered in debris, which created a deep trench running along the edge of the shield. Suddenly, the northwestern pyramid cracked down the middle. The vibration from the earth knocked the two pieces over and it broke into several massive chunks.

"Three pyramids should be enough, right?" asked Conway.

"Not if they're networked," said Dunbar. "If one fails, they all fail."

The sensor image become suddenly obscured by a red cloud, which took some time to disperse. When the dust thinned, Blake saw that the Estral energy shield had collapsed, depositing several billion tonnes of rubble onto the two western pyramids and nearly burying them. The eastern pyramids and the central building were not left completely intact. The Vraxar continued firing for a few moments after the failure of the shield and their missiles and particle beams obliterated much of the remaining structures. The damage was tremendous and when the last of the explosions died away, Blake couldn't imagine there was anything left to salvage from the Estral base.

"The seismic activity is reducing," said Hiven-Tar. "I expect aftershocks will continue for days or perhaps weeks."

"And you believe there's plenty of that facility underground?" asked Conway. "I wouldn't like to be in there."

"The Vraxar believe," said Ran-Lor.

Four of the ten Vraxar spaceships accelerated to full speed on their gravity engines. Blake had no doubt as to their target.

"They're about to land and take a look."

"There's no sign of a troop transport," said Lieutenant Decker. "The reports I've seen on other Vraxar wreckage suggests they don't carry huge numbers of soldiers on any of their craft bar the Neutralisers."

Blake had seen those reports too. "That was in comparative terms, Lieutenant, and much of it was based on guesswork. There are likely to be several thousand troops on these four spaceships. Remember, we believe they were sent here with the express purpose of acquiring the Estral missile technology. They'll need bodies on the ground for that."

"True."

The four Vraxar cruisers – each comparable in size to the *ES Cataclysm*, made best speed for the surface. At an altitude of two thousand metres, they hovered to one side of the base, waiting.

"Is it too rough for them to land?" asked Dunbar, scratching his head.

"It can't be and since when did the Vraxar give a damn about health and safety?" said Conway.

There were few things capable of troubling a ten billion

tonne spaceship, but it appeared as though an exceptionally strong earthquake was a step too far for the Vraxar. Their ships waited in the air for five minutes, before they abruptly descended. A few seconds later, they were in a surprisingly neat row, with the closest one parked adjacent to the remains of the eastern two pyramids and a little way inside the original perimeter of the base energy shield.

"What happens next?" asked Dunbar.

"What happens next is the Vraxar unload twenty thousand troops, who try to find a way into the base. Once they kill everyone and locate the main data array – not necessarily in that order – they will call down the cargo ship and it will carry off their spoils, probably by taking it to the Aranol."

"Are you planning to follow the cargo ship?" asked Dunbar.

In truth, Blake was working on an alternative plan, though it was one which involved a certain amount of destruction, rather than meekly following a cargo vessel to its mothership.

"There might be another way," he said, stepping towards the bulkhead screen and tracing his forefinger along the length of each Vraxar cruiser, one by one. "Look at them there," he said. "Parked up so neatly and tidily. It would be a shame if something happened to them."

"Enough of the games, sir," said Lieutenant Conway. "What do you have in mind?"

Blake smiled nastily. "Overcharge repeater."

"There are ten enemy warships," said Dunbar.

"That's right. Ten."

"And if we somehow manage to destroy a few of them, won't it bring the Aranol here to investigate?"

"That's the idea."

From Dunbar's expression, he had numerous objections to the plan, yet couldn't quite conjure up the words to articulate them.

"I'll prepare for our inevitable short-range transit," he said. "Loading up across four cores."

Lieutenant Decker had a warning. "I'll remind you the over-charge repeater carries the possibility of burning out our Obsidiar-T core, sir. No core means no going home."

"I checked the design sheets. The repeater draws a lot of power, but it's only a fraction of that used by the catapult. It's a calculated risk."

"Yes, sir. A calculated risk involving experimental hardware."

"This is what we're doing, Lieutenant. We'll kill the Vraxar, deny them access to valuable missile tech and draw in the Aranol."

"I have no objections, sir."

Blake entered some details into the *Cataclysm*'s tactical system. "Lieutenants Decker and Conway, I am providing you with a list of priorities," he said. "Let's see how many we can knock out."

"The cruisers are out of range," said Conway. "We've got a fifty thousand klicks maximum on the repeater."

"I'm going to bring us in closer."

"Assuming you plan to prevent the enemy's deployment, you will need to act soon," said Hiven-Tar.

On the sensor feed, Blake saw a tiny, dark snake moving away from the nose of one of the Vraxar cruisers.

"There they go," he said.

"I estimate there to be several hundred enemy troops already on the ground," said the Ghast.

"Let's see what we can do give them a surprise."

Blake took a firm grip on the control rods and fed in full power. The *Cataclysm* responded with effortless grace, accelerating to its highest speed in a few short seconds.

"Bring the overcharge repeater online," he said.

"It is online and ready to fire, sir."

"Let's give them hell."

At fifty thousand kilometres, the activation pad for the weapon lit up.

"Fire," said Blake, not quite sure what to expect.

He was not disappointed.

CHAPTER THIRTEEN

THE OVERCHARGE PARTICLE beam turret gave a familiar whine. The sound climbed and then stabilised at a level which was not uncomfortable. It held for a second or two, which was just long enough for Blake to become concerned that something was wrong.

"What...?" he began.

The weapon fired. Blake's expectations – taken from the design documentation – were set for a five-second interval between each discharge. Instead, he got something closer to a one-second interval.

The beam dome gave a heavy thump and a line of pure energy arced from the front of the *ES Cataclysm* to the first of the four Vraxar cruisers. In the place of impact, the target's armour and engines were heated to several million degrees. The heat spread outwards, until the entire spaceship glowed white and it split apart.

The beam fired again and again with a thump-thump-thump. Each expulsion of energy destroyed one of the Vraxar cruisers and set the rocky ground alight with the incredible heat.

Blake swore, Decker swore and Conway swore. Lieutenant Dunbar had been brought up better and he kept his eyes locked to his console.

"We've lost the stealth modules!" he said. "The repeater's done something to them."

"Get them back," said Blake. "Now."

"I'm working on it."

On his console, Blake watched the needles jump crazily on the Obsidiar-T core. The utilisation on the warship's processing clusters was nailed on one hundred percent and showed no sign of falling. The die was cast and it was too late to worry about the short-term consequences. With an expression somewhere between a grimace and a snarl, Blake brought the *ES Cataclysm* away from the surface. With its stealth cloak gone, the *Cataclysm* was about to become the target of a great deal of attention.

The Vraxar spaceships in the skies above Jonli didn't take long to react. Several particle beams lanced into the *ES Cataclysm*'s energy shield, knocking a chunk out of its reserves. The Vraxar also launched a few hundred missiles, which streaked through space.

"Where's our repeater?" said Blake.

"I'm not sure, sir. I'm trying to get it online again."

"How long?"

"I'm not sure."

"Fire whatever we have that *is* working."

The *Cataclysm*'s Havoc cannons boomed and six Shimmer missiles burst from their tubes, along with Lambdas and several thousand shock drones. Many of the Vraxar missiles were fooled by the drones and they exploded before reaching the cruiser.

The drones had no effect on energy weapons and the Vraxar fired their disintegration beams alongside their particle beams.

"Since their cargo vessel isn't shooting at us, it's only five versus one," said Conway.

"We're not a Hadron or a Galactic," said Dunbar. "Our shield wasn't designed to take this much punishment."

Blake's tactical screen showed him the mountain they had to climb. Two of the remaining enemy vessels were huge, whilst the other three were merely the size of heavy cruisers. Ran-Lor had locked a main sensor array onto each one and divided the images across the bulkhead screen. Each of the enemy craft looked as though it had been made to a different design by a different species. The largest was ten thousand metres long, dark grey and V-shaped, whilst the others were a mixture of shapes and sizes.

"I was expecting more than four shots out of the repeater," he said, shouting over the reverberation of the Havoc cannons. "Where is it?"

"I'm working on it!" said Conway. "I thought it was a heat issue, but it's something else. The weapon still won't activate."

Lieutenant Decker wasn't idle. "It's no longer tied into the Obsidiar-T core," she said. "There's a failsafe mechanism which has identified the repeater as a power leak and disconnected it from the power source."

"Fix it and quickly!"

"I'm trying."

A series of attacks brought the *Cataclysm*'s energy shield below forty percent. The Vraxar warships remained stationary, as if they were confident the cruiser was already a spent force. The thought made Blake angry and he brought the spaceship higher from the planet's surface until each of the enemy craft was in range of the overcharge repeater.

"Now would be a good time," he said.

"Tie-in complete!" said Decker.

"It's ready to fire," confirmed Conway.

"What are you waiting for, Lieutenant? You have your targets."

"Firing."

The overcharge repeater thumped and then again. The largest Vraxar ship became molten but it didn't break up. The repeater fired for a third time and pieces of the enemy battleship were hurled across the sky.

"Something's up with the Obsidiar-T core," said Decker.

The repeater fired again and Blake heard a new sound – there was an underlying rumble coming from the front of the ship. To his horror, he noticed that his hands had the same out-of-phase appearance as the time they'd fired the Lightspeed Catapult. He turned and noticed the others were also affected – their outlines were blurred and their movements looked out of synch.

"What's going on, Lieutenant Decker?" he shouted.

"I don't know, sir!"

Lieutenant Conway was seemingly oblivious. She activated the overcharge repeater twice more, this time reducing the second-largest Vraxar ship into so many billions of tonnes of molten alloy and liquid Gallenium.

The underlying rumble was joined by a shriek of something stressed far beyond its limits. "Cease fire!" yelled Blake. His words sounded distant and they came just as the Havoc cannons fired.

Conway either didn't hear or she was having so much fun she pretended. The repeater dome thumped twice, scoring another kill.

"Shut it down!" said Blake.

He saw Decker's hand drift across her console towards the emergency shut-off. Conway tried to fire and this time she was too late. The shrieking noise dropped away from its crescendo, becoming a part of the background rumbling. Blake watched the outline of Decker snap immediately into focus and he turned his head both ways to reassure himself there would be no repeat of what happened to Lieutenant Trudy Flynn. To his relief, everyone on the bridge was back in the same phase.

The overcharge repeater had brought great destruction to the Vraxar, putting seven of them out of action and leaving three behind, one of which was a cargo ship. The two warships didn't let up and their particle beams continued to take chunks from the *Cataclysm*'s energy shield. With the overcharge repeater unavailable, the odds were considerably diminished.

Blake weighed up their chances. "We'll lose if we stick around," he said.

"Should I activate an SRT, sir?" asked Dunbar.

Options and possibilities whirled in Blake's head. He tried desperately to think of a way to turn it around. In the end, he came to a realisation. *I just don't like to lose.*

After that, it was easy to make the decision.

"Activate the SRT. Take us anywhere that isn't here."

"Activating."

Blake readied himself for the feeling in his guts that would indicate the transit had taken place. It didn't come.

"The SRT failed, trying again," said Dunbar.

The second attempt also failed. It didn't take Dunbar long to figure out the cause. "All of our cores are at maximum utilisation," he said. "Something squeezed out the pre-loaded SRT."

"Can you reload it?"

"There are no spare processing cycles, sir. It'll take hours to calculate."

"Can you clear up some cycles?"

Dunbar didn't answer straight away. "I'm checking. All this new hardware has been wired in without proper testing. Every system should run in isolation so that it can't interfere with other systems. Whatever they've done to get the Lightspeed Catapult installed, it's made everything else go screwy."

While the conversation took place, Lieutenant Conway did her best to offer a suitable response to the Vraxar attacks. She launched every available Shimmer and Lambda missile, and created overlapping waves of shock drones to thin the salvoes of enemy missiles. It wasn't going to be enough – the only weapon the *Cataclysm* was equipped with which could bypass energy shields was the repeater and that was no longer on option.

At least it hadn't been an option when Blake thought the short-range transit was available.

"We'll have to use the repeater again," he said.

"I shut it down, sir," said Decker.

"Un-shut it down, then."

"I had to completely power it off – there was no other way to prevent Lieutenant Conway firing it. It'll take a few minutes to go through its warm-up self-tests."

Blake glanced at the *Cataclysm*'s energy shield. "Fifteen percent," he said through gritted teeth. "We don't have a few minutes."

"I'll begin the warm-up in any case."

As soon as Decker gave the instruction to bring the over-charge repeater online, the shrieking sound, which had dropped so low as to be near-inaudible, climbed higher and higher until Blake became convinced something was going to explode.

"Shut it off!"

"Roger."

Decker complied and the shrieking receded. Blake felt like punching something and he swore repeatedly at the twists of fate. The Vraxar were almost victorious and the only weapon capable of defeating them wasn't functioning properly. He flicked his eyes to the sensor feed in time to see a volley of the *Cataclysm*'s missiles detonate against the shield of one of the Vraxar warships. The plasma glare faded and the enemy craft was left intact. The *Cataclysm* lacked the brute force to finish the job.

Four more Vraxar particle beams knocked the *Cataclysm*'s energy shield reserves to zero.

"There's our shield gone," said Dunbar.

"We're out of shock drones," Conway announced.

"No shield, no drones and no SRT," said Blake bitterly. *I made the wrong call,* he thought. *I should have let the Vraxar get away with the Estral tech. Those missiles were a secondary objective and now I've blown the primary ones.*

"We've taken a particle beam hit," said Dunbar. "It's dispersing, but the next one is going to hurt us."

Blake felt utterly helpless. The *Cataclysm* had punched significantly above its weight but now it was out of answers. Its conventional weapons weren't enough to take out one of the larger Vraxar spaceships, let alone both. There was no escape into lightspeed and the gravity engines weren't sufficient to escape the enemy. His mind drifted to the Lightspeed Catapult and then he remembered the ramp-up time. It wasn't an option.

A second particle beam lanced into the cruiser's upper section, generating four amber alerts and one red alert on Blake's console. He saw Conway attempt to use the disruptors in the hope of shutting the Vraxar spaceships down even for a second or two. The *Cataclysm*'s core clusters were so busy the weapon refused to fire.

"At least we kicked the crap out of a few of them," said Decker.

"It doesn't make me feel any better," Conway replied.

A third particle beam shut down two of the *Cataclysm*'s main sensor arrays and disabled one of the Havoc turrets. Blake did his best to ignore the slew of warnings on his console and aimed the cruiser towards Jonli again, wondering if he might buy them some breathing room by flying around the planet. The Vraxar followed immediately, accelerating hard to match the fleeing cruiser's speed.

"Bastards," said Decker.

The closest of the two pursuing spaceships was six thousand metres long and boxy in shape. A salvo of the *Cataclysm*'s missiles crashed into its shields, engulfing the ship and leaving a trail of burning plasma in its wake. Something erupted in the midst of the explosions and, to Blake's immense surprise, the Vraxar battleship was ripped apart.

Before he could ask what the hell was going on, the second of the two enemy ships – this one only a little bigger than the *Cataclysm* - was lit up in whites, oranges and reds. It didn't break off the pursuit and continued the chase. A huge crater appeared in the middle of the hottest part of its hull and, a moment later, there was a second. The Vraxar ship veered off course and its tail overtook its nose. It entered a spin and its trajectory diverged further and further from that of the *Cataclysm*'s.

"They're out of action," said Dunbar. "Their shields are offline and their engines are shutting down."

"I have no idea what happened," said Blake. "Anyone else?"

"Something destroyed those two enemy warships," said Conway.

"There is an anomaly, forty thousand kilometres to starboard," said Hiven-Tar.

"What kind of anomaly?" said Blake.

"I don't know, Captain Charles Blake. There is a vessel in our vicinity which is using stealth technology to deflect our sensors."

Before Blake could wonder if this was a friend or a new foe, the answer was revealed. A familiar shape appeared on the bulkhead screen.

"How?" asked Conway.

The *Ulterior*-2 was in a bad way and there was not one part of its hull which remained undamaged. Vast areas of the battleship's armour plating were either burned away or crumbled into dust. It was blackened and pitted, with a thousand metres of its gravity engines exposed and spilling positrons into the surrounding space. Only two of its Havoc turrets remained operational and Blake thought he could see the gleam of the forward

Shimmer hatches. Most importantly of all, the Hadron had two functioning overcharge particle beam turrets, without which there was no way it could have finished off the two Vraxar spaceships.

The sight of this battle-scarred warship made Blake's chest swell with pride. The *Ulterior-2* was indomitable and no matter how much of a beating it took, the spaceship refused to bow to the inevitability of its demise.

"Hail them!" he shouted, jumping from his seat.

"I am trying," said Hiven-Tar. "There is no response."

"Maybe they lost comms," said Blake. "Can you confirm?"

There was still the matter of the Vraxar cargo ship to deal with before they could fully investigate what was going on with the *Ulterior-2*. The final enemy vessel was on the tactical screen, travelling rapidly in the opposite direction. It was well inside missile range and Blake opened his mouth to order a full launch. The red circle representing the cargo ship vanished.

"They've gone to lightspeed," said Dunbar. "I can't say I blame them."

"The battleship *Ulterior-2* has taken substantial damage," said Hiven-Tar. "Even so, its actions indicate the presence of a crew. From that, we can assume they are no longer able to use their comms system."

"Point taken. What are they doing?"

"They are stationary," said the Ghost.

The *Ulterior-2* had lost three of its four shuttles during the deployment inside *Ix-Gastiol*. The final shuttle was used to transport injured soldiers back to the warship. The last transport was badly damaged at the time and it was unlikely anyone had enacted repairs.

"We should assume they have no way to reach us," said Blake.

"Sir, what about the Aranol?" asked Conway. "It could be

only a few minutes away from here. It's unlikely they've given up on the Estral facility. Maybe they'll come here with everything."

Conway was right – they couldn't hang around for any longer than was necessary. However, Blake wasn't quite ready to run without taking a shot at the main enemy spaceship. The best course of action would be to execute a short-range transit away from here in order to buy enough time to rescue whoever was left on the *Ulterior-2*. Unfortunately, the lack of comms made the plan unworkable.

The other option was to head away on the gravity engines. The crew on the *Ulterior-2* would definitely follow, but it was unlikely they could make enough distance to escape if the Aranol showed up somewhere close by. That left one thing.

"I'm going to come in close to the *Ulterior-2*. Once we're within a hundred klicks, deploy Shuttle One. Send it over on autopilot to the Hadron. We know they aren't sensor blind because they're here and because they shot down two enemy warships, so they should see the shuttle coming. Hiven-Tar, there's a chance the crew can receive comms, yet without being able to transmit their own. Assume they can hear us and keep them informed."

"I will do so."

"Ran-Lor and Lieutenant Dunbar, keep your eyes glued to your stations – the first hint you get of anything inbound, I want to know about it."

"Sir, our cores are still loaded. I don't think we're ready for an SRT."

Blake grimaced. There was more than just the *Ulterior-2* and the Aranol to think about. There were numerous faults affecting the *ES Cataclysm*. Some of the heat alerts from the particle beam strikes had returned to amber, but the processing core clusters remained fully loaded, the stealth modules remained offline and he could still hear the whining sound from either the Lightspeed

Catapult or the overcharge repeater. He had no idea which it was. On the plus side, the energy shield had recharged as far as ten percent and it climbed slowly upwards. In another fifteen or twenty minutes, it would be at one hundred percent.

"We're still in the shit, aren't we?"

"That's putting it mildly," said Dunbar.

Blake got his bearings and aimed the ES *Cataclysm* towards the *Ulterior-2*. The cruiser was a little down on power, but not significantly enough to worry him. The distance between the two vessels reduced rapidly and Blake used the opportunity to give further instructions.

"Lieutenant Decker, do you think you can figure out what's going on with the stealth modules? I'm sure it's some of this new kit that's caused the problem. The stealth modules and the overloaded cores are our priority issues."

"I will work with Lieutenant Dunbar to resolve these matters, sir." Decker grinned. "Maybe I'll request a transfer back to a warship when we get home. This is far more exciting than working in the lab all day."

"And somewhat more dangerous," added Conway.

The ES *Cataclysm* completed the forty-thousand-kilometre journey in twenty-five seconds and Blake swung the cruiser around so that its shuttle launch bay was parallel to the one on the *Ulterior-2*. At this close distance, the sensors picked up additional details which betrayed the extent of the damage suffered by the Hadron. In parts it was still hot from particle beam strikes and there were dozens of missile craters along its length.

"They have no energy shield," said Dunbar.

"And more than half of their missile clusters are either melted shut or destroyed," said Conway. "They've taken a real beating."

"Deploying shuttle," said Ran-Lor.

Shuttle One sped across the intervening space, a tiny speck of grey against the flank of the battleship. The *Ulterior-2*'s bay doors opened halfway and then stopped. It was enough for the shuttle to enter and also enough to reassure Blake that there was someone alive to operate the doors. He closed his eyes and waited.

"Shuttle One reports it has successfully docked," said Hiven-Tar.

"Patch it into the Hadron's internal comms and find out what the crew's status is."

The Ghost struggled with the instruction – it was easy to forget he wasn't trained in the use of Space Corps equipment. "I am unable to patch," he said. "The limitation is not my own."

It was unthinkable for the internal comms to be unavailable – they were hardwired and robust. Blake felt himself going cold. Perhaps everyone *was* dead and perhaps it was the battle computer directing the spaceship's actions.

It was a few minutes' run from the *Ulterior-2*'s bridge to the shuttle bay and there was the additional likelihood that some of the people onboard carried injuries, assuming there was anyone alive. Therefore, it came as no surprise when the shuttle didn't immediately emerge from its berth.

Five minutes passed. Blake needed to get up to stretch the tension from his muscles, but there was no way he could leave his seat for even a second. The *Ulterior-2*'s half-open shuttle bay transfixed him, daring him to avert his eyes from the rectangle of blue-white light.

"How are you getting on with those stealth modules, Lieutenant Decker?"

"I'm disconnecting each of the tie-ins between the original warship and the new parts. I've got to go slowly so that I can fix it later if required."

"The core clusters are at ninety-five percent," said Blake. As he watched, two of the nodes burned out within a second of each other. "We're losing our processors."

"I'm cutting the ties with the Lightspeed Catapult, sir. It's nearly done."

"Does this mean we can't get home?" asked Conway.

"Ask me that later."

"I'm asking you now!"

"Quiet!" said Blake, louder than he intended. "Lieutenant Conway, we require stealth and we require an SRT capability. We'll handle the consequences."

"Fine."

"Yes, it is fine!" roared Blake. "This is my decision, do you understand?"

"Yes, sir."

It was difficult for Blake to bring his temper under control. Conway was stirring up crap when she should be offering support. *The stress is getting to me. I want my crew back.*

"Ten minutes," said Dunbar.

"How long until the Aranol gets here?" said Blake, keeping his voice even.

"Based on what we know, I would say they are overdue," said Dunbar.

It wasn't the answer Blake wanted to hear, though secretly he'd guessed it before he spoke the question. He was certain the Aranol was coming and he had no desire to be sitting here, waiting for a shuttle to return.

"There is the shuttle," announced Hiven-Tar.

The transport appeared as a dot against the interior lights of the shuttle bay. The craft accelerated rapidly along a trajectory that would bring it straight to the *ES Cataclysm.*

"Two minutes to dock," said the Ghast.

Blake's heart pounded. "Get me a channel."

A familiar voice came onto the comms. "You took your time, sir," said Lieutenant Caz Pointer.

Hearing her voice brought Blake close to tears. He fought

them back. "Looks like you could handle things well enough. You'll be docked in two minutes. How many are you carrying?"

"One hundred and ten. The crew made it, but we lost a few of the soldiers we took off *Ix-Gastiol*."

It was far better than Blake could have expected. "See you soon."

"Roger."

There was much to say, but the talking would wait. Shuttle One's autopilot cut it fine and applied the brakes at the last moment. It entered the docking bay, travelling at many metres per second and came to a halt adjacent to one of the gravity clamps. The clamp attached, locked in place and then it was done. A green light appeared on Blake's console.

"Shuttle One is safely docked," he said.

It was a momentous achievement, but the bridge crew were too drained to cheer.

CHAPTER FOURTEEN

THE CREW of the *Ulterior-2* were safely onboard, but there was no let-up. Blake was increasingly certain the Aranol was inbound and the *Cataclysm*'s stealth modules were still unavailable. Lieutenant Decker's most recent update was the same as the previous – she was *nearly* finished severing the links between the Lightspeed Catapult and the rest of the cruiser. There was no guarantee it would reduce the processing core utilisation and she was careful not to sound too hopeful. Two more cores burned out and shut down. The *Cataclysm* had a crapload of them, as well as a dozen spare in the stores, but Blake wasn't eager to lose any more.

Another problem reared its head and the solution was going to be a painful one.

"We can't leave the *Ulterior-2*," Blake said.

Ran-Lor understood. "It would not be wise to leave a Space Corps battleship for the Vraxar to salvage. They might be able to copy your overcharge technology."

"And they cracked open the *ES Determinant*'s data arrays," said Blake. "The *Ulterior-2* carries a more recent snapshot of our capabilities and plans. I don't want it to fall into the enemy's hands."

"What if its sensors obtained details on the Aranol that we could make use of?" asked Decker.

Blake was aware of the possibility. The trouble was, he couldn't justify another shuttle run in order to try and pick up some of the physical data arrays. In other circumstances, he would have used the comms to extract the data, something which wasn't currently possible.

"The occupants of Shuttle One are now within the *ES Cataclysm*'s interior," said Hiven-Tar.

"Tell the bridge crew to come here and send the soldiers to the troops' quarters. Give Lieutenant McKinney a heads-up so he knows they're coming."

The Ghost got on with it, while Blake considered waiting for his crew to arrive so that he could interrogate them about the *Ulterior-2*'s databanks. Sadly, he realised there was nothing they could say which would divert him from his course. The over-charge technology was the only real advantage the Space Corps held over the Vraxar and it was imperative for it to stay that way.

"Lieutenant Conway, please lock onto the *Ulterior-2*. Lambdas only – we'll save the Shimmers for the stuff that can fire back."

"Will its battle computer respond?" asked Conway nervously. "I should probably know the answer, but I don't."

"No, Lieutenant. It won't fire back."

"We're locked on."

"Fire Lambdas."

The *ES Cataclysm*'s launch hatches opened and two hundred Lambda X missiles flew across the short gap between the two spacecraft and exploded within a second. The *Ulterior-2* was engulfed in white plasma, which concealed the damaged structure beneath. When the fires subsided, the Hadron was there as before, with its flank torn up and glowing with heat.

"Its engines are still online and operational," said Dunbar.

"Fire again."

Another two hundred Lambdas followed the initial salvo. Blake couldn't take his eyes from the sensor feed. This time, the damage was more extensive – much of the Hadron's thick plating was gone, revealing the matte grey of its Gallenium engines. There were so many blast craters they overlapped, and, in places, there were holes several hundred metres deep.

"It's not breaking up."

"Fire again."

Blake heard the bridge door open and guessed who it was. He turned and saw his crew enter as a group. They were dressed in spacesuits, though they'd removed their visors. His eyes sought out one member of the team and he found her. Caz Pointer caught his eyes and he was shocked at how drawn she appeared. Whatever had gone on since *Ix-Gastiol*, it had taken its toll.

"What the hell?" said Hawkins. "Why are you shooting at the *Ulterior-2*?"

The third salvo was not enough to break up the battleship. They'd built this one strong and stubborn, and it refused to succumb even when its service was finished and its duty fulfilled.

"We have to," said Pointer quietly. "The Vraxar can't get their hands on it."

After the sixth wave of missiles, the *Ulterior-2* had no resistance left. It split into several pieces, each of which burned with plasma heat.

"Target the largest sections and fire," said Blake.

It took another three salvos before he was satisfied there was nothing worth salvaging from the wreckage. The debris was strewn across a thousand kilometres of space, forever lost.

But not forgotten.

It was a moment of sadness which Blake filed away inside his mind, to be experienced when things weren't so urgent. The Hadron's crew milled around, not quite sure what to do with themselves. The ever-practical Lieutenant Hawkins had obtained a tray of something from the bridge replicator. She chewed on what might have been pizza and offered a second slice to Ran-Lor.

"Better than one of your grey pastes, huh?" she asked, doing her bit for inter-species diplomacy.

"I am not hungry," said the Ghast.

"Suit yourself."

Blake hurried over to his old crew and shook their hands in turn. "I thought I'd lost you."

"Not us, sir," said Quinn. He had a can of Hi-Stim in his hand, which was, strictly speaking, banned for on-duty officers. The man looked exhausted, so Blake wasn't about to complain.

Lieutenant Maria Cruz was as polite as ever, though there was a hardness behind her eyes which spoke of her weeks labouring with the burdens of worry and fear.

"Lieutenant McKinney will be glad to see you," said Blake. Cruz went pink and she did her best to affect nonchalance.

Lieutenant Caz Pointer was last in line. She refused his hand and jumped in for a hug, which he returned without embarrassment.

"Thought you'd get out of that date, did you?" she whispered.

"Not a chance," he said. He stepped back and evaluated the new arrivals. They didn't look ready for duty, no matter how much he would have liked them to get involved in the running of the *Cataclysm*. "Get some rest," he said. "That's an order."

It was testament to their exhaustion that they offered only perfunctory arguments. They filed off to the crew's quarters to find empty rooms in which to crash. No sooner had the bridge door rolled shut than Lieutenant Dunbar threw another shovelful of crap onto the pile.

"There's something incoming," he said. "It's trying to mask its signature, but there's no way something this big is going to escape notice."

Blake took three long strides and jumped into his seat. "Where?"

"Halfway between here and the fifth planet. Thirty million klicks away."

"We're exposed out here, Lieutenant Decker. How are you getting on? Don't tell me *nearly* again."

"Okay, I won't," she said. "Three, two, one and...done!" she exclaimed with triumph.

The effect was immediate. The utilisation on the *Cataclysm*'s cores dropped from their peak.

"Eighty percent," said Blake. "Seventy. Lieutenant Dunbar, do we have stealth?"

"No, sir. The modules won't activate."

"Damnit! I thought they would come online!"

"So did I."

There was usually only a gap of a few seconds between the detection of an inbound fission signature and the arrival of the spaceship. In this instance, the delay was longer.

The Aranol is so big it must push far more particles ahead of it, thought Blake.

The core utilisation fell to fifty percent.

"The Aranol is here," said Hiven-Tar.

Forty percent.

"Activating stealth," said Dunbar.

"Shit, were we in time?" said Conway.

Blake didn't want to remain here in order to find out. He fed power into the *Cataclysm*'s gravity engines and brought them away from the wreckage of the *Ulterior-2* at thirty percent of maximum speed. He estimated the delay between the Aranol's arrival and the stealth activation at five or six seconds. Whilst the *Cataclysm*'s crew knew the Aranol was coming, the Vraxar could only make assumptions and they had a lot of space to scan in such a short time.

"There's a chance they don't know where we are," said Blake. "I'm keeping our speed down in any case, to reduce the likelihood they'll detect us."

The seconds passed and the Aranol stayed exactly where it was and there was no sign of hostile activity. If it decided to fire weapons towards the *Cataclysm* the range was extreme, though Blake wasn't especially keen to discover what its capabilities were.

It waited, a sphere cased in near-black metal, the size of a large moon and with a surface covered in countless towers, structures and weapons placements. It was speckled with lights and it looked like any other planet in the Confederation when viewed at night and from far up in space. Except this was the Aranol and it was the driving force of the Vraxar war machine.

"It has no satellites and I suspect that many of its outer structures are redundant," said Hiven-Tar. "As if they were constructed long ago and are now superseded." The Ghast highlighted a few areas on the bulkhead screen with red circles. "These are docking hatches. You will note the size of this largest one."

"Two hundred klicks in diameter," said Blake. "Not quite wide enough for *Ix-Gorghal* or *Ix-Gastiol* to squeeze through, but plenty big nonetheless."

"You won't be astounded to learn they are protected by an energy shield," said Lieutenant Dunbar. "Equally, it won't cause you any shock when I tell you the magnitude of it. Do you want the numbers?"

"Not just now, Lieutenant. I understand from your words

that we won't be breaking through with two hundred Lambdas and a few Shimmers," said Blake. "Get Lieutenant Hawkins on the internal comms. Her break is cancelled – I need her to tell me what this thing can do."

Hawkins hadn't gone far and she returned to the bridge after a minute, still carrying the tray of pizza.

"It showed up, then?" she asked, still chewing.

"What are its capabilities?" asked Blake. "We're carrying an Obsidiar bomb and I'd like to deploy it inside their shields." He turned his head towards Dunbar. "We can load up for an SRT, right?"

"Yes, sir. I'll get the SRT ready to go."

"Lieutenant Hawkins?" repeated Blake.

"We didn't see too much of it, sir. Most of that damage the *Ulterior-2* suffered came from inside *Ix-Gastiol*'s coil. By the end they were sending so much crap through we lost comms, most of our weapons and they knocked out the Obsidiar core. I'm not sure why we decided to go through the portal."

"You weren't sure?" Blake scratched his head.

"The heat of war and all that, sir. We made our choice."

"I wasn't criticising. Well, maybe a small amount of criticising. I assumed you had a plan."

"Not really. We went through the portal and activated an SRT to get the hell away from that thing. We called it *Planet Bastard*."

Blake smiled. "It's the Aranol."

"I don't think I can accept any other name now, sir."

"Call it what you will. It didn't fire at you?"

"We didn't give it the chance, sir. I don't believe they were expecting two-way traffic through the portal."

"How did you find the *ES Cataclysm*? Your arrival was greatly appreciated, by the way."

"Think nothing of it, sir. We were following Planet Bastard.

When you're stuck in Estral space, there's nothing much else to do. In truth, we didn't have a clue how to get home, so we used the fission modelling to keep after them. We thought that maybe there'd be another portal to fly through if we stuck close enough. We got to this solar system and stayed to watch the fighting between the Estral and the Vraxar. The Vraxar lost plenty of ships here."

"I doubt they care," said Blake.

"What was holding the portal open at this end when you first entered Estral Space?" asked Hiven-Tar.

"Nothing," said Hawkins. "The portal was just there, floating in space."

"Was it wide enough for the Aranol?" asked Blake. "I've been trying to guess why the enemy ship is still here, rather than in Confederation Space."

"I don't know, sir. Maybe they have a different way of travelling."

"Or maybe they have unfinished business with the Estral," said Blake. "Did you see what the Estral base launched?"

"Yes, sir. Missiles that fly happily through energy shields. The significance wasn't lost on us."

Blake rubbed his chin. "The overcharge tech was stolen from the Estral in the first place and we thought that was the only weapon capable of bypassing a shield. I wonder what other uses the Estral have come up with."

"It would be nice to pay that base a visit," said Lieutenant Decker. "If there's anyone alive, they might want to shake our hands and spill the beans on how they got those missiles working."

"We can't land with the Aranol where it is," said Blake. "It must have come to finish the job its spaceships failed to complete. I wonder why they haven't got on with it."

Hiven-Tar gave a deep laugh. "They are scared!" he said.

"They are scared the Estral still have concealed missile launchers on Jonli and they are scared in case the ES *Cataclysm* hits them with a hundred shots from an overcharge repeater! The Aranol is waiting until it is reassured."

"The Estral missiles were powerful, but they aren't going to destroy something so large as the Aranol. It would take thousands of shots to do significant harm," said Blake. "The same with the overcharge repeater, if it were actually working."

The Ghost tapped the side of his head with his forefinger, which was another startlingly human action. "What does this tell you about the consciousness controlling the Vraxar, Captain Charles Blake?"

Blake nodded in acknowledgement of the point. "It tells us a lot, Hiven-Tar. The Aranol has existed for so long it is wary of direct confrontation in case it tastes even the possibility of defeat."

"That is what I believe," said the Ghost. "If your enemy commander fears for himself, there is a weakness to exploit."

"The psychology of our enemy will not matter for long," said Blake. His seat creaked as he leaned forward to enter his command codes.

> SORROW ACTIVE. DEPLOYMENT AVAILABLE. TIMER AVAILABLE. STAND DOWN AVAILABLE.

"Are you planning to use the bomb on them, sir?" asked Conway.

"The enemy are here and now, and we have the capability to destroy them. Lieutenant Dunbar, how far does the Aranol's shield extend above its surface?"

"Five hundred klicks, sir."

"That's plenty of room for us to SRT inside and then let off the Sorrow bomb."

"It takes five seconds for the bomb to deploy from its chute," said Conway.

"This is why I hoped Lieutenant Hawkins would give us some idea of what weaponry the enemy can bring to bear. On the sensor feed I can only see gauss turrets. It's hidden stasis emitters I'm worried about."

"The bomb has been designed to free-fall," said Conway. "As long as we have a split-second to open the chute hatch, it'll fall out and detonate."

"I would prefer if we were able to escape, Lieutenant."

Conway blinked. "Me too, sir. We might not have that luxury."

In spite of their angry words earlier, Blake was impressed that Conway hadn't even considered her own death important. She had a fear of being stranded far from home, yet she was willing to die if it meant the Aranol was destroyed.

The plan wasn't especially elaborate. Blake wanted to lure the Aranol into a position where he could use the Obsidiar bomb against it and here it was. It felt a bit sudden and he found it difficult to grasp the enormity of what success would bring. Without guidance, the Vraxar would wither and die. Hundreds of billions of lives would be saved.

And here I am dithering, he thought.

"Right, let's do this!" he said, forcing enthusiasm into his voice. "Lieutenant Dunbar, wind up short-range transits on six cores. There's an area here on the Aranol which I believe has no stasis towers and that's the spot we're aiming for. We launch and I deploy the bomb within their shields. We launch out and come back ten minutes later to see what's left."

"Sounds like a plan," said Decker.

"One of their launch hatches is opening," said Ran-Lor. "Warships are emerging."

Whatever it was keeping the Aranol from making its move on the Estral facility, it was evidently no longer an issue. Vraxar warships streamed from the darkness within the Aranol and this time they didn't hold back.

"How many?" said Conway in wonder.

"Neutralisers as well," said Blake. He counted five of the huge spaceships, amongst the dozens of others.

"They think we're still here, without knowing where we are," said Hawkins. "They're not taking any chances against the overcharge repeater."

"They are desperate for what's in that facility," said Decker. "I'm getting pretty excited myself now that I've seen how much they want it."

"Less talk, we're ready," said Blake. "Lieutenant Dunbar, you will activate the first SRT on my command. Once I have deployed the bomb I will give you a second command, at which point you will get us the hell away from here. Do you understand."

"Yes, sir. In, out, boom."

Blake took a deep breath. "Let's go and get those bastards. Lieutenant Dunbar, activate the SRT."

"SRT activating."

With the hum of unleashed power, the ES *Cataclysm*'s deep fission engines fired up.

CHAPTER FIFTEEN

THE PLAN WENT AWRY.

The *Cataclysm* reappeared, thirty million kilometres from its starting point. The two Ghasts followed procedure and brought up feeds from the sensors. Blake paused, with his finger hovering over the deployment button for the Obsidiar bomb.

The Aranol was visible on the forward feed, like a sheer, dark cliff extending for an eternity above and below. Against it, the cruiser was nothing – less than nothing. A mote upon a mote. The Aranol gave off an aura of incredible power which produced a deep thrumming in the solid metal of the *Cataclysm*. Blake didn't like to think how much Obsidiar was inside the Vraxar's main spaceship to produce such a reaction.

There was something wrong. The SRT was meant to bring them to within a hundred kilometres of the Aranol. They were further – much further. With a sinking feeling, Blake knew.

"We're outside their shield."

His navigational screen was still populating with targets and there were dozens of them – spaceships and areas the battle computer classified as ground-based targets, whether or not it knew what their capabilities were.

"Our Gallenium engines are offline," said Dunbar.

"Neutraliser," said Blake. The backup Obsidiar core would keep things running. That's what it was there for.

"Deploy, sir," said Conway.

Time came to a standstill for Captain Blake. The choice was his to make. They were outside the Aranol's shield, but surely there was nothing capable of withstanding the blast from an Obsidiar bomb. Except, he didn't know. This might be the first and the last chance.

Hold the deployment. Order the SRT and find out what went wrong, spoke a voice in his mind.

With a certainty that went beyond mere hunch, Blake knew that nothing had gone wrong with the SRT. Somehow, the Aranol was able to deflect spaceships coming through lightspeed to prevent them from doing exactly what Blake was trying now.

We can't have been the first species to try this against them. They've learned how to defend themselves against it.

He pressed the launch button for the Sorrow bomb.

> FIVE SECONDS

"Why aren't they shooting at us?" asked Conway.

> FOUR SECONDS

> THREE SECONDS

A gauss slug the size of a building crashed into the *Cataclysm*'s shields. The reserve bar dropped to three percent and bleeped its soft alarm.

There might not be enough left in the Obsidiar core to activate the SRT, thought Blake.

> TWO SECONDS

"They're powering up one of those towers," said Dunbar.

"Missiles inbound," said Conway. "Lots of missiles."

> ONE SECOND

> DEPLOYMENT SUCCESSFUL

"Get us out of here!" shouted Blake.

Lieutenant Dunbar was waiting for the order and he stabbed a finger at his control panel. Blake felt the transit in his stomach and expected it to pass away. It didn't and the feeling stayed for several seconds before it receded. He guessed what was wrong. The power gauge for the backup Obsidiar core flashed at zero: fully depleted.

"The fission engines only half-fired," said Dunbar. "We entered low lightspeed and we've just been dumped out of it."

"How far did we go?" asked Blake. "Quickly!"

The Ghasts were calm and collected. "We are seventy-two million kilometres from our point of departure," said Hiven-Tar. "During our re-entry, we missed the fifth planet by nine kilometres and now we are in an unoccupied area of local space."

With the Neutraliser's negation field gone, the cruiser's Gallenium engines were running smoothly once more.

"Put us into stealth mode," said Blake, pointing at Dunbar. Then, "Where's the Aranol? Did the bomb go off?"

Ran-Lor had the answer. "The bomb exploded as expected."

The unspoken words told Blake what he didn't want to hear.

"It didn't work?"

"Our sensors obtained a recording," said Ran-Lor. "They do not function during lightspeed, so there is a brief period where the feed was interrupted."

"Let me see it."

The bulkhead screen showed the feed from the rear arrays, slowed down to a frame-by-frame replay. The Space Corps' latest sensors captured half a million images each second and even so, it wasn't enough to provide a smooth stream of the initial explosion.

The Obsidiar bomb appeared as a silvery cube, with the Aranol filling the entirety of the background. Blake saw two Vraxar warships in the distance, as well as the energy sparks from a Neutraliser. There was something else, a grey blur on the left-hand corner of the image, which lasted only a single frame before it vanished.

"Gauss projectile," said Hiven-Tar. "There are many noughts after the decimal point if you wish to know by how much it missed us."

The next frame showed the bomb explode - it happened with such speed that the blast simply appeared on the image, with no sign of its expansion. With a feeling of emptiness, Blake watched as the feed jumped, before resuming with the Aranol much further away.

"Here is where we entered lightspeed for approximately two seconds," said Hiven-Tar. "The sensor arrays take a moment to re-focus."

The Obsidiar bomb produced a blast sphere of incredible magnitude. It was as black as the Aranol, yet the energy from it was cleansing rather than filthy. The sphere reached its maximum and then receded as quickly as it came.

At the end of it, the Aranol was exactly where it was before the bomb exploded, and seemingly unaffected by the immense unleashed energies of the Obsidiar.

"The explosion had a diameter of one-point-two million kilometres," said Ran-Lor. "I am impressed."

Blake slumped in his seat. "It wasn't enough. Give me the live feed."

The live feed wasn't far ahead of the recording and it showed no change. The Aranol hung in space, unaffected by the largest explosion from any device the Space Corps had ever produced.

"I believe the Vraxar lost sixty-two of their warships in the explosion. Those which were not within the Aranol's shield," said Hiven-Tar. "Five of those were Neutralisers. This is a bad result for both sides."

"The difference is, we care," said Hawkins. She looked miserable, leaning back in her spare seat next to Lieutenant Decker.

"They're up to something," said Lieutenant Dunbar.

"What do you mean?" asked Blake sharply.

"They are preparing to enter lightspeed." Dunbar shook his head in astonishment. "I've never seen the like."

Whatever the technical data which had captured his engine man's imagination, Blake had other priorities. "Are they coming here? To us?"

"I can't give you a prediction based on anything other than guesswork, sir."

Blake fancied the idea of pissing the Vraxar off by executing a transit towards Jonli at the same moment as they came this way. However, the *Cataclysm*'s processing cores had dropped their SRT calculations the moment there wasn't enough power to sustain them and it would take eight seconds to prepare the SRT. It didn't appear as if they'd have that much time.

The Aranol disappeared and the crew waited silently to see what their fate might be. One second was enough to be certain. Blake gave it two.

"They've gone," he said.

"Where?" said Conway. "And why?"

Blake had an idea which he wasn't ready to divulge quite yet. He gave orders for Ran-Lor and Hiven-Tar to perform a series of super-far sweeps of the solar system, to see if the Aranol's lightspeed jump had taken it somewhere close, yet out of sight.

"It could have hidden behind a planet," said Ran-Lor. "I cannot understand why they might do so."

"Subterfuge," said Blake. The Ghasts were an up-front kind of species and struggled with the notions of subtlety or trickery.

"We need to get in there quickly, sir," said Hawkins. "Planet Bastard, I mean, *The Aranol* leaves behind a strange type of fission cloud and we should probably try and run a model off it."

It was another risk – the Aranol could be anywhere close by, waiting for the ES *Cataclysm* to emerge from hiding. There again, the Vraxar were no more subtle than the Ghasts. *Less* subtle, thought Blake.

"Take us to the Aranol's departure point, Lieutenant Dunbar. Make sure we have the means of escape and activate a second SRT the moment something happens you don't like. No need to wait for the order."

Dunbar gave a half-salute in acknowledgement. "Here we go," he said.

This time, the SRT was completed without an issue. The *Cataclysm* entered local space only a few hundred metres from its target.

"Capture the data you need for the fission model," said Blake. "We'll take it somewhere else for analysis."

"Sir, can I make a suggestion?" asked Decker, with the easy charm of a time-served captain who was going to make the suggestion anyway.

"Fire away."

"We could take a look at the Estral facility."

Blake drummed his fingers, instinctively drawn to the idea of doing something his enemy would prefer he didn't. "What if the Aranol comes back?"

Decker had plenty of insight. "They've gone because they don't know what other weaponry we're carrying. The Obsidiar bomb didn't destroy them, but we must assume it weakened their shields significantly. The Aranol does not know if we are carrying another fifteen such bombs in our hold and it doesn't want to find out."

"Maybe it is close by and will send more ships," said Blake, looking to be convinced that Decker's suggestion was the right thing to do.

"Nope, they didn't embark on a short trip, sir," said Dunbar.

"It'll be a while until I can provide you with a destination, but they intend to be at lightspeed for an extended period."

"Could they abort it early and come back here?"

Dunbar's expression suggested he thought it was a daft question. "They could. Why on earth would they do something like that?"

"Never assume your enemy will act like you want them to," said Hawkins. "Particularly enemies that are the size of a moon and filled with thousands of warships."

"Let's try to establish contact with the Estral first," said Blake. "Hiven-Tar, find out if they respond to our comms."

"There are no live receptors anywhere within range," said the Ghast. "Their antennae were certainly destroyed when the base shield came down."

"Is there any chance they will hear a broadcast from us, without being able to respond?"

"No."

Blake grimaced. "It would be nice to know what they think of us."

"We just rescued them," said Hawkins. "They will be ecstatic to see us."

From the expression on her face, Blake could tell Lieutenant Hawkins wasn't being entirely serious. The Estral were known to be a *shoot first* species and there was no guarantee they'd be happy to find Space Corps soldiers knocking on their heavily-damaged front door.

"Get Lieutenant McKinney on the comms," said Blake. "I'd like him to do a job for me."

McKinney listened to the orders with stoic acceptance. For the first time, Blake thought he detected the smallest hint of reluctance in the other man's demeanour. The reason was easily guessed – McKinney had found something he thought was lost and now he feared losing it again.

"We need this, Lieutenant," said Blake. "The Aranol's shields were too strong for an Obsidiar bomb. The Estral have something the Vraxar are afraid of and it's in the facility on Jonli."

"Jonli?" asked McKinney, perking up at once.

The response left Blake completely baffled, though he didn't ask the reason for McKinney's sudden enthusiasm.

"Take Shuttle One and depart at once. The facility site is extensive, so you might want to take everyone you can muster."

"So we simply go in and look for data arrays?"

"That's about it." Blake hesitated. "We're expecting them to be big, so you'll need to siphon off whatever you can into portable databanks. There are a few of them in stores."

"I know them, sir."

"The Ghosts will come with you. If there are any Estral left alive, you may be glad to have someone along with you who looks familiar."

"I thought they hated each other?"

"It sounds as if the Ghosts want to be friends again."

Hiven-Tar and Ran-Lor jerked at the words and Blake realised it wasn't a matter for jokes. He muted the comms for a moment in order to apologise. Neither of the Ghosts appeared offended and Blake hoped they weren't concealing any anger.

He resumed his conversation with McKinney. "Is there anything else you need, Lieutenant?"

"No, sir. I'll organise the troops."

The sight of Hiven-Tar raising his hand for attention distracted Blake. "What is it?"

"A shuttle has lifted off from the surface of Jonli. The Estral must have an escape route."

"Lieutenant McKinney, hold those orders. I'll get back to you," said Blake. He cut the channel and went to see what the Estral were up to.

"One shuttle," said Hiven-Tar. "A small one."

"Any sign of more shuttles escaping?"

"None."

The Estral shuttle flew away from the surface at what Blake assumed was its highest speed. The transport was silvery in colour and sleek, with rounded edges and landing skids in place of legs. It was only a shuttle, but it made the Space Corps' equivalent look like the work of a clumsy child.

"I heard they went in for the fancy designs," said Hawkins, leaning over. "And there it is, right there."

"Do they know we're here?" asked Blake.

"I assume so," said Hiven-Tar. "They are coming straight for us."

"Hail them and see what they have to say."

"They have sixty-three passengers onboard and request permission to dock."

This was completely unexpected and it took Blake a moment to evaluate the options. He couldn't abandon the Estral, nor could he permit sixty-three potentially hostile aliens to enter the ES *Cataclysm* without reassurances.

"If we let them dock, the life support units will be near capacity when we activate the Lightspeed Catapult," said Decker.

"They may be willing to share information about their missiles," said Conway.

"If we destroy their shuttle, we could take the data from their facility," said Ran-Lor. "That would be the most practical solution."

The idea of shooting the alien shuttle out of the skies did not sit easy with Blake. On the other hand, they might easily be lying about their numbers and have two hundred onboard. The ES *Cataclysm* was equipped with ceiling-mounted miniguns, so they couldn't take over the ship, but he didn't want to be in a position of having to deal with them if there were too many for the life support modules to cope with.

To his great relief, the choice was taken out of his hands. As soon as the Estral shuttle reached an altitude of two thousand kilometres, a single, huge explosion tore through the surface facility. Orange-white flames spouted upwards and outwards until they billowed a hundred kilometres into the air. The oxygen content on Jonli was low and Blake dreaded to think how far the blast would have extended in an oxygen-rich atmosphere.

"Scan them for explosives and if they're clear, let them dock," said Blake. "Warn them our internal defences are active and they are to remain on their shuttle."

"There is no indication the shuttle is carrying explosives," said Ran-Lor.

Blake got hold of McKinney. "Your mission is cancelled on the basis the Estral just blew their installation to pieces. They have an escape shuttle coming to dock with the *Cataclysm* in ten minutes. They are to stay onboard their vessel, but I would like a head count. If any try to escape, either shoot them or retreat and we'll contain them with the miniguns."

"Yes, sir, I'll take a squad and we'll deal with it."

With McKinney gone, Blake prepared for an anxious wait and he busied himself with checking on his crew's progress.

"How is the fission modelling coming along, Lieutenant Dunbar?"

"Still narrowing down their vector, sir. The modelling always starts out slow and gets quicker as it approaches a conclusion."

"Any idea how long?"

"Even with four cores burned out, we've got plenty in reserve. Unfortunately, the longer the lightspeed jump, the harder it is to predict."

"If they aren't staying here in Estral Space, there's only one likely destination."

"I'm aware of that, sir. You'll know as soon as I do."

Blake went to see how Lieutenant Decker was getting along. She'd been morose over the last few hours and he wasn't sure if it was because she felt responsible for the failings in the new hardware, or because her free spirit was rooted in the days where the Space Corps was at peace and there was room for officers who didn't take everything seriously.

I'm thinking like an old man again, he thought. *Worse – I've accepted that I'm miserable and strait-laced with it.*

He forced a smile to his face. "We're going to need the Lightspeed Catapult soon, Lieutenant. That means bringing it back online."

Decker studied him carefully, as if she could read his mind. "I kinda figured out a few of the things which went wrong on the first jump and I'll take steps to avoid them this time."

"I trust you'll get us home, Lieutenant."

"Don't put that on me, sir."

"I mean it."

She sighed. "There's a permanent instability in our Obsidiar-T unit which wasn't present the first time we used the Lightspeed Catapult. The Obsidiar-T is turning out to be far more volatile than I was informed and next time we use it, I don't want to think about what could happen. I think there's a fault with the Lightspeed Catapult which is causing it to screw around with its power source."

"The worst thing that can happen is we die so quickly we don't feel it."

"Or get trapped out of phase forever."

"Really?"

"There's a chance of it. I don't know what the hell it would mean for us. This stuff can take years to research with a full team and unlimited resources. Here?" Decker shrugged.

Lieutenant Dunbar called over. "Sir? The Aranol is going to the Origin Sector."

Decker gave Blake another of her perfect smiles, though it didn't reach her eyes. "Looks like we're going to find out soon enough what happens."

"It was going to come to us at some point, Lieutenant."

With that, Blake hurried across to see what it was Dunbar's modelling had concluded.

CHAPTER SIXTEEN

"I DON'T KNOW what the hell they use for propulsion, but there are traces of Obsidiar and something else in their fission cloud," said Lieutenant Dunbar. "They're travelling fast – *really* fast."

"Two weeks until they reach the Origin Sector, you say?"

"Give or take."

"Where are they aiming for?"

"Well, that's the thing, sir. According to my data, they aren't going directly for one of our planets. There are two possible solar systems they could end up in, neither of them too close to anywhere populated."

"The Aranol is cautious," Blake reminded him. "And if we're right, it contains many of the Vraxar ships they left in Estral Space. They know where our planets are located – once they arrive, they could unload their fleet and annihilate us. If they no longer have an interest in converting us into new Vraxar, there is nothing to stop them destroying everything."

"They haven't finished fighting here," said Hawkins. "Strikes me that they're easily distracted. One minute they want to be in Estral Space, the next they want to attack the Confederation."

There was an obvious reason for their behaviour and Blake didn't like it. "We've pissed them off so much they're going to launch a punitive strike on humanity," he said.

"They can't be that easily riled," said Hawkins. "Then again, they're full of it, aren't they? All this Vraxar talk about *children* and what-have-you ended up being a crock of shit."

"The Aranol got sick of us turning up in places we weren't wanted and maybe now it's decided it's had enough."

"You may be on to something, Captain Charles Blake," said Ran-Lor. "The war against the Estral has produced a similar outcome, in that the Vraxar seek the extermination of our forebears. When there is no logical reason for behaviour, we must assume there is an illogical one."

"I'm not sure it is illogical," said Blake. "The Vraxar are simply acting to take out a perceived threat. The fact that their actions are abhorrent does not necessarily make them illogical."

"We are going to fly back to Confederation Space ahead of them," said Hawkins. "And kick the crap out of the Aranol when it arrives."

"With Obsidiar bombs which don't penetrate their shields," said Dunbar.

"I'd rather be there than be here."

"How long before the Lightspeed Catapult is ready to fire?" asked Blake. "The sooner we get back, the longer the Space Corps has to prepare. It's a real shame we can't even get a comms message home inside two weeks."

"I could have the catapult online within the hour, sir," said Decker. "That's if you want to take the quick *switch it on and see* route. If you want risk mitigation I'll do a staged power-up of each individual subsystem to isolate any faults."

"How long will that take?"

"At least a week, with no guarantees."

"That's too long. Will it start chewing on our processing clusters like the overcharge repeater?"

"I don't think so. Not immediately at least. We may end up replicating the circumstances that caused it to happen, but it shouldn't be straight away."

It wasn't the most reassuring answer. There again, this mission had been a huge risk from the outset.

Lieutenant Hawkins had another thought. "The Vraxar have fission modelling – *Ix-Gorghal* used it to follow us before," she said. "Won't they assume we'll figure out where they're going?"

"They might," Blake replied. "They either won't care, or they won't expect us to arrive ahead of them. I doubt they know about the Lightspeed Catapult."

"Let's get going then!" said Hawkins.

"Lieutenant Decker, bring the catapult online and let me know once complete."

"Yes, sir."

"The Estral shuttle has entered our docking bay," said Hiven-Tar.

"Repeat the instruction for them to remain onboard and let them know we have someone coming to do a headcount." Blake got through to McKinney. "The Estral shuttle is docking. Are you in position?"

"Yes, sir. We've got the area secure. Even if they have a thousand soldiers waiting to assault the ship, they won't get past the airlock."

"That's good to know. The Aranol is going to Confederation Space and will be there in two weeks. Those Estral might know a way to help us fight it."

"I take it we're going to use the Lightspeed Catapult again?"

"That's right. Its power source isn't as stable as we'd like. It might be a bumpy journey."

"Better than forty years at lightspeed, sir."

"I fully agree," said Blake with feeling.

While Decker got the Lightspeed Catapult ready for its second firing, Blake waited impatiently for McKinney to get back to him. The interior of the *Cataclysm* was comprehensively blanketed in sensors, but it wasn't quite the same as being there. Consequently, Blake felt remote as McKinney, Raxil-Ven and Tren-Fir spoke to the occupants of the shuttle, who were out of sensor view.

After five minutes, McKinney came onto the comms.

"All done, sir. They're happy to stay on the shuttle. I have informed them they are prisoners of the human Confederation."

"Good. They sound cooperative."

"I'm hopeful, sir. There are sixty-three of them as they reported, with no injuries."

"There's something you aren't telling me, Lieutenant McKinney."

"They're all female, except for eight of them, sir."

"The Estral must have lost most of their men in the conflict," said Blake. "Or maybe their women are simply better at weapons research. Keep an eye on things and let me know at once if there's any sign of trouble."

"Will do, sir."

With everything settled, Blake felt himself descend into a state of calm, from which he could focus on the remaining issue – the upcoming operation of the Lightspeed Catapult. He spoke to Decker to find out if she required any assistance. She expressed dismay at the dryness of her mouth and Blake found himself at the replicator fetching her a cup of orange juice. Upon his return, he discovered Lieutenant Decker was hungry, so he made a second trip to the replicator to obtain a cheese salad sandwich. After that, he left her alone.

With nothing specific to occupy him, Blake remained deep in

thought. The war against the Vraxar had always been a case of fighting the tide. Their endless waves rolled in against humanity's wall of sand, forever lapping close to the sides or threatening to spill over the top. The Aranol was a discovery which showed how little effort the Vraxar had really put in so far. This time they were sending potentially thousands of their fleet, as well as the biggest damned ship in known space. They would roll straight over that wall of sand and wash away everything hiding behind it.

Blake didn't like to dwell on potential failure, so he cut off that line of thought. Instead, he pictured Lieutenant Pointer and told himself how nice it would be to find her and speak with her alone for just a few minutes. The idea made him smile, but there was no way he could leave the bridge, even for a short break.

He looked around for the dozenth time to make sure everyone was wearing a spacesuit and had a visor close by.

"Does anyone need an injector?" he asked, looking at his own with distaste. No one responded.

Eventually, the time came.

"I've got the Lightspeed Catapult fully running in isolation, sir," said Decker. "I'm just about to switch it over onto our live systems. As soon as that happens, it has access to the Obsidiar-Teronium."

"Do it."

The background whine which had never gone away since they'd shut off the overcharge repeater suddenly increased in volume and harshness.

"That's it done," said Decker.

"When can we go?" asked Blake.

"Any time you choose, sir."

He checked his main console. The Lightspeed Catapult was once more listed as one of the *ES Cataclysm*'s critical systems. Its entry was highlighted in red and he touched it to find out more information.

> LC CRIT SYS 4: UNKNOWN ALERT; UNKNOWN
ALERT; UNKNOWN ALERT.

"Three unknowns?"

Decker smiled ruefully. "One of them relates to the instability of the Obsidiar-Teronium. The other two appeared as soon as I finished tying in. If we're lucky, they're false positives."

"I am feeling lucky!" said Ran-Lor. "It is a day for good luck!"

"I never heard of an optimistic Ghast before," said Hawkins.

"We are neither optimists, nor pessimists," said Ran-Lor. "We eat our pastes and we exist."

Hawkins was already tuned in to the Ghast sense of humour and she laughed. The sound served as a distraction and Blake was happy that Hawkins' ordeal in Estral Space didn't seem like it would have a long-term effect. He hoped the same would be true of the others.

One of the monitoring gauges was misbehaving.

"The utilisation on the Obsidiar-T is rising," he said.

"The Lightspeed Catapult requires a certain amount of power to keep warm."

"It wasn't drawing this much on the first run."

"No, it wasn't."

At that moment, Blake realised how much everything was in the balance. The Obsidiar-T core was unstable and the Lightspeed Catapult was far from a finished product. Relying on both at the same time would be utterly stupid were there any other choice.

There *was* no choice.

"Lieutenant Dunbar, our target is Prime. Enter the coordinates."

"That's done, sir."

"Ran-Lor, please advise our passengers that we're about to attempt the return journey to Confederation Space. It might be a good time to keep fingers crossed."

The sound of the bridge door caused him to turn in irritation - it wasn't a time for distractions. Lieutenant Pointer was there, and she was one distraction he didn't mind.

"I couldn't sleep," she said. "What's wrong?"

"We're going home, Lieutenant," said Blake.

She came over to the front of the bridge.

"I missed you," she whispered

Blake's stomach clenched tightly and he did his best to smile. "We'll get through this, huh?"

"It's going to be that bad, is it?"

"Pretty much. We're ready - take a seat, please."

Pointer found herself a spare seat near Lieutenant Hawkins and the two of them let the active crew get on with it. There wasn't any more preparation to be done.

"Lieutenant Decker, we're as ready as we'll ever be."

It wasn't strictly true, but no one objected.

"You know the drill – there'll be warmup and then we fire. This might be a good time to inject."

Ran-Lor used the internal comms to pass the warning to everyone on the ship. There were plenty of the injectors spare, as if the Space Corps expected the Lightspeed Catapult to be a roaring success capable of a hundred uses without a single hiccup. Blake jabbed himself in the thigh and grimaced as the fluid entered his veins.

"I'm commencing the warmup," said Decker.

The words hadn't left her mouth before one of the monitoring indicators shot all the way from left to right. A second gauge changed to maximum a second later. Blake didn't waste his breath asking if the behaviour was expected – it probably wasn't, but they had to make this trip whatever it took.

The noise began and the *ES Cataclysm* shook like an old aeroplane in the middle of turbulence. A booming from the vessel's nose echoed through the bridge and the shrieking of over-stressed Obsidiar rose steadily to prominence.

The entire bank of monitoring needles jumped around for a few seconds and then steadily converged on the far-right of their gauges.

Everything nailed on one hundred percent, thought Blake. *That core better hold together.*

He looked at his hands and his eyes traced a path to his shoulder. The blurriness was back and his movements left a faint trace in the air as he operated his console. He knew if he turned around, everyone else would look the same. He remembered Lieutenant Flynn and closed his eyes in hope that it wouldn't happen again.

We've got a lot more onboard this time. Men and women rescued, only to find they have to go through this.

The noise increased in volume until it felt to Blake as if a sharp implement were scraping against his ear drum. The control rods buzzed against his palms and fought against his grip. The bulkhead wall screeched and Blake's eyes searched for the tear in the metal he was sure the sound indicated. He refused to succumb to the easy acceptance that failure was coming.

We're going to make it. We will not fail.

The blurring of his flesh became progressively more pronounced, until each movement produced a hundred reflections, which trailed a moment behind. It was a peculiar sensation, as if he existed in an infinity of different places, each one diverging by the tiniest of fractions.

"Firing!" shouted Lieutenant Decker.

The monitoring gauges on the Obsidiar-T core redrew with completely new scales, hundreds of times higher than they had been a second before. The power of the refined Obsidiar was beyond anything Blake had experienced in the past.

The power to transcend.

The different, overlapping sounds which came together into a single whole, cut out, leaving only the incessant, painful whining. Blake's mind begged for the release granted by unconsciousness or death. He wouldn't permit either and forced himself to stay awake, using every ounce of his willpower.

The Lightspeed Catapult gave one thump, loud and deep like a hundred overcharged particle beams heard from close range.

A wormhole opened in front of the *ES Cataclysm* and the spaceship went through.

CHAPTER SEVENTEEN

BLAKE WAS sure he'd remained conscious throughout the transit and he was equally sure they'd gone *somewhere*, wherever that was. He turned his head towards the navigational system, to see if they were close to Prime. Something wasn't right.

"What the hell?" he asked, his words slurred.

When he tried to stand a drum beat inside his head and his spacesuit injected him. The pain of the needle was dull and remote, like his skin was made from rubber. He got to his feet, leaving echoes of his movement hanging in the air behind him. The first person he laid his eyes on was Lieutenant Pointer. She looked asleep.

"Wake up!" he shouted. "Anyone?"

"I am awake," said Ran-Lor.

"Where are we?"

"We have arrived," said the Ghast.

The alien had the same languid movements as Blake saw in himself. Hiven-Tar was also awake and when he leaned across his console, the echoes clung to him.

"We're out of phase," said Blake. "It should have stopped."

"I think we are in phase, while the ship itself is out of phase," said Ran-Lor.

That didn't sound right – everything on the *Cataclysm* was completely in focus.

"Where are we?" repeated Blake. His brain was slowly getting its act together and it told him he should be sitting in his chair, in case there were any dangers nearby.

"We are six hours from the Confederation world Prime," said Ran-Lor. "We arrived exactly where we intended."

"Lieutenant Decker? Wake up!" shouted Blake.

"Mmph."

Blake got into his seat again. The Lightspeed Catapult was offline and unavailable, the same as it was after the first trip. The Obsidiar-Teronium core monitoring tools were reporting so many errors and red alerts that he didn't bother trying to read through them. The core was generating sufficient power to run a dozen planets. It couldn't last and it wasn't safe to wait here any longer.

"We need to get away."

"I agree," said Ran-Lor.

Blake's feet carried him to where Lieutenant Decker was trying gamely to rouse herself. True to type, his spacesuit had squirted him full of battlefield adrenaline and Blake already felt more alert. The echoes refused to leave and he saw them in the movements of Lieutenant Hawkins and Dunbar as they jerked awake.

"Caz?" said Blake. He patted her cheek gently and then shook her. Panic gripped him and he shook her again.

Lieutenant Pointer wasn't dead and her eyes opened. "I feel like crap. The Vraxar portal was a lot smoother than that."

There was a distant quality to her words which Blake didn't think was entirely attributable to the transit.

"Get up! We have to go!"

"What's so important?" She looked as if she wanted to fall

asleep again. "Ow!" she said. "Stupid spacesuit just gave me a shot."

Blake couldn't micromanage everyone and he shouted encouragement to try and get them moving. When he was reassured the crew were making their best efforts, he went to stand next to Ran-Lor.

"Get a signal out to the Space Corps. It's imperative they know the Aranol is coming."

"I took the liberty of advising both our navy and the officers on your Raksol base," said the Ghast. "However, I did not receive a response and I am not sure if the comms are operating normally."

"What do you mean?"

"I think the ES Cataclysm is dislocated from its time stream, Captain Charles Blake. We are separate from our usual place in the universe."

"That's a good enough explanation," said Lieutenant Decker. She was on her feet, though she didn't look steady.

"Are we affected as well?" asked Blake.

"I don't know, sir. We should get away from this ship as soon as possible. The Obsidiar-Teronium has changed state – I have no idea what's happened to it, but I'm sure it's completely unstable. This is something totally outside of anything I've seen before – the Obsidiar-T is holding the Cataclysm in the wrong phase. I'm sure of it, and I don't want to be here - whatever it decides to do."

"I agree - we will abandon ship. Ran-Lor, are we close to anywhere we can set down?"

"The nearest solar system will require lightspeed."

"I wouldn't recommend setting down anyway," said Decker. "Leave the Cataclysm here in the middle of nowhere where it can't do any harm."

Blake nodded once and opened a channel to Lieutenant McKinney. "Have you any casualties to report?"

"No, sir, no casualties."

The words were unexpected and Blake had been prepared for far worse.

"That's excellent news, Lieutenant, but we can't celebrate quite yet. We're abandoning ship."

"Is it something to do with this weird stuff that's affecting everyone down here?"

"Yes – we have to get away from here. We're taking our two shuttles and the Estral are coming with us. Put as many soldiers on their shuttle as you need to ensure they don't try anything."

With the order given to abandon ship, Blake handed off to control to the *ES Cataclysm's* battle computer. It would look after the ship until the cruiser's fate was decided.

"We're going to lose so much valuable data," said Lieutenant Decker.

"It's all in your head."

"True."

They left the bridge in a group and made a run for the shuttle bay. It was one of the strangest experiences Blake could remember – every movement left a trail after it and the faster the movement, the longer the trail. In addition, there was an ethereal quality – a serenity that made him feel they were running in slow motion. His mind was anything but serene and it churned through recent events. It appeared as though they had survived a second firing of the Lightspeed Catapult, but that success brought another series of problems. It was ever thus.

There was no direct access to the Shuttle bay. Instead, airlock tunnels led to the docking irises on the vessels in the bay. The system was compatible with more or less anything and the Estral shuttle was clamped at the end of the third tunnel.

McKinney waited, his visor raised. He shouted orders at the soldiers, directing them to their shuttles. He saw Blake.

"Would you like to see the prisoners, sir?" he asked. "I've got a squad of twenty in there with repeaters."

"Yes, I'd like to see them," Blake confirmed. "Lieutenants Decker and Pointer, you're coming with me, so are you Ran-Lor."

"It's a squeeze, sir," warned McKinney.

"That's fine. Where are the rest of my crew?"

"They're on their way."

The third airlock tunnel was at the far end of the long access room. Two soldiers stood at the entrance, with their repeater barrels lowered into the firing position. Blake ran past them with the other three coming after. There were two more soldiers at the far end, both of whom he recognized.

"Welcome aboard the Estral Express," said R1T Jeb Whitlock.

"Please mind the gap," added Huey Roldan.

There was no gap, just a faint seam where the Estral shuttle was attached to the airlock tunnel. Blake stepped over it and into the blue-lit interior of the transport craft. Dozens of Estral stared at him, with their wide, pale grey eyes. Blake had never seen a Ghast woman in the flesh, let alone an Estral one. Compared to the males, they were two feet shorter and slender, with the same grey skin and a disturbingly similar range of humanlike expressions. He felt the need to say something.

"We are leaving," he said.

"Best introduction ever," whispered Pointer.

"Shh."

The interior of the shuttle failed to match the sweeping design of the exterior. In fact, it looked arguably less comfortable than a Space Corps model, a thing Blake had, until now, not thought possible. There was seating which was clearly designed to dissuade anyone from sitting and there wasn't even a view screen to keep the passengers occupied. The Estral weren't complaining, though there was a squad of human soldiers pointing plasma repeaters straight at them.

"Who's piloting this?" asked Blake. "We're leaving as soon as everyone's onboard."

"There's an Estral lady at the controls, with Sergeant Li keeping watch," said Ricky Vega, indicating an open doorway in the front bulkhead. "The translation modules can just about keep up and I think she knows what the plan is."

"They don't seem too bothered about these streamers we're leaving behind," said Clifton, lifting his arm and leaving a hundred fading copies in its wake. "It's like they've seen it all before."

The words struck Blake as oddly insightful, but he didn't want to spend time asking the soldier to explain why he'd reached that conclusion. Instead, he entered the cockpit to find Sergeant Li and Casey McCoy combining speech and exaggerated gestures to communicate with the Estral at the controls. If it wasn't for the fact that these were trained, experienced soldiers and this was a potentially bloodthirsty alien prisoner, Blake would have sworn the two of them were trying to flirt with the captive. The Estral turned towards him, blinked her almond-shaped grey eyes and spoke. Her voice was light and feminine, even if the sounds didn't make sense. The language modules gave it a go.

"[Translation unclear: Hello.]"

"Hello," said Blake, his eyes more on the controls than the captive. Everything looked standard and he was sure he could pilot the shuttle himself if required.

"I think she's called…" McCoy replicated a sound he evidently thought was the Estral's name.

It didn't take a polyglot to recognize the low quality of the reproduction and Blake wondered if he caught the hint of an upturning at the side of the alien's mouth. Then, Ran-Lor put his head into the cockpit.

"I have located their most senior member," he said. "She is a researcher from the facility."

"Will she talk?"

"Our conversation was a brief one and I do not know the extent of her willingness to volunteer secrets."

"Thank you," said Blake. He pointed at the Estral in the pilot's seat. "Can you make sure this lady here understands what is required?"

Ran-Lor spoke a series of short sentences. The language modules didn't offer an understandable translation and Blake asked himself how the Ghast could still communicate after several hundred years of language divergence. The important fact was that they could.

The Estral responded and Blake listened hard to see if she was hostile, scared or whatever else she might be. When the captive stopped talking, Blake found himself non-the-wiser.

"She is waiting for your warship to detach its gravity clamps and then she will follow the other two shuttles."

It was a good enough answer.

One of the soldiers in the passenger bay shouted that everyone was onboard. Sergeant Li lowered his visor and Blake did likewise. There were several channels for the troops to use and Blake joined the open one in time to catch McKinney confirming everything was in place.

"Everything is set, can someone get Captain Blake into the....hello, sir. We are ready to depart."

Blake used the visor to send a command to the ES Cataclysm's battle computer. It didn't respond immediately and he became concerned that whichever of them was in the wrong phase, it was now an impediment to communication. He breathed out when he heard the gravity clamps disengage from the shuttle's hull.

The pilot moved her hands nimbly across the flight console and brought up a sensor feed. On it, Blake saw the *Cataclysm's* docking bay door sliding upwards into its recess.

"Will this go away when we leave the ship, sir?" asked McCoy, moving his repeater barrel in a circle to produce a trail.

"If it doesn't, we're screwed," said Blake.

"Will we be invisible to other people and stuff?"

"He's asking if he can start breaking into houses without getting caught, sir," explained Li.

"Hey, Sergeant, that's not what I'm asking at all!"

Blake would have normally enjoyed the banter. Now, he was too apprehensive to get involved. The sensor feed showed the *Cataclysm's* two shuttles speeding away from their berths, travelling far faster than during a usual departure. The Estral pilot used a pair of vertical silver bars to take the shuttle sideways from the docking clamp. The vessel's engine was smooth and the effects of its acceleration were well-damped by the life support.

They exited the *ES Cataclysm's* bay and McCoy continued to wave one arm around, to see if he was returning to normal.

"Aw, shit," he said.

There was also a rear feed and through it, Blake watched the cruiser recede along with his hopes.

"Damn," said Li.

The Estral pilot turned to check if the words meant she was being given new instructions. Blake shook his head, not knowing if it would get the message across.

"Keep going," he said and the language module in his visor squawked something out.

Blake left the cockpit. Lieutenants Pointer and Decker were sitting on the metal floor, with their backs to the bulkhead wall.

"I don't know what to do, sir," said Decker. She tried a smile.

"At least we made it home, even if no one will be able to see us or hear us."

"Or learn about the Aranol," said Pointer bitterly.

Blake felt their dismay affecting him and he hated the feeling. There was nothing he could say or do to put the situation right. He'd been sure it was the *Cataclysm* itself which was in the correct phase – after all, the spaceship was as stable as it had ever been.

And then, he heard a ragged cheer break out across the open channel. The words mingled into one and he couldn't tell what anyone was saying. More cheering joined in and Blake felt the first tingling of excitement. He connected to the officer channel, but he didn't need to hear McKinney's words to realise what was going on. Blake waved his arm in front of Lieutenant Pointer's face. The echoes were there, fewer in number and barely visible. Then, they were gone.

"We did it!" he shouted into the comms, letting the moment wash away the lingering numbness of the journey home.

When the noise died away, Blake spoke to McKinney on Shuttle One.

"Send a message to the Raksol base on Prime. Tell them the Aranol is coming and request an immediate pickup from our current location. Whatever ship they send, it has to stay the hell away from the ES *Cataclysm* and make sure you get an acknowledgement."

"Yes, sir, I'll get that sent right away. Just so you know, the phase effects ended at five thousand klicks from the *Cataclysm*."

"Thank you, Lieutenant."

There wasn't much room to stand, let alone sit. Nevertheless, Blake managed to hunker down next to Lieutenant Pointer. She smiled at him and he smiled back. Decker caught the look and winked at the two of them. Blake didn't care if she knew and he laughed.

The message reached the Raksol base and the closest warship was sent to complete the pickup. The wait wasn't a long one. Within the hour, a huge shape appeared from nowhere and surged towards the three shuttles. At the last second, it slowed and swung around to bring its docking bay near to the transports.

"Oblivion," said Blake. "Another new one."

"The pride of the fleet," said Ran-Lor. "That's the *Rusor-Nilfar.*"

"You kept that one secret. Fifty billion tonnes?"

"Nearer sixty."

"I hope it can take a beating."

The Ghost nodded. "It can."

The captain of the *Rusor-Nilfar* gave clearance to land and, fifteen minutes later, Blake was off the shuttle and heading for the battleship's bridge.

CHAPTER EIGHTEEN

VIEWED FROM THE AIR, the Destiny plant looked as if it could fulfil any one of a dozen functions, from food processing to storage. It was a long building, a few kilometres from the outskirts of the Raksol facility, clad in a concrete shell to hide the hardened alloy walls underneath. The plant was anonymous by design and built in such a manner that deep space surveillance wouldn't highlight its strategic importance. Most significantly, its modular construction meant it could be moved elsewhere if a threat was identified.

Fleet Admiral Duggan watched the ongoing work for a few minutes from the cockpit of a Raksol shuttle. They were making a few modifications to the facility and the time constraints meant it was tough to complete the changes without it being obvious. The time for subtlety was gone and the area was a hive of activity.

"Cerys, please access the latest revision of the project plan and confirm the most recent estimate for completion of the works."

"Eight days, three hours, Fleet Admiral."

Duggan frowned. "It was seven days twenty-two hours when

I checked an hour ago. The Aranol is predicted to arrive in nine days."

"There has been slippage on the refinement of module 3B."

"A lot of slippage. Slippage they didn't warn me to expect."

Cerys was human enough to know when it wasn't expected to provide an answer and it remained silent. News of the delay angered Duggan and he swung the shuttle away towards its landing pad on the military base. The Destiny plant was a critical element to his plans and it was already in grave danger of being ready too late to have an impact. There was a Plan B, which he did not wish to implement if he could avoid doing so.

Duggan landed the shuttle and got into the waiting gravity car, accompanied by the two soldiers who acted as his escort. He was mid-way through telling the vehicle to return him to his office, when he had a change of mind.

"Take me to the central holding block."

The car's navigation system didn't respond verbally, since Duggan had instructed it to be silent so that it wouldn't disturb him with its inane chatter. It floated away from the edge of the landing pad and waited until it was safe to enter the traffic moving along one of the busy streets. After a few minutes, the car stopped at the outer gates of the walled compound which surrounded the holding block. The guards stationed outside didn't recognize Duggan but their handheld check-in device did. The men's eyes widened and they saluted, before waving him through.

The external gate moved aside and Duggan's gravity car took him into the parking lot in front of the ugly cube of concrete which was the above-ground section of the holding facility. It was generally referred to as a prison, but it was designed to offer safe storage for anything which could be dangerous or, perhaps, sensitive in nature.

There was nothing prison-like about the lobby - it was as

bright and open as the reception area in the central administration block. Cerys had evidently caught up with Duggan's movements and the base AI had sent advance warning to the personnel. Consequently, every seat at the main desk was occupied, with the staff trying their best to look focused.

There was a woman standing at the desk, smartly dressed and with her dark hair held back from her forehead by a silver band. She moved to intercept Duggan and he recognized her as 2nd Lieutenant Moya Florentine, the on-shift officer in charge.

"Fleet Admiral Duggan," she greeted him. "Are you here to see the new arrivals, sir?"

"I am. Have they given you any recent cause for concern?"

"None whatsoever, though that does not mean we are less vigilant."

"That's good. Has the equipment arrived?"

"Most of it was installed three days ago as you are aware. The final processing cluster arrived late last night and is working as expected."

"Is Lieutenant Jacobs on site?"

"I don't think she's been anywhere else since the Estral came, sir."

Duggan gave a half-smile. "I would like to see her."

"She's on level Sub-9, sir. I'll take you there right away."

They entered an airlift and Lieutenant Florentine spoke their destination. The lift made no sound as it dropped into the below-ground area of the holding facility. The door opened.

"Level Subterranean 9," announced the lift computer.

There was another reception area here, smaller than the one on the surface, but with considerably more bodies squeezed inside. Some of these were grey-skinned and in excess of seven feet tall. When it came to this particular task, it was one-hundred percent collaborative between humans and Ghasts.

There were six passages leading away, each sealed by the

type of metal door which could be found in many other types of military buildings - doors which were designed to withstand extreme levels of force.

Florentine spoke to a woman hurrying by with a diagnostic tablet in each hand.

"Where is Lieutenant Jacobs?"

The woman was in a world of her own and it took her a moment to respond. "Along there in the monitoring room, with Lieutenant Paz."

Duggan knew exactly where he was going and he thanked Florentine. He beckoned the two soldiers to follow and set off along one of the corridors, which was filled with personnel brought here to study the Estral.

The monitoring room was second-left and Duggan went through the door. There were consoles and wall-mounted screens, many of them recently-installed. There was plenty of space in the holding facility, which made it the ideal place for the task in hand.

Allison Jacobs and Charissa Paz were a few metres away, talking to a couple of the technicians. Paz saw Duggan first and raised her hand in greeting.

"Good day," said Duggan. "What is our progress, Lieutenant Jacobs?"

It was an open-ended question and he waited to see what Jacobs would prioritise.

"Everything is installed, sir. We are struggling with the language modules. Ran-Lor's assistance is invaluable, but he is acting as both interpreter and technical liaison with the alien languages teams. He can't be everywhere at once."

Ran-Lor was, amongst other things, a scholar in the early language of his people from the time of the schism. There weren't many like him and he was in a unique position of being able to understand much of what the Estral said, though still imperfectly. For all his knowledge, he was still a large step removed from being fluent in modern Estral. The other Ghosts could speak to the Estral more effectively than the human language modules, but it was slow going and prone to errors.

Duggan asked the most important question.

"Is there any sign they are willing to help us?"

Jacobs chewed on her lip. "There are factions within the Estral, sir. It is our impression that some wish to help, whilst others are either suspicious or outright hostile. Everything is set up for them if they wish to share their technology."

"There was nothing of any use in their shuttle databanks," said Paz. "Captain Blake's report said they left the Jonli facility in a hurry and there's no evidence they managed to hide any of their weapons research data on their escape vessel. Whatever they know, it's all in their heads."

"Are we even sure they have something useful to tell?" asked Duggan.

"Absolutely, sir. They tried to keep it quiet, but one of them let it slip that she was the lead scientist for the entire facility. These aren't soldiers trained to resist interrogation."

"If there's an impasse, we need to resolve it, Lieutenant. The Aranol's shields withstood an Obsidiar bomb and we must assume there's a strong chance they will resist multiple bomb detonations. Therefore, it's imperative we have this extra string to our bow – if we can modify our missiles to go through the Aranol's shields, we might be able to drive the enemy away."

"Drive away, not destroy," said Paz sadly.

"That's the current thinking," said Duggan. "I don't like it any better than you do."

"We have people studying the Estral physiology in preparation for the administration of truth drugs," said Jacobs.

"They're too blunt an instrument, Lieutenant. Not only that, it'll ruin any trust we might otherwise engender."

"I don't know if we have the time to worry about trust," said Paz.

Jacobs took a deep breath. "Sir, the Aranol is predicted to arrive in nine days. In that time, we need to obtain the cooperation of our captives and extract details of how to convert our missiles. It is likely to require the manufacture of new components which will need to be retro-fitted to a hundred thousand of our missiles. It will not be quick or easy."

Duggan knew Jacobs to be a realist. "Is there any way we can accomplish our aims?"

"If the Estral spill the beans – with or without truth drugs - in the next few hours and it turns out we only need to adjust the guidance programs on our missiles, we'll have plenty of time."

"Except there's no way this can be fixed with programming," said Paz. "At some stage, we're going to require a production line for new missile parts. We're pretty good at doing this stuff, but nine days is a tall order."

"The updates to the Destiny plant are slipping," said Duggan.

"Irrevocably?"

"Not that I've been told. I'll be speaking to the project manager once I'm done here."

"We could do with Debbie Peterson now, huh?"

"I'd feel happier with her in charge."

PM Debbie Peterson was amongst the thousands killed during the Vraxar attack on the Tucson base. She wouldn't be helping out this time.

"We're left with spaceships, bombs and guns," said Paz. "Same as it ever was."

"And same as it'll always be," Jacobs replied.

Duggan took them by surprise. "I want to speak to the lead Estral. Right now."

His staff knew when he was beyond persuasion.

"It'll take five or ten minutes to arrange, sir. Where would you like to speak to the captive?"

"There's a meeting room three doors along. Take her there."

The monitoring room was secure enough to conduct an interview and there was no way a lone Estral would be able to escape. However, there were plenty of staff working here and Duggan didn't want them eavesdropping.

Jacobs hurried off, leaving Duggan, Paz and the two soldiers to find their way to the meeting room. There was a meeting breaking up and Duggan waved the last few personnel out into the corridor. There were chairs in the room, but he didn't feel it appropriate to sit.

"I recommend you stand back when she arrives, sir," Paz advised. "She might punch you on the nose."

Duggan chuckled. "I've suffered worse, Lieutenant." He saw she was serious. "Point taken – I'll stay out of easy punching range."

The door opened and Ran-Lor walked through.

"I will act as translator," said the Ghost.

"Do the Estral find lying as difficult as the Ghosts?" asked Duggan.

Ran-Lor's eyes glittered. "I cannot be certain. There have been no signs of deceit, yet I do not wish to promise certainty."

"I understand."

The door opened again and this time a female Estral entered the room. She was flanked by armed guards, with two more following behind. Lieutenant Jacobs walked in front and didn't once look at the captive, as if turning around would be a show of weakness.

"Stop," said Ran-Lor, with the captive three paces away from Duggan.

The Estral stopped. She was about Duggan's height, though slender. There were lines on her forehead and at the corners of her eyes, which suggested she was in her middle years. There was an undeniable beauty about her, like the alien features combined perfectly with the humanness of her expression. She met Duggan's gaze and he saw a coldness behind her grey eyes which might have come from fear, disdain or hostility, or perhaps none of those things.

"I am Fleet Admiral John Duggan. I command the human military."

The Estral spoke a few short sounds in a voice which was far more pleasing to the ear than that of the male Ghasts.

"Her name is Liyan-Evera," said Ran-Lor.

"Tell her I know she was in charge of the weapons facility. Tell her the Aranol is coming and that we need her assistance to destroy it."

It took one or two attempts to get the message across. The Estral responded.

"If the Aranol is in human territory, then it is not in Estral territory."

"This is how our earlier efforts progressed," said Lieutenant Jacobs. "They are distinctly reluctant to help."

Duggan nodded and raised a hand to request Jacobs remain quiet.

"The Vraxar are determined to eradicate the Estral," he said.

Liyan-Evera's mouth tightened and she uttered one brief syllable. "Yes."

"The Aranol will destroy humanity and then it will return to exterminate the Estral."

"We will destroy our foes."

"You haven't managed it yet. The Vraxar have thousands of spaceships in their fleet." Duggan narrowed his eyes. "Many of them are within the hold of the Aranol. If the Aranol is defeated, much of the Vraxar fleet will fall with it. Then, the odds will be much better for the Estral."

"We are not friends, human."

"We may never be friends. The wormhole which linked our territories is gone and the distance between us is great. There is no reason for us to fight."

There was no sign of Liyan-Evera warming to the idea of any form of relationship that didn't involve conflict between humans and Estral. "Two of your spaceships came into our territory."

She was spoiling for an argument and Duggan couldn't figure out why. The Estral were known to be warlike, so maybe it was in their nature.

"Which is the greater threat? The human Confederation or the Vraxar?"

Some of the coldness faded from Liyan-Evera's face. "The Vraxar do not stop and there is no reason for them to continue killing us. We are too far spread for them to make us extinct unless they pursue us for another hundred years."

Duggan had no idea if the Vraxar would persist or if they'd eventually give up on the Estral and focus on the as-yet-undiscovered Antaron species.

"Whatever commands the Vraxar, it is the embodiment of madness. Are you willing to gamble that it will tire of its efforts? We could stop the Aranol here and remove the guiding force behind our opponents."

There was uncertainty in Liyan-Evera's face and she didn't try to hide it. Duggan didn't know much about the Estral or their motivations and he guessed they believed themselves superior to other species. His past experience taught him they were murderous bastards in the same way as the Vraxar. The methods were different, but the intended end result was the same. It didn't matter – the Vraxar were a major threat to humans, Ghasts and Estral alike. Once the Vraxar were out of the equation, the Confederation could look to the future, even if that future eventually involved another war with the Estral.

"What do you propose?" she asked.

"You show us how to modify our missiles so they will penetrate the Aranol's shield."

"And have you use the technology against the Estral in the future?"

"That is for another day. This is today."

Liyan-Evera suddenly looked lost and out of her depth. Her shoulders slumped and she nodded. "I will instruct my team to assist you."

Duggan's heart jumped. "Thank you."

"The shield-penetrator modules are delicate and it will require specialist equipment to make them. Your missiles will require new propulsion sections. How long until the Aranol reaches here?"

"Nine days."

Liyan-Evera blinked in surprise. "I did not expect it would take so little time for the Vraxar to travel from Estral Space to human space."

"How long do you need?"

"The installation on Jonli was a dedicated unit for shield-penetrator ballistic research and we would require a similar facility here. Nine days is not enough."

"Perhaps we have existing technology you can use?" said Duggan, his newfound hope already gone.

"If you send your weapons scientists to us, we will speak with them. The chance of you possessing what we need is extremely remote."

Duggan didn't want to reveal how much of a setback this was, so he kept his expression neutral.

"You will have everything you require and you will have it today."

After Liyan-Evera was led from the meeting room, Duggan sat heavily in one of the chairs, whilst Paz and Jacobs watched him with concern.

"Well," he said at last. "It was always a remote possibility we'd get something from this. Lieutenant Jacobs – keep hard at the Estral and see what they come up with. In the meantime, it's spaceships, bombs and guns."

"And the Destiny plant."

"It was never meant to be converted into a bomb. I'd rather we weren't relying on it."

"I've seen the projections, sir."

"So have I, Lieutenant. It makes me fear success as much as I fear failure."

The Space Corps had built fifty Obsidiar bombs, many of which had failed during construction and been dismantled for safety. The Destiny plant was bomb number fifty-one and it was the first using Obsidiar-Teronium. If the bomb worked and the projections turned out anything close to the truth, the results would be unimaginable.

It was better than extinction at the hands of the Vraxar, but Duggan had no desire to carry the guilt on his shoulders. Until this morning, his hopes were pinned on *conventional* Obsidiar bombs or shield penetrating missiles. Now he only had one of those hopes left before he'd be required to test out 000051.

CHAPTER NINETEEN

THE *ES FULMINATOR* was one of the three Hadron battleships completed shortly after the *Ulterior-2*. The *Fulminator* was built from the same blueprint, which meant it was capable of kicking the crap out of the smaller members of the Vraxar fleet, assuming the aliens didn't already shit themselves when they saw it coming.

After almost two weeks of continuous debriefing, Captain Charlie Blake and his original crew were reunited and assigned to escort duties. This wasn't an ordinary escort mission and they were bringing an important cargo into the Rangel-3 system, where the Aranol was expected to arrive at some point in the next twenty hours. The journey to Rangel-3 was a long one and they were cutting it fine. It was only two hours ago that Blake had received a call telling him the cargo was ready to go and that he should get his warship into position.

"When is the *Atlas* due?" said Lieutenant Pointer, checking her watch.

"It's overdue," replied Blake.

"You don't think...?" said Lieutenant Quinn.

"No, I don't think," Blake replied sharply. "Delays happen."

Except they didn't happen very often and certainly shouldn't happen during an operation as critical as this one.

Blake kept a close eye on the updates rolling in across his command console. There was so much happening it was hard to keep on top of it. If the Aranol came in earlier than expected, he dreaded to think what effect it would have on the preparations.

"The comms man on the *Rusor-Nilfar* asks what's causing the hold up."

"Tell him there's no hold up."

"He doesn't believe me."

"I thought the Ghasts were meant to be gullible?"

"Not this one, sir."

"Tell him it won't be long."

The Ghast battleship was in a parallel stationary orbit above Prime and barely twenty kilometres from the *Fulminator*. If there'd been a viewing window on the portside, Blake knew he'd see the hulking shape of the Ghast warship, with its particle disruptor, endless missile launch tubes and the massive dome of its stasis nullifier.

As it was, there was no viewing window and Blake had to content himself with a sensor image of the Oblivion. Both warships were at a low altitude and the *Rusor-Nilfar* was amongst the clouds. Every so often, a bolt of lightning would hit the hull of the Ghast vessel and illuminate its outline against the dark grey. Rain came down in torrents and the wind blew in strong, unpredictable gusts. Against the Oblivion and the Hadron, the wrath of nature was insignificant.

Ten minutes after its scheduled arrival time, the Military Heavy Lifter *Atlas* broke out of lightspeed, fifty thousand kilometres away from Prime. It fired up its gravity drive and came in at what was – for an *MHL* – an exceptionally high speed of eighteen hundred kilometres per second.

"Any reported problems?" asked Blake.

"Its battle computer has checked in with us. Other than that, it's saying nothing."

The *MHL Atlas* wasn't carrying a crew. It would have been easier to manage if it was, but under Admiral Duggan's orders, it was unmanned.

The lifter slowed as it reached the upper atmosphere of Prime. It rotated smoothly and rapidly and descended directly between the *Fulminator* and the *Rusor-Nilfar*. The *Atlas* was easily the largest of the three in terms of volume, though in weight it was similar to the Hadron and lighter than the Oblivion.

The lifter was the Space Corps' newest model and was designed to carry unimaginably heavy loads from one place to another. It was twelve thousand metres in length and cuboid, with rounded edges and massive cargo doors underneath. Unlike earlier generation lifters, it was heavily armed and armoured and could likely go toe-to-toe with a Vraxar cruiser and stand a realistic chance of coming out on top.

"Nearly in place," said Lieutenant Cruz.

"How long is the lift scheduled to take?" asked Quinn.

"It's planned to take thirty minutes. Let's see if the ship claw back some of the lost time and do it in twenty."

"This thing the *Atlas* is picking up, it's going to work, isn't it?" asked Lieutenant Dixie Hawkins. "I mean, what if it just goes *pop* and the Vraxar laugh at us?"

"You think of some strange questions, Lieutenant. We won't be trying out the Destiny bomb immediately. The Alliance Fleet has five other Obsidiar bombs distributed amongst its warships. If they fail to take out the Aranol, that's when we get to see if the Destiny bomb works."

"I heard they had to use a separate Obsidiar bomb as a detonator," said Quinn. He shook his head. "This whole thing it's just madness from start to end. We only figured out how to produce

Obsidiar-Teronium a few weeks ago and now we're making a bomb out of it? With another bomb as a detonator?"

"What else could we do?" asked Hawkins. "This is endgame and we either win or we die."

"Yeah, I know the stakes," said Quinn. He threw his hands up. "I just want those Vraxar bastards to die whatever it takes and if we need to build a tower of Obsidiar-Teronium bombs and throw them like hand grenades, then I'll be ecstatic to help out with the lifting."

"There is more bad news," said Blake. "The Destiny bomb isn't equipped with a timer – only a warmup period."

"That shouldn't be a problem. We treat the warmup as the timer," said Quinn.

"We don't know exactly what the warmup is."

"You're kidding me?"

"Nope. The initiating routine sets off a reaction in the Obsidiar-Teronium and until that's complete, the detonator won't do anything more than blow the whole thing into pieces."

"How long are the estimates for the warmup?"

"Anything from ten seconds to sixty. That's what why we're here with the *Rusor-Nilfar* – to keep an eye on things during the preparation period."

"How will we know when it's time to hit lightspeed?" asked Hawkins. "Or are we crossing our fingers and hoping for the best?"

"No. We have a half-second window to escape. Our battle computer is set to recognise the trigger moment and it'll take us to lightspeed."

"So I won't be required to sit with my finger over the button?" asked Quinn. "That's a relief."

"This is *really* new technology, Lieutenant. We don't even know if it's going to work."

Neither Quinn nor Hawkins appeared especially convinced

by the arrangements. There again, they'd been around long enough to know when it was time to get on with things. Quinn gave a nervous laugh of acceptance and Hawkins pulled a face. Blake gave them a genuine thumbs-up to indicate he was happy he could rely on them so much.

"Look," said Pointer. "The *Atlas* is in place."

It wasn't every day Blake got to watch an *MHL* in operation and he kept his eyes on the sensor feed. The Destiny plant was three thousand metres in length and twelve hundred wide. Blake didn't know exactly how much Obsidiar-T was inside it, but he was sure the Confederation didn't have anything like enough to fill the building. If they were required to detonate the bomb, this was a significant sacrifice of the Confederation's resources and Blake was aware the Ghasts had offered to stump up some of their own reserves in replacement. Given this was their war as much as humanity's, it was only fair.

The operation didn't take long. The area around the plant was devoid of personnel, so there was nothing to prevent the lift happening quickly. The invisible gravity chains connected the *Atlas* to the walls of the bomb in hundreds of places. The *Fulminator*'s sensors picked up the power emanating from the chains and Blake gave a low whistle when he realised what they were capable of. The *Atlas* could likely pick up the sixty-billion-tonne *Rusor-Nilfar* if it needed to.

The Destiny bomb weighed somewhat less than sixty billion tonnes and it came up from the ground with serene ease. Once the bomb was fifty metres off the ground, the *Atlas* adjusted its chains in order to better balance the load. It resumed the lift and Blake saw pieces of concrete cladding fall away from the building's exterior as they fractured under the stresses. Underneath it was hard alloy which hardly flexed as it was hauled progressively higher.

Twenty-three minutes after its arrival, the *MHL Atlas* closed its cargo bay doors and sent a message to the ES *Fulminator* advising itself ready to go.

"That's the check-in point," said Blake. "Lieutenant Pointer, please contact Admiral Duggan and advise him we're ready to depart."

"Admiral Duggan wishes to speak to you, sir."

It was no surprise in the circumstances.

"Sir, we're ready," said Blake.

"I would like you to repeat your orders, Captain Blake."

The request betrayed the depths of Duggan's concern.

"We will fly to the edges of Rangel-3 and await the Aranol. Once there, the *Fulminator* and the *Rusor-Nilfar* will await the outcome of the engagement between the combined human and Ghost fleet. If our Obsidiar bombs fail to penetrate the enemy shields, we are to take whatever action is necessary to detonate the Obsidiar-Teronium bomb close to the Aranol."

"Sounds easy, doesn't it?" said Duggan with a bitter laugh. "Remember that the ES *Devastator* carried an Obsidiar bomb against *Ix-Gastiol* and that didn't work out as we planned."

"This time we have propulsion systems for the bombs and stasis nullifiers, sir."

"There's much that can go wrong. *Earth's Fury* and her sister ship *Earth's Vengeance* are based on planets Tunde and Larno respectively. They are fully loaded with Obsidiar projectiles and should give the Aranol something to think about, if they are given the chance to fire unhindered."

"Admiral Talley is in charge from the *Maximilian*," said Blake.

"You are outside of his command and Henry is aware of the fact. Once the engagement begins, you'll be best-placed to determine what to do and when. I'm trusting you with everything."

"I understand that, sir. I won't let you down." He paused. "What of the *Rusor-Nilfar*?"

"Tarjos Kol-Faran has been asked to follow your guidance. His seniority within the Ghast navy permits him to treat orders as advice only. I have met him several times and he is a sound officer."

Blake had also met Kol-Faran, though only once and that was two days ago. The Ghast captain was huge, even amongst his species, and he spoke with an eloquence that betrayed the existence of a fierce intelligence beneath the brawler's exterior. Blake had liked him immediately.

"I'm sure he'll do what is right, sir."

"It will take the *MHL Atlas* sixteen hours to reach Rangel-3," said Duggan. "That doesn't give you much leeway. Is there anything else before I go?"

Blake hesitated in asking something to which he was sure the answer was *no*. "Sir, are we far from obtaining results from our collaboration with the Estral scientists?"

"We've learned the theory behind how their shield penetrators work. Believe it or not, they pack modules into their warheads which knock the entire missile out of phase for a miniscule amount of time, yet without going into lightspeed. The modules are huge, expensive and they burn out after a single use. We're a long way from being able to implement the technology and the Estral themselves only install it on their largest missiles."

"The base on Jonli fired very large missiles," agreed Blake.

"Even our newest Shimmers are small in comparison. Anyway, we're wasting time. Perhaps if we had another six months I would be hopeful. As it is, we will have to rely on our Obsidiar bombs bringing down the Aranol's shield and hopefully the enemy with it. Otherwise, it's going to be a dirty fight."

"Let's see what our future holds, sir. In twenty hours, we'll have a better idea."

"It's going to be the longest twenty hours of my life."

Duggan closed the channel and Blake looked at his crew in

turn. They'd been through so much that not one of them looked scared. There was worry and concern, but they'd lost their fear bit-by-bit, each time they fought the Vraxar.

"Send a polite message to Tarjos Kol-Faran on the *Rusor-Nilfar* informing him we are ready to depart and ask him if he would like to accompany us on our journey."

Lieutenant Pointer laughed. "I will use those exact words, sir."

"Lieutenant Quinn, I have just this moment put the MHL *Atlas* into slave mode and it should mimic our lightspeed warmup. Please check and make sure nothing goes awry."

"Yes, sir. The *Atlas* is tied in and I foresee no problems."

Blake allowed himself a few seconds before he gave the order. He glanced at the sensor feed and saw the enormous hull of the heavy lifter, filling the skies to the left. Beyond it, the Oblivion battleship was still visible, with its upper decks wreathed in clouds. The rain fell unceasingly and drummed against the spaceships. Two of them were the most capable weapons of war built by their respective navies. The final one was an unknown – a bomb with the potential to annihilate stars if it fulfilled its potential, or to ensure the death of humanity if it was called upon and failed to achieve its purpose. It was a terrible thought to imagine that everything might come down to this single device and Blake felt his heart quicken.

"Sir?" said Hawkins. "It's time to go."

"Synchronise with the *Rusor-Nilfar* and the *Atlas*. I'll bring us to forty thousand klicks above Prime, warm up the fission engines and take us to Rangel-3 on my order," said Blake.

"Roger that," said Quinn. "We're synchronised and ready to go on your command."

Blake pulled on the *Fulminator*'s control bars. The warship's engines lifted it easily away from the surface and it accelerated steadily until the clouds and the beating rain were left far, far below.

"We're at forty thousand klicks, Lieutenant. Take us to lightspeed."

"Lightspeed in seven seconds."

The three spaceships jumped into high lightspeed, with the Hadron and Oblivion travelling at seventy percent of their maximum velocity in order to ensure they didn't leave the heavy lifter behind.

"Sixteen hours until we arrive in the Rangel-3 system," said Quinn. "We are targeting the ninth planet, which is called Felspar. It should be far enough out that we can watch, without being shot to pieces by any Vraxar who might be waiting."

"There are no Vraxar waiting, Lieutenant. We've killed the ones that made it to Confederation Space," said Blake. "There's only the Aranol."

"What if it arrives early?" asked Hawkins.

"If it does, we'll act as necessary. They've combed through the modelling data a thousand times and we know when it's coming. All we've got to do is blow the Vraxar to pieces and then we can go home. Until the Estral resume hostilities with us."

When it was spelled out so plainly, Blake felt depressed about the future and he wished he'd kept his mouth closed.

"Gee sir, I thought you were meant to be the optimist."

He spun in his seat to find Lieutenant Pointer grinning at him and he was reminded that not every future was predetermined and that some of them were worth fighting for. He grinned back.

CHAPTER TWENTY

THE FLIGHT to the Rangel-3 system was tough for the crew. They had fought the Vraxar for so long – coming from their early beginnings on the *Juniper* orbital and from there into the middle of the conflict on Atlantis – that it was almost impossible for them to imagine they might play a part in this final showdown with the enemy. Assuming this *was* to be a final showdown, Blake thought to himself. The Vraxar had existed for so long and they always seemed to have something in reserve. The Aranol had to be the last.

"There are 271 ships in the Alliance Fleet," said Lieutenant Pointer, at the halfway stage of the journey. "Plus another three if you add the *Fulminator*, *Rusor-Nilfar* and the *Atlas*."

"It doesn't leave us much elsewhere," added Hawkins. "Look at what we've got! Hadrons, Galactics, and near enough every Imposition in the fleet."

Quinn read through the ship roster. "The Ghasts are pulling their weight too. They don't have so many ships, but I reckon the overall tonnage isn't much different from the Space Corps' contribution."

"This is the moment, folks," said Blake. "All or nothing. Show the Vraxar we aren't pissing about any more."

"What if the Aranol simply opens its bay doors and a thousand of their ships come out?" said Cruz. "How will we combat it?"

"We'll meet them with Obsidiar bombs, Lieutenant. Failing that, missiles and particle beams. Their Neutralisers won't be anything like so effective now that all of our fleet have backup power cores and their comms jammers are useless now that we've fitted the latest comms arrays to our spaceships. The enemy have the numbers but we have something to fight for. When they first came to Atlantis, the evidence suggested they were technologically superior to us and they were. Now we've caught up and in places we're ahead."

"Whoever or whatever runs the Aranol doesn't like to be on the frontline," said Quinn. "What if they simply go to lightspeed and start blasting our planets into pieces?"

Blake knew something his crew didn't know. He owed them the truth.

"They beefed up the fission modelling on a few of our warships. They fitted a couple of dedicated number cruncher bots into the *Maximilian*. If the Aranol makes a short lightspeed trip, such as would be necessary to reach a Confederation world, we'll know their destination in a few seconds."

"And then we follow them and what comes next?" said Hawkins.

"Obsidiar bombs."

"Even in proximity to one of our planets?"

"Those are the orders."

Quinn looked haunted by the revelation and he slumped. "Shit."

"It's nothing unexpected, Lieutenant. They'd have done the

same at Pioneer when *Ix-Gastiol* came. No one wants to make a sacrifice of this magnitude."

"Yeah, I know that sir, Still, it's awful to hear the decision is on a strategy planning document somewhere, written out like it's an order for pizza."

"The Confederation Council were in full agreement. They're in this with us and not one of them has chosen to go into space."

"Everyone together," said Cruz. "The way it should be."

"When your enemy is twice as big and twice as strong as you are, it's the only way to win."

Quinn stared into the distance. "Who loses out on this one? Who are the unlucky billions? Does the Space Corps have any idea?"

"They anticipate Old Earth will be the primary target. This is a punitive attack by the Vraxar, so where better for them to go?" Blake replied. "However, there's hope, Lieutenant. The Aranol knows the location of Old Earth, yet it has chosen the Rangel-3 system. Do you know why that is?"

"They have to recharge their batteries."

"That's the assumption we're making. It's why much of the Alliance Fleet is spread in orbit about the sun – it's where we believe the Aranol will go."

"And we're going to drop enough bombs to wipe out a star."

"Like the Falsehood bomb," said Pointer. "Only this time there'll be no coming back for Rangel-3. One bomb was almost enough for Anxiar-Rho and Rangel-3 is a lot smaller than that one."

"I keep telling myself that they're only stars," said Hawkins. "That there are trillions of other ones out there. And yet, looking up at the stars when I was a kid is what made me join the Space Corps in the first place. It's hard to think I might be party to their destruction."

"We don't know what's going to happen," said Blake. The words didn't sound convincing.

With four hours to go, Blake found himself drinking coffee, though his mouth didn't crave it, and reading through the list of hardware which would soon be facing the Aranol. The Obsidiar bombs carried by the Alliance Fleet were numbered 000045 through to 000049 and they came from the same design documents as the Sorrow bomb which had failed to deplete the Aranol's shields only two weeks ago. Five was better than one, assuming they were able to land successive detonations near enough to the enemy.

And then, he discovered a classified report titled Theoretical Area of Effect Report: Destiny Plant Bomb Conversion. The report hadn't been amongst the files while they were waiting for the *MHL Atlas* to complete its pickup, so it must have populated into the *Fulminator*'s databanks moments before it entered light-speed. Blake skimmed the details, his eyes wide. There was a whole lot of Obsidiar in the plant, so the predicted magnitude of the explosion was incredible.

At the end of the report was another document, with the title Addendum: Obsidiar-Teronium Refinement of the Destiny Bomb. Blake felt his entire body shake when he saw the projections and he closed the file, wondering if this was too much responsibility for humanity to shoulder. This was the path of gods, with everything that entailed.

"Who just walked over your grave?" asked Hawkins.

Blake smiled weakly. "It's finally hit home what the *Atlas* is carrying in its hold."

"A big, terrible bomb."

"And so much more."

Blake watched the cogs in Hawkins' mind turn. He saw she wanted to ask the question, but she backed away from it. Sometimes it was better to pretend something didn't exist until you had no choice other than to use it. The Destiny bomb was an aberration on the universe and there was no requirement for her to learn the details until she saw it with her own eyes. If the five Obsidiar bombs did what they were supposed to, they could fly back home and nobody would ever know.

With an hour to go, the *Fulminator* dropped out of lightspeed in order to pick up the latest information on the Space Corps network. The *Atlas* and the *Rusor-Nilfar* appeared within thirty thousand kilometres and checked in.

"Any significant news?" asked Blake.

"There is no sighting of the Aranol," said Pointer. "I guess we'll be in plenty of time for the party."

"What about the Alliance Fleet?"

"Every warship is on patrol in the Rangel-3 system and we should join their network as soon as we complete the final stage of our journey."

"Good. Now speak to the Ghasts and make sure they haven't received any conflicting orders we might like to be aware of."

"Tarjos Kol-Faran advises there are no changes and everything can proceed as planned."

"Then what are we waiting for? Lieutenant Quinn, take us into lightspeed."

The three craft left the empty area of space and resumed their flight. Blake tipped his last coffee away unfinished and tried to keep himself busy. He asked someone to add a timer to one corner of the bulkhead screen so that he could keep a track of when the Aranol would arrive.

"Four-and-a-half hours," he muttered.

"Anyone want a game of backgammon?" asked Hawkins. "I hear it clears the mind."

"I didn't know you played," said Cruz.

"I don't. What about you?"

"Nope."

Blake had no idea how to play backgammon and he wasn't planning to start. In fact, he had no idea why he was even thinking about it and he took his seat once more in order to brush up on the technical capabilities of the warships in the arena. There was nothing new – the Space Corps had plenty of missiles and particle beams, whilst the Ghasts had plenty of missiles and incendiaries. In another five years both navies would be packing an assortment of more advanced weaponry, though Blake doubted any of it would be enough to sway the coming engagement were it available immediately.

"Two minutes!" shouted Quinn.

The warning startled Blake from his reverie.

"Battle stations! Assume we are entering a combat situation!" he said.

The crew didn't need the reminder and they were ready for whatever might come. In a way, Blake found himself hoping the Aranol would have arrived before them and that they would be pitched straight into the fight. It would be preferable to another four hours of waiting.

The ES *Fulminator*'s fission engines switched off and the Hadron entered local space. Blake prepared himself for a cacophony of urgent comms chatter. What he found was plenty of chatter, but it was standard inter-ship communications.

"We're shielded and our stealth modules are active," said Quinn. "The *Rusor-Nilfar* has activated its own shields and stealth."

"Leaving the *MHL Atlas* looking like a juicy, sitting duck," said Hawkins.

"The Aranol isn't here," said Pointer. "There probably isn't a single person in the entire fleet that isn't crapping themselves, but it doesn't look like the Vraxar are going to be rushed."

"I'm disappointed," said Hawkins.

"Did you really think it would be early?" asked Quinn.

"Maybe. Not really."

"That's enough idle talk," said Blake. "We're here to do a job."

"Yes, sir."

"Here's Felspar," said Pointer. "We're half a million klicks away from the ninth planet."

"It's a big old place to be so far from its sun," added Cruz. "We're seven-point-three billion miles from the expected zone of engagement."

Felspar was cold and empty – a grey, imperfect sphere which nevertheless held beauty of a kind. It was rugged and its five-billion-year-old surface would never see a visit from anything living. The sun, Rangel-3, showed as a bright pinprick of light upon a carpet of sheer black and when he looked upon it, Blake couldn't imagine a lonelier vista than this one.

With the *Fulminator* connected to the local network, the tactical screen was constantly updated with the positions of the individual spaceships in the Alliance Fleet. There were a lot of ships and a lot of area to cover. Most of the biggest guns were close in to Rangel-3, in anticipation of the Aranol's arrival.

"Three of the ships carrying Obsidiar bombs are in orbit about the sun," said Blake. "Rangel-3 has a twenty-five million klick diameter. It's not going to survive if all three go off close by."

"I've got Admiral Talley on the comms, sir."

"Bring him through."

"Good to see you, Captain Blake," said Talley. "Is there anything you need to know?"

"No, sir. I have been well briefed."

Talley laughed. "As much as it's possible to be briefed."

"We're going to hang back here and watch as the Alliance Fleet destroys the Aranol, sir."

"There will be no hesitation this time. *Ix-Gastiol* took us by surprise and we've learned from our mistakes. As soon as the enemy arrives, we will give it hell."

"Is there a chance we might destroy some of our own fleet if our bomb carriers get the timing wrong on the short-range transits?"

It was obviously a question which had come up before.

"This is war, Captain. You know as well as anyone that we can't predict every outcome. We've done our best to mitigate – we have pre-arranged attack formations which are intended to ensure our spaceships don't get caught in the detonations. It will have to be enough."

There was nothing more to be said and Talley closed the channel.

"This is going to be a real shitstorm, isn't it?" said Hawkins.

"Did you expect a round of gentleman's fisticuffs, Lieutenant?"

"No, sir, I expected to kick the Vraxar in their cold, shrivelled balls and fly off home to collect my medal."

Blake laughed. "I like that."

With the Aranol not yet due, Blake found himself looking at the clock on the bulkhead more often than was healthy. It was tempting to order it switched off, yet it was too fascinating to watch the minutes erode.

"One hour to go," said Quinn. "How accurate is the modelling prediction?"

"To within three minutes, apparently."

Whoever in the Space Corps had gone over the fission modelling prediction, they'd forgotten to carry the two when doing their sums.

"There's something wrong," said Quinn. "I'm reading signs of an inbound vessel."

"We have nothing due, Lieutenant." Even as he spoke the words, Blake knew he was wasting his breath.

"This is something else, sir."

"The Aranol."

Given the enormity of such a conclusion, Quinn spent a couple of seconds making absolutely certain. "The fission cloud matches the data Lieutenant Dunbar gathered at Jonli, sir. They're trying to mask their size."

The Aranol was far too massive to conceal its path through lightspeed and its signature appeared midway between the fourth and fifth planets.

"Everyone ready!" shouted Blake. "Lieutenants Cruz, Pointer, make sure the rest of the fleet is aware!"

The crew of the *Rusor-Nilfar* were definitely aware and they began feeding power into their particle disruptor. The members of the Alliance Fleet were only a second behind and they began loading their cores for short-range transits.

The Aranol emerged from ultra-high lightspeed and the rupture it made through the fabric of space continued spilling positrons into the vacuum as the fissure slowly healed. The Vraxar planetship remained motionless for a few seconds, as though it was taking in its surroundings. Then, one of its bay doors opened and warships emerged, one after the other.

The Aranol was in no mood to run.

CHAPTER TWENTY-ONE

AT ITS HEART, the approach was a simple one: attack until one side was defeated. The officers in charge had devised a strategy involving staggered SRTs in order to minimise the effectiveness of an area stasis weapon such as *Ix-Gastiol* had employed so devastatingly in the past.

The Hadron *Stars of Home*, accompanied by the Galactics *Fearsome* and *Brick Wall*, alongside the Ghast Oblivions *Rawklond*, and *Lunfak-Z* activated their short-range transits to bring them within twenty thousand kilometres of the Aranol.

The *Stars of Home* deployed bomb No. 000045, Tears of the Dead, on a short timer. The *Rawklond* activated its stasis nullifier, just as the Aranol emitted a vast wave of energy that filled a sphere a million kilometres across. The stasis wave failed to shut down the Alliance Fleet warships, which launched a wave of several thousand missiles and two dozen particle beams, directed at the Aranol.

With reactions far beyond that of the best human captain, the synchronised battle computers of the five warships triggered a second series of SRTs, but not before the *Brick Wall* took a thundering strike from a gauss slug launched from a turret on the Aranol. The heavy cruiser – known more familiarly by those who served onboard as the *Brick Shithouse* - shrugged off the blow. Its fission engine fired and it emerged with the other four, several million kilometres away.

The wave of missiles required four seconds to reach the enemy shields, which was not sufficient. The Tears of the Dead detonated with 130% of its expected efficiency. The sphere of dark Obsidiar energy flooded in all directions, until it reached a diameter just shy of 700,000 kilometres. Two Vraxar Neutralisers, one huge battleship and three cruisers which had already emerged from the planetship's bays were utterly obliterated, reducing them to atoms.

On the bridge of the *Fulminator*, the crew watched the grainy sensor feed, to see what the outcome would be.

"We will cry no longer," said Blake, remembering the words from the bomb's nameplate.

The dark sphere vanished – one moment it was the largest feature in the solar system after Rangel-3, the next it was gone as though it had never existed.

"Shit," said Quinn. "Not enough! I don't think that bothered them one bit."

The Aranol hadn't moved, nor did it show indication that it was damaged. Suddenly, two huge explosions appeared on the shell of its energy shield. Against the dark metal of its hull, the blasts were hard to see and Pointer worked hard to clean up the image.

"Shots from the *Earth's Fury* and the *Earth's Vengeance*," said Blake. "Their projectiles have a few seconds' travel time."

"And a long reload," said Hawkins.

Another wave of Alliance Fleet warships initiated their SRTs. This second group was larger than the first and it swarmed around the perimeter of the Aranol's shields. There were several bay doors open on the planetship and Vraxar spaceships raced away, firing their particle beams into the allied ships.

It was getting busy and Blake tried to identify which of the attacking Space Corps vessels had an Obsidiar bomb onboard. There wasn't one.

"Good planning," he said. "We don't know what the Aranol is keeping in reserve and our ships are trying to lure it into using whatever unknown weapons its equipped with."

A second stasis pulse swept outwards and again there was a Ghast warship close enough to block the effect. There was a short, punishing exchange of blows. Several thousand missiles struck the Aranol, leaving much of its shield speckled with plasma light. In return, the Vraxar ship unloaded with dozens of its immense gauss turrets. Two Galactics and a Ghast Cadaveron were punched into lumps of crushed Gallenium.

"They're staying too long," said Blake.

He needn't have worried. The Alliance Fleet warships jumped away, emerging in random locations designed to make it harder for the Aranol to hit them with an area-effect weapon. Two more Obsidiar projectiles thundered into the planetship, creating splashes of darkness a hundred kilometres across. Against the Aranol, the explosions appeared tiny.

"Something's coming," said Quinn. "They're charging up a weapon."

"The fleet is aware," said Pointer. "They will act with caution."

"It's not the right thing to do," said Blake. "We've got to push the bastards."

At one time, Admiral Talley had been known as a prudent officer. A safe pair of hands. Blake had met the man on a few occasions and concluded that there was now a streak of the impetuous in Talley. And so it turned out.

"There goes the third wave," said Cruz.

The *Maximilian* and the *Stars of Home* appeared near to the Aranol, in the midst of eighty more heavily-armed warships. The stasis pulse engulfed them, once more countered by the nullifier from the Oblivion *Rawklond*. The *Lunfak-Z* scattered its payload of two thousand incendiary bombs, whilst the other ships spewed missiles and shock drones.

Blake watched it unfold. The area surrounding the Aranol was suddenly aflame with the fires of the *Lunfak-Z*'s incendiaries. A million streaks of white from the Ghast Vule cannons and Space Corps Bulwarks traced lines in all directions.

The Vraxar ships engaged and Blake saw at least fifteen of their V-shaped battleships. The *Maximilian* vanished inside a cloud of high explosives and he held his breath until he saw it burst free at maximum velocity, its overcharged particle beams cutting through the Aranol's shields and igniting the metal beneath.

"Holy crap," said Hawkins.

The brutality of the contest was appalling to behold. Any vestiges of Talley's caution had been washed away by his experiences near planet Roban at the start of the war. He kept his spaceships in range for as long as he dared. The Aranol punished the Alliance Fleet with its gauss turrets, destroying eight and forcing another nine to SRT out of the fray. Only the heaviest ships had strong enough energy shields to resist a single blow.

Although the Aranol's guns had a formidable impact, they were comparatively sparse in overall numbers. As the seconds went by, Blake started to believe the planetship was more of a defensive platform, designed to shelter the Vraxar fleet in safety and take them from place to place.

He was wrong.

A message flashed up on Blake's tactical screen, one amongst a thousand other updates.

> FINALITY DEPLOYED. ACTIVATING SYNCHRO-NISED RANDOMISED SRT.

"000046. The end is nothing more than a new beginning."

The Obsidiar bomb exploded at precisely the same moment as the Aranol fired. Finality achieved 2300% of its expected blast radius and the explosive sphere reached a peak diameter of eleven million kilometres. Dozens of Vraxar spaceships were unmade, along with the Imposition class *ES Never Say Die*, whose captain gambled with the timings and lost.

A thick beam lanced out from the midst of the Obsidiar explosion and struck the fourth planet – Tunde – where the *Earth's Fury* was based. For a few moments, it appeared as if nothing happened. Then, Blake noticed the outline of the planet wavering as if it were seen through a fine mist. With horror, he realised the Vraxar weapon had caused the entire planet to disintegrate and, gradually, it began to separate as it drifted on its orbit around Rangel-3.

The blast from the Finality bomb receded.

"The bastards are still there!" said Cruz. "What will it take to finish them?"

Blake studied the feed, trying hard to discover any sign that the planetship had suffered damage, or that its shields were failing. Visually, there was no change.

"Lieutenant Quinn, are they even struggling?" he asked. "Can you obtain readings that give us some kind of clue about whether we're hurting them at all?"

"There hasn't been a flicker, sir, except for the build-up before they fired at Tunde. I'd say..." Quinn hesitated, causing Blake to face him.

"What is it?"

"Sir, we've been operating on the basis that we gave the Aranol a fright when we hit it with the Sorrow bomb. What if it isn't frightened? What if its behaviour is nothing more than a result of the madness we are sure it is possessed by?"

"I think I could believe anything, Lieutenant. Why do you say it now?"

"I don't believe we can harm it with Obsidiar bombs, sir. The Aranol could be made from solid Obsidiar, able to withstand a thousand bombs, but it would still need to draw on that power for its shields. There should be a fluctuation – something to indicate it's been attacked."

"What if our instruments simply can't measure the change? It could have different shield technology to our own."

"That isn't how it works, sir. To maintain a shield requires a source of energy. If there's a source of energy, our sensors can read it, even if they don't know exactly what is producing the energy."

The fervour in Quinn's voice made Blake start to believe the words.

"Do you believe this is already lost?"

"Sir, I do not believe we should stop trying."

"What about a refined Obsidiar bomb?" asked Blake. "Maybe it's time we tried out what's in the hold of the *MHL Atlas*."

Quinn faltered. "I don't know, sir. I'm just an engine man. I have no idea what they've done to the base product in order to refine it into Obsidiar-Teronium."

While they talked, the combat resumed. The Alliance Fleet changed tactics and used their SRTs to attack in waves of fifty. They jumped towards the Aranol, unleashed their missiles, incendiaries and particle beams, before jumping away to safety. Each wave lost three or four of its numbers to a combination of gauss turrets and beam attacks from the newest Vraxar space-ships to leave their bays inside the Aranol.

Blake counted the enemy ships.

"They're only letting out thirty at a time," he said. "And then they stop."

"The Aranol isn't as reckless as we thought," said Hawkins. "It knows our Obsidiar bombs can finish off any number of its fleet and it doesn't want to lose more than it needs to."

"In a battle of attrition, we're going to come out on the losing side," said Blake.

He tried hard to predict the flows of the engagement. The Aranol couldn't be immune to Obsidiar bombs – surely it couldn't. And yet, there it was, undamaged by the catastrophically large blast of the Finality bomb. A message came onto his screen.

> ATTACK PATTERN C: INITIATE.

"They're going in properly," said Blake.

One hundred and thirty spaceships from the Alliance Fleet executed their SRTs. They ignored the Vraxar Neutralisers, battleships and cruisers and directed everything at the Aranol. Blake could understand the tactic – the Aranol was the key and if they could smash through its shields and destroy the controlling force of the Vraxar, anything left of the enemy fleet would lack direction.

The Oblivion *Sandarvin* got off a shot from its particle disruptor and a beam of blue connected the Ghast battleship with the Aranol's shields. The incendiary fires circled the planet-ship, crackling with ferocity and reaching hungrily into space.

"That's produced a big spike on their power generation!" said Quinn excitedly. "Maybe we need a few more like that."

The *Givose-12* fired a second particle disruptor after the first. The blue sphere wrapping the Aranol expanded further still, forcing some of the closest spaceships to break away. The Vraxar ship fired its stasis weapon. The Ghasts nullified the first one, only for the Aranol to use the stasis emitter again.

"They've knocked out most of the fleet!" said Pointer. "Why aren't the Ghasts breaking the stasis field?"

"Their nullifiers have a cooldown, Lieutenant. They require a long interval between each use."

More than one hundred of the Alliance Fleet drifted without power and the sight of it sickened Blake. It reminded him how powerless he'd felt watching as *Ix-Gastiol* did the same thing only a few weeks ago. This was something he hoped never to see again.

The Aranol was here on a mission of punishment and it had no desire to capture the helpless spaceships. With a contemptuous lack of haste, it targeted the fleet spaceships four at a time and directed its gauss turrets at them, destroying one group before moving on to another.

The *Lunfak-Z* wasn't involved in Attack Pattern C and it flew amongst a wide-spread cluster of other spaceships, sixty million kilometres away. The Oblivion activated an SRT, and used its stasis nullifier immediately it came out of lightspeed. The disabled spaceships of the Alliance Fleet recovered from the stasis emitter's effects.

"They're moving under their own steam," said Pointer, her voice thick with emotion. "I thought we'd lost everything."

Blake breathed out noisily. "I hate being out here, away from it."

"I've got the *Rusor-Nilfar* on the comms, sir," said Cruz. "Tarjos Kol-Faran advises he will leave us in order to join the Alliance Fleet. It is his opinion they require another warship equipped with a stasis nullifier."

It was something Blake had been half-expecting and he had no intention of arguing with the Ghast captain. In truth, he was envious that Kol-Faran was served up this easy chance to take a more direct role in the conflict. There was no doubt the *Rusor-Nilfar* was the most capable allied warship in the field.

"Wish him good luck and tell him to give the bastards hell."

"Kol-Faran expresses his hope that we will be given the chance to join him."

> REMEMBRANCE DEPLOYED. ACTIVATING SYNCHRONISED RANDOMISED SRT.

Blake opened his mouth to repeat the words from its nameplate. *No. 000049. Never Forget.* With horror, he saw one of the gauges on his screen, which was monitoring the *Rusor-Nilfar's* engine output. *They haven't noticed the deployment.*

"Lieutenant Pointer, tell Kol-Faran to abort!" he yelled.

"Sir?" Pointer stuttered but didn't allow her confusion to interfere with her attempts to open a channel.

"The bomb!" shouted Blake.

"*Rusor-Nilfar*, this is *Fulminator*. Please abort, I repeat...." Pointer raised her head. "They've entered lightspeed, sir."

Three billion miles away, the pride of the Ghast fleet exited lightspeed four hundred kilometres from the Remembrance bomb, just as the spaceships involved in Attack Pattern C departed. The device detonated, destroying thirty Vraxar spaceships as well as the *Rusor-Nilfar*. As tough as they'd built the Oblivion, it couldn't resist the might of an Obsidiar bomb and it was reduced to particles, the crew onboard gone in an instant.

"Oh crap," said Hawkins, close to tears.

It wasn't as if they'd known the crew of the battleship, but there was something uniquely upsetting to see such a proud vessel lost to a terrible accident like this one.

Judged on blast radius, the Remembrance bomb was a success. In terms of the damage it inflicted on the Aranol, it was no more a triumph than the two bombs which preceded it.

After this briefest of lulls, combat resumed.

215

CHAPTER TWENTY-TWO

THE ALLIANCE FLEET warships swirled around the Aranol like insects seeking the exposed flesh of a huge, armoured beast. Missiles hit the enemy shields in a constant rain, the explosions tiny when viewed against the enormity of the planetship. A projectile from *Earth's Vengeance* smashed into the Aranol, producing another huge output spike from the enemy spacecraft. Far away to the side, the planet Tunde began fragmenting as though the Vraxar weapon interfered with the forces of gravity holding the pieces together. Grit and stone smeared across space like grey paint on a mad artist's canvas.

"If we had another ten guns like the *Earth's Vengeance*, we might get somewhere," muttered Quinn, pushing sweat-drenched hair away from his forehead. "The Aranol has increased the power to its shields fivefold to account for our missiles, but it's the big hits from Larno and the particle disruptors that are causing them problems."

The only thing Blake took from Quinn's words was that the Aranol would shortly destroy the planet Larno in the same way it had done with Tunde.

"This is nothing but a show of strength," said Pointer. "A parent bringing unruly children into line."

"Yeah," said Hawkins. "Look at us, we've got a massive spaceship and we're going to kill you all because you've pissed us off."

Blake shared the same feelings. He was certain the Aranol intended to stay in Rangel-3 until it either wiped out the fleet or it got bored and flew to the nearest populated planet. If it needed to recharge its power source any time soon, it wasn't giving any impression of urgency. In hindsight, the Aranol could likely store so much in its tanks, it probably never ran close to dry and if the controlling entity was as cautious as he imagined, it surely kept plenty in reserve for confrontations such as this one.

So many assumptions, so many of them wrong, he reflected bitterly.

> NO EVIL DEPLOYED. ACTIVATING SYNCHRONISED RANDOMISED SRT.

The fourth Obsidiar bomb had no more effect than the other three, or, indeed, Sorrow before them. Thirty of the smaller Vraxar spaceships were destroyed, only for the Aranol to deploy thirty more. This time, five of them entered lightspeed and emerged near to Larno, where they engaged with the Alliance Fleet spaceships assigned to guard *Earth's Vengeance*. The Obsidiar cannon managed to get off one final shot before its main armament was destroyed by a Vraxar dark energy beam.

Blake swore. "Get me Admiral Talley."

Talley was busy and it took a few moments for him to enter the comms channel. Blake kept it brief.

"Sir, our conventional armaments are not troubling the enemy. I am preparing to deploy the Destiny bomb. I assume you are aware of the possibilities."

"I am well aware. Please synchronise with the Alliance Fleet. I have given you broadcast priority – when you transmit, the battle logs will display only your message until you are done and the ships in Alliance Fleet will respond to your orders."

"Thank you."

"I hope this does not become a burden for you, Captain Blake."

The words struck Blake hard and, for the first time, he got a real glimpse of what it was like to carry the weight of a momentous decision like this one. There were others who carried so much more than this and he wondered if he could cope as well as they did.

"I will do what must be done, sir."

"I know."

The connection ended and Blake put the conversation from his mind. He accessed the battle computer on the *MHL Atlas* and sent it a series of command codes.

> NO. 000051: DESTINY. ACCESS GRANTED.

"The bomb has accepted my codes," he said. "We're going to SRT to within a quarter of a million klicks and initiate warmup."

"What if the bomb underperforms, sir?"

"The chance of underperformance is precisely why we're going in close - we're relying on the Aranol having no defence against an Obsidiar-Teronium blast. The attributes of the explosion are expected to be entirely different to that of a standard bomb."

"It's got to work."

"Don't we know it, Lieutenant."

Once the bomb accepted his access codes, it was remarkably simple to initiate the warmup. Blake was merely required to access the final option on one of the menu screens and type in a command. He felt eyes upon him and he looked to find his crew and the two ensigns staring at him.

"This is it, folks."

"Ready when you are, sir," said Quinn.

"We're holding for an SRT?"

"Yes, sir. Eight cores are loaded."

"Ten seconds or sixty. Let's find out which."

He sent a message over the shared battle network.

> INITIATE ATTACK PATTERN D. *MHL* ATLAS PRIORITY 1. STASIS BLOCK PRIORITY 1.

The effect was immediate. The remaining warships in Alliance Fleet activated their short-range transits and within seconds, the Aranol was surrounded by more than two hundred craft and the bombardment on its shields began.

With a deep breath, Blake entered his next command, the text of which would appear on every single tactical screen in the fleet.

> DESTINY WARMUP: BEGIN. SET TIMER.

That was it done.

"Lieutenant Quinn, take us to the stated distance. Full attack upon arrival, hold the stealth modules – we want to be the target instead of the *Atlas*."

"Roger."

The ES *Fulminator* and the *MHL Atlas* departed local space for the briefest of moments. They reappeared, on the edges of what was a full-scale engagement. Immediately the two ships arrived, the Aranol fired its stasis weapon, only for the battleship *Rawklond* to nullify the effects.

Pointer and Cruz worked the sensors, trying to pre-empt the moves of the Vraxar and identify the most likely threats. Blake pushed the *Fulminator* to half speed, keeping it a constant distance from the Aranol. The *MHL Atlas* followed along the same path, five thousand kilometres behind.

Along with piloting the warship, Blake tried to make sense of the tactical screen. The individual details were lost to him – thousands of missiles and hundreds of beam weapons raked through space – so he tried to focus on the overall picture. It was tough going.

> TEN SECONDS.

"Four hundred Lambdas away, full broadside," said Hawkins. "Thirty-six Shimmers in pursuit. Impacts in seventy-eight and fifty-nine seconds respectively."

They would never reach their target.

"Set the Bulwarks to full auto."

"Bulwarks on full auto."

The *Fulminator* was armed to the teeth and its warheads plunged towards the Aranol, joining the thousands already in flight from the rest of the fleet. The Space Corps ships with over-charged particle beams stayed close, hitting the planetship time after time. The Aranol was incredible in size, but there were a few visible areas where the overcharge beams were doing plenty of damage. For each few hits the enemy took, it gave one in return and the Aranol's gauss turrets continued to inflict heavy – often terminal – damage on everything they targeted.

"Come on!" said Quinn. "Get those bastards!"

> TWENTY SECONDS.

The power from the *Fulminator*'s main Gallenium engines shut off and the warship switched smoothly onto Obsidiar backup. It would put strain on the Hadron's energy shield if it came under any sort of sustained attack.

"We've entered a negation field," said Hawkins.

Blake located the source – a Neutraliser was a hundred thousand kilometres away, coming clockwise from the far side of the Aranol. The spaceship's nullification spheres sparked and flashed against the darkness of its alloys.

"That's the new target!" ordered Blake. "Shoot it down!"

The Neutralisers were tough and it was easier said than done. The *Fulminator* was equipped with eight Havoc cannons, only five of which could currently target the enemy vessel. The

Havoc barrels thumped into their turrets, producing a dense thunder of sound. The entire battleship seemed to shake and creak with the tremendous recoil.

The projectiles were far faster than any normal missile, and they crashed into the Neutraliser's shield. The blue jagged lightning criss-crossing its fore and aft spheres changed briefly to green and glowed with a sharper intensity.

From somewhere else, an overcharged particle beam struck the Neutraliser, cutting directly through its energy shield. A moment later, the craft was completely engulfed in plasma explosions - missiles fired from a different source. Blake had no idea which other ships were targeting the Neutraliser and there wasn't a necessity to find out.

> THIRTY SECONDS.

"How long is this damned warmup going to take?" said Hawkins angrily.

The Aranol fired its area-effect stasis weapon again, only for the Oblivion *Sandarvin* to block the effect. The Vraxar followed up by using the same beam weapon it had used against Tunde, except this time it fired it directly into a group of eight Alliance Fleet warships which flew within two hundred kilometres of each other. The craft vanished within the beam and when the weapon was shut off, they were gone.

"That main beam came from those towers," said Cruz, adding a highlight to the sensor feed.

"Surface amplifiers," said Quinn. "There are more of them clockwise and anticlockwise. Seems like they can fire that weapon from one of multiple points."

Blake glanced at the structures on the feed. The towers were two thousand metres high and thicker at the base. They curved inwards, such that they reminded him of talons and they were arranged around the edges of a circle many kilometres across. There was a smooth, domed area in the centre, from which the disintegration beam came. As he watched, the Aranol fired once more and then again from a different place a few hundred kilometres away. A dozen more warships, and their crew with them, were reduced to dust. Time was running out.

The *Fulminator*'s Havoc cannons boomed again and this time they punched clean through the Neutraliser's damaged energy shield and struck it in a line across the front nullification sphere. A row of deep impact craters appeared and the flow of energy stuttered, died and then re-established.

> FORTY SECONDS.

The Neutraliser was suddenly struck by enough high-explosives to destroy it twice over. The ship was torn in two and the aft sphere crashed into the Aranol's shield at high speed. The Neutralisers were mostly solid and the sphere flattened, before it deflected into space, throwing out fading sparks of lightning as it went.

Blake held his breath, gripped by the thought that the nullification sphere would somehow open a path through the planet-ship's shield. A few of the Alliance Fleet captains had the same idea and they directed missile and cannon fire at the area of impact.

"Damnit!" Blake swore when he saw the Aranol's shields remained solid.

"They're using progressively more power to maintain their shields," said Quinn. "They're starting to feel it. I just don't think it's going to be enough."

> FIFTY SECONDS.

Disaster struck. A ball of solid Gallenium weighing in excess of 250,000 tonnes, hit the *MHL Atlas*'s energy shield at a velocity slightly below the speed of light. The *Fulminator* was linked to the other ship's battle computer and Blake saw the alerts warning of a full depletion of the *Atlas*'s Obsidiar core.

A second Gallenium slug followed the first. With no energy

shield to stop it, this projectile demolished the front third of the lifter, leaving the vessel's nose crumpled and unrecognizable.

Blake felt his chest tighten. "Into which bay did it lift the bomb?" he yelled.

He didn't wait for an answer. The damaged lifter was only five thousand kilometres away, dutifully trailing the *Fulminator* on its orbit of the Aranol. Blake pulled the battleship's control bars hard towards him and felt the vessel respond at once. It slowed rapidly to a standstill and then began flying backwards, straight towards the *Atlas*.

It was a difficult manoeuvre to pull off in a 37 billion tonne warship travelling at 2500 kilometres per second and Blake knew he'd got lucky when the Aranol's third projectile struck the *Fulminator*'s shields instead of hitting the *MHL Atlas*. He was doubly fortunate when he realised the slug had caught the Hadron at an angle, allowing the shields to deflect the blow without causing significant drain on the Obsidiar core.

While was making the fine-tuning required to keep as much of the *Fulminator* between the Aranol and the lifter, the battleship was hit again. This time, the Obsidiar core dropped from 93% all the way to zero.

"We don't want to take another," said Hawkins.

> SIXTY SECONDS.

That was the problem with the theoretical stuff - the estimates were as unreliable as the projected detonation sizes of the conventional Obsidiar bombs. The Destiny warmup should have finished by now and here it was, still going.

"Firing Shimmers," said Hawkins. "Target – the Aranol."

And then Blake saw it on the sensor feed – the gauss turret which had them in its sights was a hulking cuboid with a wide, protruding barrel. The barrel jerked back with the recoil from another round aimed straight at the *Fulminator*. The damage would be devastating when it struck the unshielded Hadron.

A scant few hundred kilometres from the *Fulminator*, the inbound gauss projectile was blown apart by the pure flames of a massive plasma warhead.

"It got hit by one of our Shimmers," said Hawkins. "What were the chances of that?"

"Thrice lucky," said Blake, hardly able to believe it.

Blake couldn't imagine there was any hope of rescue from the next shot. The Aranol's turret rotated, keeping track of the *ES Fulminator*. Blake hadn't kept a note on the firing interval, but it surely wouldn't be long until the Hadron received severe or terminal damage.

> SEVENTY SECONDS.

The text disappeared, to be replaced by something new.

> DESTINY WARMUP COMPLETE. ACTIVATING SRT.

The *ES Fulminator*, along with the remaining 172 warships of Alliance Fleet, went to lightspeed, leaving the *MHL Atlas* alone with its cargo.

The Obsidiar-Teronium bomb exploded.

CHAPTER TWENTY-THREE

THE LIGHTSPEED TRANSIT was scheduled to last twenty seconds. Within the first second it became obvious something was wrong. A series of reports came up on Blake's console, advising him of catastrophic hull damage. The entire spaceship shook as if it were in the grip of a violent and petulant god.

"What's going on?" said Quinn, trying to locate the problem.

Blake didn't know. At lightspeed, a spaceship was safe from everything. It could ignore solid objects and there was no weapon that could damage a craft once its fission engines fired up.

Until now.

"Destiny," said Blake.

"That's impossible," said Hawkins. "It can't happen."

With a shudder, the *ES Fulminator*'s fission drive switched off and the battleship entered local space, many billions of kilometres from Rangel-3. The external sensors kicked into life, revealing the extent of the damage to the Hadron's outer hull. The hardened alloy plates along the rear half of the spaceship were entirely gone, revealing the Gallenium underneath. The engines themselves were deeply pitted and uneven, as though they had been bathed in something enormously corrosive. The external temperature of the hull was at the expected level, so whatever caused the damage had done so without heat or cold.

"We got caught in the blast," said Blake. "It expanded so fast, it caught the ship and did this."

"Where is the rest of the fleet?" asked Pointer. "I've only had check-ins from 112 out of 172."

"That can't be right, Lieutenant."

"It is right, sir. There are only 112 spaceships on the network."

Blake closed his eyes. The warning signal from the *Fulminator*'s battle computer would have taken the smallest fraction of a second to reach the rest of the fleet. From there, another fraction of a second to process the message and to act on it. There was only one conclusion.

"They're gone," said Blake. "Caught in the blast as we tried to escape."

"Impossible," said Quinn, repeating what Hawkins said moment ago.

"What have we unleashed?" asked Cruz. "There's nothing capable of this."

Blake shook his head sadly. "There is now. We've still got work to do before we can think about the consequences. Lieutenant Cruz, find out if any of the fleet requires our direct assistance. Lieutenant Pointer, find out what's happening at Rangel-3. Check the sensor logs and see if they picked anything up."

Cruz responded first. "Admiral Talley is alive and has taken charge, sir. He will deal with matters relating to the fleet. The *Fulminator* is equipped with the newest sensors and he would like us to perform a super-far scan of Rangel-3."

"Sir?"

It was Pointer and Blake knew her well enough to detect the fear.

"What is it?"

"There is no Rangel-3."

Blake wanted to ask her to repeat the words and after that he wanted to ask for confirmation – a second opinion from another competent officer. He knew he'd be wasting his breath.

"We destroyed a sun."

"No, sir, we destroyed the Rangel-3 *solar system*. Felspar is gone."

"What about Lox-Pion?" he asked numbly. The planet Lox-Pion was the eighth planet and on the far side of the Rangel-3 sun at the time of the conflict.

"Gone as well, sir."

The numbers weren't hard to add up. Felspar and Lox-Pion were approximately thirteen billion kilometres apart when the bomb exploded and now both planets were gone.

"Thirteen billion klicks," he said.

"Minimum," said Hawkins. "The maths guys will probably be able to come up with a number based on the *Fulminator*'s speed and the amount of damage we sustained."

Blake sat down. "The blast sphere could conceivably exceed one hundred billion klicks."

"Conceivably."

In the context of the universe as a whole it was nothing. An insignificant event lost in the infinite. It was the promise which was important. If an unstable, imperfect Obsidiar-Teronium bomb could do this, what would be next, when they worked out how to properly refine Obsidiar? And when they managed to fuse it with something else that made it a trillion times more efficient? What sort of bombs would humanity control by then?

Better we have them than somebody else, thought Blake. *Humanity has had its wars and now we're one of the few species that isn't trying to kill every other poor bastard out there in the universe.*

In his mind, he pictured the file image of the Destiny bomb. This one had a nameplate in the same way all the others had their own nameplate. Except this one was blank, as if nobody had dared come up with suitable words to capture the essence of what Destiny meant for the future.

"At least we won, huh?" said Hawkins. "We took a kicking, but the Aranol came off worse."

"Yeah, maybe it's time for celebration instead of acting like we lost," said Quinn. "How about you get us a round of drinks from the replicator, sir?"

Blake wanted to share in the optimism. In the wake of the bomb's detonation, he'd almost forgotten what it was designed to accomplish. What it surely *had* accomplished. Until he knew for absolute certain, there would still be that nagging doubt.

"How are you getting on, Lieutenant Pointer?" he asked. "Rangel-3 is gone. What about our enemy?"

Pointer stared at the reams of sensor data on her console's centre screen. She spotted something which caused her to jerk as though she'd been touched with a live cable. "We haven't won," she said quietly.

"I don't want to hear that, Lieutenant."

Pointer waved Cruz over for confirmation. Within moments, Cruz's face went pale. It told Blake everything he needed to know.

"There's no doubt?"

"No, sir. The Aranol is in the same place as we left it."

Blake punched the comms console. "It can't be!" He closed his eyes and forced himself calm. "Can you give me anything more? Is it damaged? Is it moving?"

"It's not moving. I can't tell you much else, sir. We're too far away from it."

"It's smaller," said Cruz. "Significantly smaller."

"That's got to mean it took some damage," said Blake. "Get me Admiral Talley."

It took less than five seconds to get hold of him.

"Captain Blake, what news?"

"We didn't destroy the Aranol, sir. It's right where we left it and I believe it has sustained damage. I can't give you specifics."

Talley didn't answer at once and Blake could picture the man summoning up his reserves of strength.

"I'll get a message to Fleet Admiral Duggan letting him know," said Talley. "We've lost far more than I hoped and now this."

"We're still in the hunt, sir. Might I provide a recommendation?"

"I think I know where you're going with it."

"We can't delay. We've been hurt, but so has the enemy. We should return immediately and finish what we started. If the Aranol is damaged it means we have depleted its shield and that gives us an opportunity."

"I understand what you're saying, Captain Blake." Talley's voice strengthened. "We have not yet deployed the Worlds Apart bomb. If the Aranol is unshielded, we may yet surprise the bastards."

"I'm sure they are already surprised, sir."

"I'm sure you're right. Damnit, I thought Destiny would be enough, but I will not permit this second chance to slip away! I will rally the fleet and we will return!" He gave a bark of laughter. "I bet John is furious at sitting this one out."

"I imagine his wife is happy, sir."

"That's where you're wrong. If Fleet Admiral Duggan is furious, I can guarantee you Lucy will be incandescent."

The arrangements didn't take long and Blake found himself impressed by Admiral Talley's organisational skills and willingness to listen to advice. There was more than one admiral in the Space Corps who Blake was sure would shy away from taking direct action having suffered such devastating losses in the first encounter with the Aranol.

"Only ninety-five ships this time," said Pointer. "The rest are too beat up to make lightspeed safely. They'll have to wait for a pickup."

"Half of the ninety-five aren't in great shape," said Cruz. "And the other half aren't much better."

"It's what we have, Lieutenant."

Blake watched the updates on the battle network as the light-speed-capable ships signalled their readiness.

"We're going all-guns blazing again, folks. Keep the stealth modules deactivated – we take the punches the same as everyone else."

"Our shield is at fifty percent," said Quinn. "We won't be taking too many punches from those gauss turrets."

The final warship checked in.

"That's us ready," said Blake.

There were some occasions which benefitted from extra preparation time. This wasn't one of them. If the enemy was weakened, it was important to strike before their shields could recharge or come back online. The ES *Maximilian* triggered a fleet-wide short-range transit and the spaceships entered lightspeed.

The journey wasn't long, but it was enough for Blake to reflect that he hadn't been expecting to fight again so soon after using the Destiny bomb. It was meant to be an all-or-nothing response to the Vraxar – a device to save humanity or to fail utterly. Instead, the indications were that the fighting would shortly continue, like a contest between too bloodied, battered opponents who'd been so exhausted by the opening exchanges they were required to rest before beginning once more.

His wandering imagination did not prepare him for the truth.

"Entering local space," said Lieutenant Quinn.

"Commencing local scans," said Pointer. "I have located the Aranol and..."

"And what?" asked Blake sharply. The enemy ship appeared on his tactical screen as a huge, red dot, surrounded by dozens of much smaller green ones representing the Alliance Fleet.

"Still checking, sir," said Pointer. "I'm not sure what the hell is going on."

"Target locked, firing missiles," said Hawkins.

Half of the *Fulminator*'s missile clusters were gone. The launchers which survived the Destiny blast slid open and missiles spilled into space. Elsewhere, the other members of the fleet unloaded with everything they had.

On the *Fulminator*'s bridge Blake was still awaiting answers from his comms team. "What about other hostiles? Where is their fleet?"

"There are no enemy spacecraft on the nears or fars," said Cruz. "Starting on the supers."

"The enemy fleet is gone," said Pointer. "I'm sure of it."

"Where?" said Blake.

"Destroyed, sir. Look at this – coming up on the main screen."

The Aranol hung motionless in what had once been the Rangel-3 solar system. The planets and the sun were no more, having been so utterly obliterated by the Destiny bomb, there weren't even detectable clouds of dust on the sensors.

The planetship was much smaller than before, with a diameter closer to one thousand kilometres than six. It was still a perfect sphere, though where it had previously been the darkest of greys, now it was a black so deep it seemed to absorb light and it stood out against the background of space like a sullen disk. The outer structures of the spaceship were gone and what remained of the Aranol was smooth like the nut at the centre of a rotten fruit.

"We took out its shield and everything else apart from the core," said Blake in wonder. "How the hell did they manage to live through that blast?"

The first wave of missiles detonated against the Aranol's shell, while the *Maximilian* fired three of its overcharge particle beams. The *Fulminator* came within fifty thousand kilometres and Hawkins discharged the two underside beams, which thumped and whined.

"Direct hit," said Hawkins. "Let's see how they like it."

"There's no sign of damage," said Cruz. "No increase in surface heat, no impact craters. Nothing."

"Is there any indication the enemy are building up for a response?" asked Blake.

"Not yet, sir. We have the *Sandarvin* and *Rawklond* with us, so we should be able to withstand the first stasis attacks. And there are no turrets on what's left of the Aranol. I don't even know if they have any offensive capabilities remaining."

"They've got something," said Quinn. "There's an incredible amount of power flowing out to the surface of their ship."

Blake didn't want to find out what the planetship was capable of. The Destiny attack *had* been at least a partial success, albeit in a different way than expected. The blast had stripped away most of the Aranol's outer structure, appearing to destroy potentially thousands of Vraxar spaceships it kept in its hangar bays, whilst leaving the centre entirely untouched.

The Aranol wasn't at all helpless and it used its stasis emitter, which the *Sandarvin* nullified. The *Rawklond* discharged its particle disruptor and the planetship was engulfed. Shimmers,

Lambdas and Ghast Shatterers ignited within the midst of the incendiaries. It was an awe-inspiring sight.

Then, from the midst of the fire, Blake saw the Aranol's immense disintegration beam lance outwards. The beam was broad enough to hit three spaceships and it was followed immediately after by a second beam which destroyed the *Sandarvin*. The Vraxar had evidently had enough of the Oblivion's particle disruptor and its stasis nullifier.

"Damnit!" shouted Blake. "What the hell is going wrong here? They should be out for the count!"

It was Quinn who realised the problem.

"Sir - I spoke to Captain Decker about her work when we were in Estral Space," he said, talking quickly. "About how the Lightspeed Catapult shifts phase when it creates the wormhole."

Missiles continued to strike the Aranol and the *Sandarvin* fired a second particle disruptor, followed a moment later by its stasis nullifier. Million-degree flames encircled the planetship, hungering fruitlessly for its destruction.

"What are you trying to tell me, Lieutenant?"

"It's out of phase, sir! We've destroyed the Aranol's outer shell, but they've got sufficient power to keep the core in a different time phase to the rest."

"We can't damage them," said Blake, realising the implications.

"Lieutenant Quinn is correct, sir," said Pointer. "What's left of the Aranol is completely untouched by our attacks."

"While they can kill us at their leisure," growled Blake. "Contact Admiral Talley and advise him, Lieutenant."

"Do you have any recommendations, sir?"

"Hold off with the final Obsidiar bomb."

"Admiral Talley acknowledges. He asks your opinion on whether or not we should break off."

Blake threw his hands in the air. "What choice is there? We have to keep up the attack in the hope something gets through."

Before they could lay down anything more than the most basic of plans, the Aranol vanished. There was no warning, or build-up – the Vraxar planetship entered lightspeed and was gone.

CHAPTER TWENTY-FOUR

THE ALLIANCE FLEET comms went crazy with questions and guessed answers about what the enemy were up to.

"Find out where the hell those bastards are going!" said Blake.

"I'm on it, sir," said Quinn. "The predictive modelling software is tapping into the sensor data. If they're staying local I should have an answer for you shortly."

The *Fulminator*'s exterior was badly damaged, but its core clusters were intact. The Obsidiar processors hit one hundred percent utilisation and stayed there for a few seconds, before the answer came up.

"They're going to Old Earth, sir," said Quinn.

It wasn't a surprise. The Vraxar were here to punish the Confederation for its resistance, so it was natural their first choice would be the home of humanity.

"Make sure Admiral Talley is aware."

"He just worked out the answer like we did, sir. He has spoken to Fleet Admiral Duggan and the advice is to pursue."

There was no other advice Duggan could have offered.

"It's ten hours to Old Earth, sir," said Quinn. "The Aranol can probably manage it in two hours unless they've lost some of their propulsion systems in our attack."

"What do you think?"

"I think what's left of the Aranol is made up from near-solid semi-depleted Obsidiar, sir. I think they've got practically unlimited power to get them to Old Earth."

"That's what I think too, Lieutenant."

"The Alliance Fleet is synchronising in preparation to depart," said Quinn. "We'll be on our way in less than fifteen seconds."

"To face an enemy we cannot possibly defeat," said Blake too quietly for the others to hear him. "Let's give it another go," he added, louder this time.

"Five seconds."

The Alliance Fleet entered lightspeed on a course which would see them reach Old Earth long after the Aranol arrived. There was a single warship left behind in the area of space which had once been home to the star Rangel-3 and its nine planets.

"Our fission engines didn't launch," said Quinn. "There's been a remote override."

"Why the hell would anyone do that?" asked Hawkins. "I didn't even think that was possible."

The cause was soon revealed.

"I've got Fleet Admiral Duggan on the comms," said Cruz.

Duggan's voice was calm on the surface, but Blake could detect the undertones of tension. It was the voice of a man who was going to say something he hated.

"Captain Blake, I used Cerys to stop your lightspeed engines firing in order that I might talk to you."

"What is it, sir?"

"Admiral Talley has provided details about your engagement with the Aranol and the outcome."

"Our weapons cannot harm them, sir. Not while they are in a different phase."

"I know and I have an idea which might help us. Do you remember what I told you about the Estral missiles?"

"Yes, sir. They go out of phase for the amount of time it takes them to pass through an energy shield."

"I conferred with Captain Decker on the matter and there are surprising similarities between the Estral missile tech and one of the control modules on the Lightspeed Catapult. They use different methods to achieve a similar result."

Duggan was clearly heading somewhere important and Blake tried to predict the course of the conversation. It clicked in his head.

"The ES *Cataclysm* was out of phase when we left it."

"And it's still out of phase. Captain Decker has been studying it."

Quinn was on top of his game today. "We are twenty minutes from the place we abandoned the *Cataclysm*, sir," he said in a loud whisper.

"Do you believe the *Cataclysm*'s weapons systems have the capability to damage the Aranol?"

"That's exactly what I believe, Captain Blake."

"We'll set a course at once, sir. I must warn you, we believe the overcharge repeater is in a state of failure and the Aranol is too large for us to inflict significant damage with our missiles. That's assuming those missiles don't return to their normal phase five thousand klicks outside their launch tubes."

There was a hitch in Duggan's voice when he responded. "I didn't expect a different response from you or your crew. However, you are unaware of what this means – what I must ask you to do."

"We are here, sir. Tell us what is required."

"Board the *Cataclysm* and use the Lightspeed Catapult to

pursue the Aranol. If you live through the transit and the catapult holds together, detonate the out-of-phase Obsidiar-Teronium power core. That should be sufficient to destroy our enemy."

There were many questions and, on this occasion, the one concerning how the *Cataclysm*'s crew would escape was of secondary importance.

"Sir, did Admiral Talley inform you of the magnitude of the Destiny blast?"

"He did and I will advise you that the Obsidiar-T in the light-speed catapult is in a completely changed state. Our projections suggest it will be vastly more potent pound for pound than the Destiny bomb."

"You are asking us to destroy Old Earth and everything in its solar system. It is a lot to carry, sir."

Duggan laughed without humour. "A part of me wishes to assure you that I would never ask another person to perform such a task. However, I swore I would do whatever it took to defeat the Vraxar and I am not a man who breaks a promise once it's made. On this occasion, I hope to avoid having to kill billions of our own people."

"Then what, sir?"

"We cannot allow the Aranol to reach Old Earth. I am certain that once it arrives, it will simply murder everyone using its disintegration beam, before moving on to the next closest planet, which happens to be Prime."

"The Lightspeed Catapult?"

"It theoretically has the capability to launch you into the centre of the Aranol whilst it is at lightspeed. That gives you an opportunity to intercept the enemy and destroy it before it enters Old Earth local space."

"The catapult is not that accurate."

"Captain Decker has been working on it. She's confident."

"I hope so. Has this been proven to work, sir?"

"No, which is why I used the word *theoretically*. Captain Decker is situated close to the *Cataclysm* and she will answer any questions you might have."

"I'm sure she'll try, sir."

Duggan laughed again and this time it was genuine. "She knows this stuff better than anyone, which is why she's coming with you."

"I'll be happy to have her onboard, sir."

"She's provided you with some instructions to look through in the twenty minutes it'll take you to get there."

"I'm intrigued."

"Now go and if I come up with any modifications to the plan, I'll let you know once you exit lightspeed." The line went quiet, with only a faint background hum to let Blake know the channel was still open. "Do whatever you can to get out of this alive, Captain Blake. You, your crew and that lieutenant you keep locked up in the troops' quarters."

"And his squad."

"Those too. If you pull this off, humanity will owe you all a debt of gratitude that can never be repaid."

"I think a few of Lieutenant McKinney's men will settle for a medal, sir."

"I'm sure they will."

The line went quiet and this time Duggan was gone. Blake turned to face his crew and they shared a moment where nobody spoke. Then, Lieutenant Pointer smiled.

"If we pull this off, it'll definitely, *definitely* be the end."

Blake smiled back. "Until the next time, Lieutenant." He raised an eyebrow towards Quinn.

"We're all set for lightspeed, sir. Target is the *ES Cataclysm*."

"We're running out of time. Let's get on with it."

The *ES Fulminator*'s fission engines grumbled and hurled the battleship across the immensity of space. Blake remembered about the instructions Decker had provided and he found them in his mailbox list, already three from the top. He skimmed over the words.

"We need to do some work, Lieutenant Quinn. In order for the Lightspeed Catapult to intercept the Aranol, it needs to open a wormhole at precisely the location of the enemy ship, which, as you can imagine, is like stabbing a pin into a map of the universe and hitting the twelfth moon of Euridio-7 on the first attempt."

"They're travelling at about a zillion klicks per second, sir."

"We have the model of their fission cloud. Use it to predict where the Aranol will be and at which moment in time. Once you have the data, we can forward it to the ES Cataclysm."

The ES Fulminator was equipped with dozens of the latest Obsidiar processors and Quinn set them to work on a series of infinitely complicated sums. The core cluster utilisation went to maximum and remained there.

"Divert cycles from whatever non-critical systems you wish, Lieutenant."

"I've already done so, sir."

"Is there enough time?"

"I don't know – it's not as if we're hunting a specific *answer* as such. The longer our cores have to work on the problem, the greater the accuracy. I have a table which gives a prediction of what our chances are of landing in the middle of an object travelling as fast as the Aranol using the Lightspeed Catapult. Do you want to know what that chance is at the moment?"

"No."

"It's seven percent. Now seven-point-one percent."

"Don't feel obliged to keep me updated, Lieutenant. I'd rather not know."

Pointer spoke up. "I hope you don't mind, but I've accessed your table, Lieutenant Quinn. I see we've gone to seven-point-two percent."

Blake narrowed his eyes in Pointer's direction and she smiled sweetly in response.

"Seven-point-three percent," said Cruz. "This is exciting."

Blake knew when he was defeated and he tried to suppress his laughter. They were on the verge of attempting something riskier than anything they'd done before and, on balance, he decided he was happy with the distraction.

"Fifteen minutes until we reach the *ES Cataclysm*," said Quinn.

It wasn't enough time to plan or predict and Blake didn't attempt any of these things. This was one of the occasions when events would carry them along and the best he could hope to achieve was to steer them through the turbulent waters of the coming encounter.

Hawkins caught sight of his expression. "We've done well to get this far, huh?"

"Better than I ever imagined."

"And now this final opportunity to poke our fingers into the dead eyes of a Vraxar god."

"That's a good way to put it," he agreed. "I bet the Aranol really does think it's a god. It has the power to grant life or death."

"It always chooses death."

"I'm sure it believes the conversion process is a gift. A better life of eternal servitude."

Hawkins' face hardened and she wasn't one to get angry. "I can't wait to blow the shit out of them, sir."

"That goes for all of us."

The *ES Fulminator* flew on and the minutes to arrival counted down with agonising slowness. The Hadron's core clusters executed decillions of calculations per second as the fission modelling software tried to plot the Aranol's location at each given moment in time.

Blake tried to let everything wash over him. The doubts and

the uncertainties assailed him in a constant barrage of what ifs. What if the Aranol was solid inside? What if the modelling software got it wrong? What if the Lightspeed Catapult didn't fire?

What if we fail and humanity dies?

"Ten minutes!" shouted Quinn.

That was the trigger moment.

"Everyone into the shuttle!" said Blake. "You can suit up once we're inside."

They made a run for it, along the cool-lit corridors of the battleship. They sprinted through the airlock room as a group and into the airlock tunnel. Ahead, the door to Shuttle One was open, revealing the few soldiers who'd been given the awful job of sitting in the depths of the *ES Fulminator* when it went into battle with the Aranol.

Blake recognized them all, but he didn't exchange words with them. Someone had already hauled out armloads of the thick spacesuits from one of the wall lockers and the crew hurriedly pulled them on. Blake grabbed a visor for everyone from a storage box and handed them out, before resting his own on top of his head. He raced into the cockpit and found McKinney already there, as calm and solid as a chunk of weather-hewn granite. Corporal Bannerman was alongside and he tipped Blake a friendly salute. The *ES Fulminator* emerged from lightspeed and, without further delay, the warship's control computer opened the outer bay door and Blake saw the carpet of darkness outside.

"Everyone is onboard, sir," said McKinney. "The outer shuttle door is closed."

"Depart immediately."

As soon as the gravity clamps released, McKinney rammed the control joystick towards the front bulkhead. The vessel rocketed through the bay door and into space.

Something was wrong.

"Where the hell is the *ES Cataclysm*?" asked McKinney.

Bannerman altered the filters on the shuttle's sensors, uncertainty clear in his movements.

"I can't find it, sir. I've got the destroyer *ES No Return* at twenty thousand klicks and one of its shuttles is three thousand klicks to our starboard. Other than that, we're in the middle of sweet nowhere. Are you sure this is the right place?"

"It's definitely the right place, soldier," Blake assured him.

"In that case, the *Cataclysm* is somewhere else."

Blake scratched his head and peered at the sensor feed, as though his own eyes would somehow see what those of Corporal Bannerman had not. However much he squinted, the outcome was the same. The *ES Cataclysm* was gone.

CHAPTER TWENTY-FIVE

THE PROBLEM DID NOT STAY unresolved for long.

"I've got Captain Misty Decker on the comms," said Corporal Bannerman. "She's calling in from that shuttle over there."

"Where is the *Cataclysm*?" asked Blake, too tense to bother with polite greetings.

"Right where you left it, Captain Blake," said Decker.

Blake caught on. "It's gone even more out of phase."

"They weren't exaggerating when they said you were the best." Decker had apparently perfected the art of combining flirtation, gentle mockery, flattery and genuine sentiment into a single sentence. "The process which started when we used the Lightspeed Catapult continued and now the *Cataclysm* is no longer visible."

"How do we find it, ma'am?" asked McKinney.

"Don't worry, Lieutenant, we won't blunder around until we crash into it. Once our shuttles are within five thousand klicks, our target should become visible."

"*Should* become?" asked Blake. "I was told you'd been studying it."

"You don't study a crocodile by putting your head into its mouth, Captain Blake. I have been taking readings and analysing the data. That's how real science works. I wasn't expecting anyone to say *You know what, Misty? It's time you jumped back onboard the Cataclysm to see how that ol' Lightspeed Catapult is working after it nearly killed you last time.*" She gave a theatrical sigh. "But here we are."

There wasn't much Blake could offer in response to such an outpouring and nor was he inclined. McKinney glanced in his direction and raised an eyebrow. Blake shrugged.

"We've got ninety-seven minutes in which to make the interception and blow up the Aranol, Captain Decker. How would you like to join us on this voyage of discovery?"

"I should be delighted."

"In that case, on we go."

McKinney held the shuttle in place while Decker flew her equivalent model into close proximity. As soon as Decker's transport was within five kilometres, McKinney set off again, aiming for the coordinates in the navigational computer.

"We arrived ten thousand klicks out, so it shouldn't take long under full power," he said.

In the two minutes it took, Blake felt himself starting to brood, something he tried hard to pull himself out of. He was grateful for an interruption from R1T Garcia, who stuck his head through the opening from the passenger bay.

"Hey, Lieutenant, maybe you could clear this one up for us? Roldan says that if we eat a plate of chow that's out of phase and then we go back into phase, the food we just ate will become immune to our gastric juices and it'll just sit there until someone cuts us open and removes it. I reckon that's bullshit and that..."

McKinney raised a hand to interrupt, opened his mouth to answer, closed it again and shook his head. "Go and ask Sergeant Li."

"Okay, sir. Will he know the answer?"

"I'm sure he'll have something to say on the subject."

"The benefits of being lieutenant, eh?" asked Blake, when Garcia had vanished. He heard the sound of laughter from the passenger bay.

"Sometimes I wonder, sir," McKinney replied.

"You got the short straw being on the *Fulminator*, Lieutenant."

"There's only one long straw to draw, sir, and I keep telling myself I'll get it one day."

"He'd be bored within a week if there were no Vraxar to shoot," said Bannerman.

"Not true," said McKinney. He chuckled. "You're probably right, but it would be nice to have the opportunity to find out."

That line of conversation was cut short. "We're closing to five thousand klicks from the target location," said Bannerman.

"Let's see what we've got," said McKinney.

Decker's words proved true. One minute there was no *ES Cataclysm*, the next it was there, waiting in space like a cross between a loaded gun and a bomb with an invisible fuse. There wasn't even a transition – it simply appeared on the sensor feed.

"The passenger bay is still open," said Blake.

"The *Cataclysm*'s battle computer says hello," said McKinney. "We have clearance to dock."

"Take us in, Lieutenant and let's see what we find."

The comms fizzed into life. "No motion-blur," said Decker. "I believe that's a good thing."

Blake lifted his arm and moved it rapidly. He thought he detected a faint ghosting effect, but the exaggerated after-images from last time were gone. "Any ideas, Captain Decker?"

"There is a wave effect to the phasing. There are intersection points where you can be in completely different phases, yet able to interact as if nothing is wrong. Maybe that's what's happening here."

Bannerman muted the comms. "That might be complete and utter crap, but it sounded believable. I'm impressed."

"She's good," said McKinney. He took the comms off mute.

"Are you talking about me?" asked Decker at once.

"Comms glitch, ma'am."

"A likely tale. Anyway, what I just said was a complete guess. Everything about this is completely new and that's how science works – you see something, guess at how it works and then iterate on those guesses until you can prove the most likely one. And then someone comes up with an even better guess which disproves all of the earlier hard work and sets everyone off trying to see if they can prove the new theory."

Bannerman muted the comms again. "She's been drinking."

"Nope," said Blake. "This is how she always is."

"Is she single?" asked Bannerman.

"Maybe you should ask her."

"Maybe this isn't a good time."

"Coward," laughed McKinney.

"You're a fine one to talk, sir."

"I asked."

"And?"

"Later, man."

The easy banter filled the short time it took for McKinney to guide Shuttle One into the *ES Cataclysm*'s vacant bay and dock against the side wall. Blake caught Bannerman surreptitiously waving his arm to check for after-images. There were none.

"Captain Decker is right behind us," said McKinney. He looked expectantly at Blake.

"I'll take my crew and go, Lieutenant. Make yourselves at

home wherever you choose – just make sure you grab a supply of those needles for when we fire the catapult."

"Half of the men believe they're filled with sugar water," said McKinney. "They haven't been brave enough to put it to the test yet."

"It's not worth the gamble, eh?" said Blake, rising and clapping the other man on the back. "Of all the things to die from, stupidity isn't the first one I'd pick."

With that, Blake summoned his crew and they sprinted through the airlock and into the *ES Cataclysm,* just in time to see Captain Decker exit the adjacent airlock corridor. She greeted them with a wave and jogged over.

"It feels like the entire ship is coiled," she said.

The words were insightful and could have only come from a person who'd spend a long time in service. Instead of the usual thrum of restrained gravity drives, the *ES Cataclysm* resonated. There was a high-pitched whine underlying everything as if the structure of the spaceship knew something was different. Not necessarily *wrong* – just not as it should be.

"Is that the sound of the catapult's power source," asked Cruz, her head tipped to one side.

"That's exactly what it is," said Decker. "It's no longer Obsidiar and it's no longer Obsidiar-Teronium. In fact, we have absolutely no idea what it is or what it does and no one has bothered to come up with a name for it yet. It's so unstable that it's actually reached a state where it's self-sustaining, if you understand what I mean."

"Stability from instability," said Quinn.

"We can talk about it later," said Blake. "We've got eighty-five minutes."

"Eighty-four," said Quinn.

Decker treated them to a smile. "We'd better get moving then."

A short while later, Blake found himself in the captain's chair. Everything was as he'd left it and the ship's battle computer had maintained a state of readiness across the many systems – all except for the Lightspeed Catapult which was completely powered down and offline. The monitoring tools for the cata-pult's power source were active and he rubbed his eyes when he saw how much it was generating.

"Is this right?" he asked.

"No one knows," said Decker. "It might be overreading or it might even be under-reading."

Blake spent a couple of minutes checking and double-checking what he could. There wasn't much to do, except to find the limitations of being out of phase with the rest of the known universe.

"The sensors aren't working right," said Pointer. "They can read everything in the five thousand klick bubble around us. As soon as I try to focus them outside I get a stream of data that means absolutely nothing."

"That's what I expected," said Decker. "We can't see in or out. I think if we had time we could make some adjustments that would allow the sensors to recognize objects in what we would call our normal phase."

Losing the sensors was far from ideal, but if everything went to plan they wouldn't need them. "We'll have to fly blind for this one," said Blake. "If anyone thinks up a quick fix, I'm all ears."

"I'll let you know," said Decker.

"The comms aren't functioning either, sir," said Pointer. "I've tried to get a message to high command to let them know our preparations are nearly over. There aren't any visible receptors to link with."

"It's expected. I assume the internal comms are fine?"

"Yes, sir, they are."

There was no point in waiting any longer. Blake connected

remotely to the ES *Fulminator*, where its core clusters were still working on the fission modelling calculations. It was time to take a snapshot of the results.

"Lieutenant Quinn, we aren't waiting any longer. End the calculations and have them streamed into the *Cataclysm*'s databanks."

"Yes, sir. It'll take a few seconds for the data to transmit."

"Acting Lieutenant Decker, bring the Lightspeed Catapult into a state of readiness."

"Will do. I'll activate the modules in isolation, the same as last time. When I'm sure we're set, I'll connect it to the main power source. When that's done, I don't want to predict what'll happen or how long we'll have. We're on the edge of a knife, here."

"And the blade is sharp," said Hawkins.

Either Blake's perception of time was skewed or Decker was getting quicker through experience, but it took far less time for her to bring the Lightspeed Catapult online than it had on the return from Estral Space.

"The catapult is fully active and waiting the switchover to live, sir," said Decker.

"What happens to our shields and stealth when we arrive?"

"I don't know. We can't resolve these issues now."

It was another of the many problems caused by having their backs to the wall and Blake didn't press the matter. "Lieutenant Quinn, have we received the modelling predictions from the ES *Fulminator*?"

"Yes, sir. We have a plot which shows where we expect the Aranol to be on its lightspeed journey. All we have to do is launch."

Blake checked the timer: seventy-eight minutes until the Aranol reached Old Earth.

"How is the accuracy of the catapult now, Lieutenant Decker? We can't afford to miss."

"If we miss, it won't be because of the hardware."

It was as good an answer as any and Blake put it from his mind. "Time to inject," he said. "Make sure Lieutenant McKinney is aware."

He pulled out another needle from its metal case and turned it over in his hand. He thought he detected the faintest signs of motion blur along the edges of his skin and he remembered Decker's words about two waves intersecting on the chart. He blinked and everything was back to normal. He jabbed the needle into his thigh and felt it inject him. *Sugar water*, he thought.

"The troops below are set, sir," said Pointer. "We can go whenever you're ready."

"Is everyone good to go?" asked Blake.

"You don't normally ask," said Hawkins.

"This time is different."

"If we're gonna die, we're gonna die. No point in putting it off," she replied.

Blake had prepared a short speech about how proud he was of them for coming so far. When he looked into their faces, he saw the words weren't necessary. They were a team and they knew it.

"Lieutenant Decker, connect the Lightspeed Catapult. Fire it as soon as we're ready."

"Finishing the tie-in," said Decker. "Let's see how this goes."

The results were not as expected.

The moment Lieutenant Decker connected the Lightspeed Catapult to the rest of the *ES Cataclysm*'s main systems, everything went quiet. The background whine and vibration, which the crew had become so accustomed to they barely noticed it, simply vanished. Blake turned his head and the only thing he could hear was the quietest buzz from his console, along with the perfect note from the warship's gravity engines.

"We're in the zone," said Decker, her voice hushed with disbelief.

Blake didn't ask her to elaborate – he got the same feeling too. He couldn't get the image of those converging waves from his head and in his mind, he saw dozens of lines intersecting at this precise place and at this precise moment in time. This was the cosmic forces of the universe coming together to give humanity one shot at survival.

On the console in front of him, he saw the power gauges for the Obsidiar-Teronium all holding absolutely steady. Whatever the power core had turned into, its atoms were in complete harmony and showing so much potential that Blake's doubts were swept aside. The catapult's power source was magnitudes in advance of anything else known to humanity. Or Vraxar.

"This is our opportunity," he said.

"Amen to that, sir," said Hawkins.

"Lieutenant Decker, fire that catapult."

"Launching."

Blake was prepared for a cacophony of noise and a physical battering from the device's warmup. What he got was a pure metallic howl, like nothing he'd heard before. He instinctively knew this was how the catapult was *meant* to sound, if only had the right power source to drive it. The howl became louder until it reached a level below the threshold of pain and there it remained.

His eyes were drawn to the console in front of him and he saw the monitoring needles swing smoothly and relentlessly to the right. The gauges recalculated and the needles dropped back, before climbing steadily and at a linear speed across what was an exponential power scale. The needles reached a level and there they stayed.

"Any second," said Decker.

The Lightspeed Catapult fired. A wormhole opened in front of the *ES Cataclysm* and the spaceship went through.

CHAPTER TWENTY-SIX

THERE WAS silence for a time measured in seconds, during which the crew came to terms with the fact that they weren't dead. Blake felt the smallest amount of lethargy, as if he'd had a fraction too much to drink the night before. Otherwise, he felt much better than he had any right to.

"What's our status?" he said.

The words snapped the crew out of their collective trance.

Decker was the first to report. "The catapult fired successfully and we are no longer where we were. The catapult remains online."

"Our instruments are recalibrating," said Quinn. "That probably means they don't have a clue about what just happened. Neither our energy shield nor stealth modules are available. I'm working on it."

"Lieutenant Pointer?" asked Blake.

"I think we made it, sir." Her voice was distant as though she was coming to terms with something completely out of the ordinary.

"Show me."

"Bringing up the feed."

An image appeared and, at first, Blake wasn't sure what it depicted. The longer he studied it, the more the details became clear.

The ES *Cataclysm* was in the centre of a vast, open space, several hundred kilometres across, with curved black walls, tinged with a sullen green glow.

"A perfect sphere," said Pointer. "With a diameter of six hundred klicks and no sign of armaments."

"We did it," said Cruz. "We're in the centre of the enemy ship."

"Are the bounds of this space definitely the inner walls of the Aranol?" asked Blake.

"It's got to be, sir. Where else could we be?"

"Our instruments have recalibrated and I can confirm we are travelling at high lightspeed," said Quinn. "A very high lightspeed. Sir, this *is* the Aranol."

Blake breathed out and tried to think. The Lightspeed Catapult had taken them to the centre of the Vraxar planetship and now all they had to do was figure out a way to blow the crap out of it from the inside. For once, the enemy was vulnerable.

"Lieutenant Decker, we must detonate the power core."

Decker looked worried. "I don't think we can. Not anymore."

"What do you mean? The Obsidiar-Teronium is the only thing big enough to destroy what's left of the Aranol and Fleet Admiral Duggan said we should trigger an explosion."

"When it was unstable we could have triggered an explosion simply by turning the overcharge repeater back on and firing it until the power core went bang. Now that the core has stabilised into its new state, that might not work. There's more than that as well."

There was a note of something else in her voice which Blake didn't recognize. "What's that, Lieutenant?"

"The power core has become something different to both Obsidiar and Obsidiar-Teronium. It's a pure refinement of raw, chaotic instability." He eyes glowed with fervour. "We're carrying the key to humanity's transcendence. You've seen the power we're generating. We need to return it safely to the Confederation for study. If we can replicate it – make more – the Confederation might advance a thousand years."

"And our possession of such a key could bring a hundred hostile species to our front door," said Pointer. "The races which have ignored us until now might suddenly see us as a threat. A threat to be annihilated."

"Which is no change to how we are treated already!" snapped Decker. It was the first time Blake had seen her angry.

The exchange was interrupted. A deep, sibilant voice came from nowhere, appearing to float in the centre of the bridge, yet without coming through the comms speakers.

"You are here," it said.

Blake met Pointer's eyes. "What the hell?" he asked.

She raised her arms in a *who knows?* gesture. "It's not coming through the comms, sir. We don't have an open channel."

"Find out where, then!" He raised his voice. "Who are you?"

"I am everything. I have brought you to this place."

"You are the Aranol."

"That is sometimes how I am named."

"You are going to destroy the Confederation worlds."

"Humanity has proven unworthy of the Vraxar. You could have become my children, yet you chose otherwise."

"Your *children* are the result of genocide."

"They will live forever, until there are only Vraxar."

"Is that the goal? A universe filled with rotting corpses?"

"That is inevitable."

"Why are you speaking to us?"

"Your spaceship carries something unique and important."

"You are correct. There are men and women onboard."

"Life is merely unique."

Blake tried to think about what was going on. It was the first time the Aranol had made direct contact with humanity and there had been plenty of earlier opportunities for it to do so. That fact it was choosing to do so now meant that the situation had changed. He would dearly have liked to confer with his crew, but he didn't want the enemy overhearing the words. This was something he'd have to work out on his own.

"What do you want from us?"

"I will take your spaceship and I will convert its occupants into Vraxar. You are the honoured few – you will be the only members of your race preserved as a record of its existence."

Blake's head swam and his earlier thoughts came back to him. The Aranol *was* a single consciousness and it was mad, or at least it was mad in terms of how humanity viewed the universe. Worse than the madness was Blake's certainty that the Aranol thought itself a god.

Maybe it is a god. Maybe there are hundreds of similarly powerful beings across the universe, each of them so different to the conventional image we have in our collective imagination of what a god might be.

"Are there more like you?" he asked.

"I have defeated some. There are others. Your spaceship will bring them here. They will smell it across the depths of space and they will come."

"Are you a god?"

There was a hint of a pause before the Aranol answered, as though it were aware of its own hubris. "I cannot be stopped. When the universe ends, I will be everything which remains."

"We hurt you. Our bomb has reduced you to this."

"I will rebuild the outer structures. This *core* which remains is immune to harm. I am Aranol and I will exist forever."

"What is so important about our spaceship?" asked Blake.

"It is a key."

The words brought back Lieutenant Decker's earlier statement and Blake shivered at the thought of what such a key might unlock if it were enough to bring entities like the Aranol in search of it.

Treat everything it says as a lie, he thought. Except he felt sure that in this, the enemy was deliberately permitting him a glimpse of the truth for its own ends. Blake guessed the many potential reasons behind this behaviour. The Aranol wanted the key for itself, but couldn't obtain it without cooperation from the human occupants of the *Cataclysm*. Maybe it was unable to touch them while they remained within its centre. There was another possibility.

It's shit scared of us and it's going to say whatever the hell it needs to in order to stop us blowing the crap out of it. Even beings with the delusion of godhood can die.

"What if I decide to destroy you?" asked Blake. "What if I detonate the power source we are carrying and, with my dying gaze, watch as you are ripped apart? It would be a fitting payment for the deaths you have caused."

"The power source you mention is dangerous, Captain Charles Blake. If you were to detonate it whilst travelling at light-speed, you would open a hole in the fabric of this universe which would never heal and which would eventually destroy everything."

"Even you?"

"I exist in many universes."

"Lieutenant Decker?" asked Blake, no longer caring if the Aranol heard. "Is that a possibility?"

She shrugged. "Maybe. We don't know what this power source is and we certainly haven't begun to explore its potential."

In truth, Blake was fascinated by the conversation with the

Aranol and he longed to speak with it and find out anything which might give clues about its origins or the reason it hungered for endless death. When it came down to it, the Aranol was going to destroy Old Earth in approximately one hour and no amount of words would change the fact.

"It's stalling for time," he said. "We're going to introduce an instability in the power core and then we're going to destroy this bastard once and for all."

The Aranol was a third of a million years old and it had different plans.

"You cannot destroy me," it said.

"Sir, there's some kind of field emanating from the internal walls," said Quinn.

"What is it?"

Lieutenant Decker had the answer. "There's a phase shift happening."

"What do you mean? Is the Aranol changing to a different phase so we can't harm it?"

"I don't think that's what's happening here. Oh, shit!"

If there were any words Blake hated to hear in combination, *oh* and *shit* were up there with the best of them.

"Sir, look at the sensor feed!" said Pointer urgently.

Blake spun towards the front bulkhead screen and watched with horror as dozens of shapes – previously unseen – shimmered into view. His eyes darted from place to place as he tried to make sense of what was going on. He saw seven or eight enormous battleships parked up in a row overhead, each of which likely displaced one hundred billion tonnes. Elsewhere, there were many smaller warships, in all sorts of shapes and sizes, but each one large enough to be a threat to the *ES Cataclysm*.

Worst of all were the two identical vessels which were directly below. Their huge hulls ran parallel to the much smaller Space Corps cruiser and their armour plates crackled with green sparks. These two spaceships weren't much smaller than *Ix-Gorghal*, though their shape was different in that they were irregular and cuboid. Blake saw plenty of armaments on their visible upper sections, in the form of gauss guns and particle beam domes.

Every one of these spaceships had a blurred outline and Blake's brain quickly made the connection.

"This entire fleet has been here all along, just in our normal phase."

"It looks that way," said Decker. "And the Aranol is bringing them into our phase."

"There is a total of ninety-seven enemy spaceships visible to sensor sight," reported Cruz.

"How long until they're in the exact same phase as us?"

"Seconds," said Decker.

"And then they start firing," said Hawkins.

"Lieutenant Quinn, where is our energy shield?"

"Sir, I'm still trying to get it online."

Blake's mind hunted frantically for a solution. There was no way the *ES Cataclysm* could take on a fraction of these Vraxar warships and there was no immediately apparent way to detonate the new power core in order to take them all out at once. And then there was the Aranol's warning that they might damage the very fabric of the universe.

The first Vraxar particle beam lanced into the *ES Cataclysm*'s hull. At the same time, The Aranol's laughter filled the bridge. It roared with mocking hatred at the plight of beings who had defied it and who were going to find out what it meant to anger a creature of infinite power. On and on it went, until it was the only sound the crew could hear.

CHAPTER TWENTY-SEVEN

THE LAUGHTER DIDN'T REDUCE Blake to a state of fear, nor did it make him beg for either leniency or mercy. Such concepts were unknown to a being which had the sole aim of removing life from the universe.

Instead, Blake found himself becoming angry and, in his fury, his mind prised an idea from the reluctant grasp of hopelessness. He looked at his command console, just in time to see a row of red lights appear as a result of a second particle beam strike. The ships of the Vraxar fleet weren't entirely in the same phase as the *Cataclysm* – once they were, the cruiser would be annihilated. There wasn't long left.

"Lieutenant Quinn," said Blake, his voice cutting sharply through the Aranol's laughter. "Switch our energy shield so that it is tapping into the Obsidiar-Teronium power source."

Quinn's face brightened as though he'd been given the answer to a problem which had eluded him his entire life. "Yes, sir. Switching across."

The shield gauge went straight up to one hundred percent,

just as the Vraxar let fly with everything they had. Blake's tactical screen filled with enemy missiles, as well as hundreds of the fleeting traces left by beam weapons. In the comparatively confined space of the Aranol's interior, the Vraxar missiles had almost no travel time and they detonated against the *Cataclysm's* shield in their thousands. The front bulkhead screen lit up in the purest white, casting long shadows against the back wall of the bridge.

Blake squinted through the light and could make out the shield level, still at *exactly* one hundred percent, as though someone had hammered a nail through the screen in order to keep the gauge from falling any lower.

The Vraxar didn't stop. They launched their missiles in a continuous stream and the *Cataclysm* was hit by forty or fifty beam weapons every second. The Aranol's laughter died away, as though it was puzzled by this unexpected resistance.

"I'm firing our weapons, for all the good it will do. I'm targeting the inner walls of the Aranol." said Hawkins. She unloaded everything the *Cataclysm* was carrying. Its missiles exploded against the closest wall, their warheads not remotely large enough to do significant damage. The single operational Havoc cannon fired once, the massive slug lost amongst the enemy fleet.

"Maybe we'll give it some heartburn," said Cruz.

Blake gave his next order, trying to tell himself he wasn't excited by what might come from it. If he was going to die, there might as well be fireworks at his funeral.

"Lieutenant Decker, turn on the overcharge repeater. Give it full access to the Lightspeed Catapult's power source."

In the stark illumination from the view screen, Decker appeared unhealthily pale, as though she had just seen a ghost and was trying hard to overcome the shock of it.

"Sir – we were forced to shut it off last time! We can't predict the result of giving it access to the stable core!"

"The Obsidiar-Teronium power core is the only thing big enough to destroy the Aranol. If the repeater doesn't introduce an instability, at least it'll take a few of the enemy down!"

"I don't know what will happen if we activate the overcharge repeater without proper testing. The core might simply fail and then we'll have lost everything."

"What choice is there? We have our mission and that mission is to do whatever the hell it takes to stop the Aranol before it reaches Old Earth!"

Decker didn't give up. "Couldn't we try to get out of here? I can activate the catapult again. We've learned so much about the Aranol – the Lightspeed Catapult will get us to Old Earth before the enemy."

"Less than sixty minutes ahead of their arrival," said Quinn.

"Time in which to think of something!"

Blake was a captain who listened to the ideas of his crew, but in this case, he didn't want to waste any more time arguing with Decker. He didn't need convincing that the new power core was important to humanity – he could see exactly what it was doing against the might of the Vraxar fleet.

"The survival of the Confederation is more important than anything else, Lieutenant Decker. I will take the path I believe gives us the greatest chance of success."

Decker wanted to talk about it more. Blake could see in her eyes that she thought he was wrong and that there was a better way. He was sure there was not.

"Sir, will you reconsider?"

"I will not. Bring the overcharge repeater online."

She bowed her head. "As you will. It takes a short while to warm up."

A light came onto Blake's console, which told him the repeater was in the process of tying in with the rest of the onboard systems. He listened carefully, expecting to hear the same tremendous noise from the first and only time they'd employed the weapon. A new sound reached his ears, except this was a humming, not entirely dissimilar to that made by the gravity engines. The humming gradually developed a metallic edge, which caused the hairs on the back of his neck to stand up.

"Whoa," said Hawkins. "That sounds a lot better than last time."

Blake couldn't take his eyes away from the status display for the repeater. It ran through its many self-checks, a routine which needed to complete before the weapon would fire. Meanwhile, the Vraxar did everything they could to break through the *ES Cataclysm*'s energy shield and Blake asked himself what was going through the Aranol's consciousness as it realised it had found something it couldn't easily destroy.

"Our shield gauge has fallen to 99.94%," said Quinn. "Absolutely unbelievable. This new stuff is at least a hundred thousand times more potent than plain old Obsidiar."

"Let us hope we don't lose it," said Decker.

"Enough!" said Blake.

The status light representing the overcharge repeater changed from red to amber and then to green. It glowed softly, alluringly. The metallic hum didn't go away and when Blake closed his eyes he could hear its whispered promises.

"That's it done, sir," said Hawkins. "I will target and activate upon your command."

When Blake gave the order, he couldn't help but feel he was about to witness something both momentous and terrible.

"Fire," he said.

"Target priorities set. Firing."

The first activation of the overcharge repeater – over the

planet Jonli – had left Blake in awe of the brutal, incredible power of the weapon. It had been like riding a wild animal of such ferocity that one could only remain in place for a matter of a few short seconds, before being thrown to the ground and torn to pieces by the beast.

This time, it was something else.

The overcharge repeater thumped once. The Aranol was the primary target and where the beam struck its internal walls, an area with a diameter of fifteen thousand metres turned instantly to brilliant white, ringed by oranges, blues and reds. An over-charge particle beam was a normally a devastating weapon, but this time the effects were amplified until the damage was far in excess of anything Blake could have imagined.

It's got a much more potent power supply to tap into this time, he thought.

It thumped once more, twice and then three times, the firing interval decreasing steadily as if the repeater were gradually warming up to its own capabilities. Within a short time, it was firing several times per second and the thump-thump-thump of its turret produced a deep note felt throughout the spaceship. It made Blake's bones ache, but he didn't care at all.

He turned his head and saw the shocked expression on Lieu-tenant Hawkins' face. The incredible power of the weapon she controlled didn't break her stride and she targeted and re-targeted, her fingers speeding over her console as she created new priority lists as quick as her brain could process the information from her eyes. Her mouth moved in the way it always did when she was completely and utterly focused.

Pointer and Cruz didn't slow either and they switched between feeds, giving Blake everything he required to build up a picture of the events unfolding. For the Vraxar, it was not a pleasant scene.

Viewed from the outside, the *ES Cataclysm* was under so

much missile bombardment it appeared to be a bright white sphere, smaller but vastly hotter than the surface of a star. Its light was enough to fill the interior of the Aranol and illuminate the walls hundreds of kilometres away.

From the centre of this new sun, invisible beam weapons jumped outwards, each one hitting a Vraxar spaceship or the walls of the Aranol. The smaller enemy spaceships weren't quite vaporised, but they were destroyed so completely, so utterly, that Blake thought the word was an apt description for what happened to them.

Some of the battleships were large and well-enough constructed that they resisted two or three strikes, before they were reduced to molten alloy. The Aranol maintained its own gravity so these ships did not crash down. Instead, they floated in place, casting out incredible amounts of heat and light.

The Aranol was far from unscathed. Five out of every six shots from the overcharge repeater hit the inside of the Vraxar planetship and within a matter of minutes, there was not a single part of its depleted Obsidiar lining which wasn't burning at a temperature of several thousand degrees.

Through it all, the repeater dome thudded, rapidly and without cease. Blake hardly noticed the aching pain it produced in his bones, but his suit computer guessed he'd had enough and it injected him with battlefield adrenaline to help out.

The last of the smaller Vraxar spaceships was destroyed and Hawkins targeted the first of the far larger vessels. It was hit dozens of times in the space of five seconds and trillion-tonne sections of its hull split and then split again.

The sensors continued to show the crew a vision of pure chaos, wrought in the hottest of fires. There was not a single part of the Aranol which was free from heat and the temperature of its interior was several thousand degrees. Here and there, darker or lighter patches betrayed the position of a Vraxar spaceship and globs of liquid metal occasionally drifted serenely by. Blake wondered if there was anything which could possibly compare to the sights he witnessed within the Aranol.

"I can't believe this," said Quinn. "This is the strangest..."

His words tailed off, though everyone knew exactly what he was trying to say. Blake wasn't sure how long he stared at the carnage outside, but when he finally looked at the core power gauge, he discovered it was down to thirty percent. The combination of Vraxar weaponry and the discharge of the repeater was taking its toll.

"We're going to run out of power soon," said Lieutenant Decker. "We've got less than two minutes at our current rate of expenditure. There is absolutely zero instability on the core – we've discovered the perfect power source and we're going to run it dry."

"In a good cause, Lieutenant."

The deep, sibilant voice from before spoke once again, catching Blake by surprise.

"You. Will. Stop."

"Are you frightened?" asked Blake. It was a petty question, but he couldn't help himself. After all the death and misery this being had caused, maybe it was time someone asked.

"I will not die. I will see the end of the universe."

"It's looking increasingly less likely, don't you think?" asked Pointer. "How does it feel?"

"Your ship is mine. Your lives are mine. The Vraxar will be everything."

Blake shook his head in wonder. He'd never spoken to a god before and he was willing to concede the Aranol was the closest thing to a god he'd come across during his many years in the Space Corps. This *god* had no concept of defeat and no realisation of what it meant to know failure. There was absolutely no connection he could make with it and he had no intention of trying.

"You will not see the end of the universe," he said. "I don't normally hate the things I don't understand, but in this instance, I will make an exception. We are going to fire our weapon until you are destroyed. Even once I am sure you are finished I am going to keep firing until there is no chance you might somehow repair yourself. After that, I am going to recommend to my superiors that we deploy an out-of-phase Obsidiar bomb on whatever is left. Soon the Aranol will discover what total eradication means."

"Your lives are mine."

"Did you listen to a word I said?" asked Blake.

"The Vraxar are everything. They are my children as you will soon be my children."

"Shut up and piss off," said Hawkins.

Whether it heard the words and cared enough to comply, or if it was too far damaged to continue the conversation, Blake didn't know. Either way, the Aranol spoke no more.

"We're at fifteen percent on the power core," said Decker.

"The inside of the Aranol is looking pretty beat up," said Quinn.

"Terminally?"

"I don't know, sir. There is easily enough heat within this space to reach the outer hull of the enemy ship and probably cause it to break apart."

"Ten percent on the power core. It's dropping faster and I don't know why."

"The outside temperature has reached ninety-five thousand degrees," said Quinn. "It's draining the shield much quicker."

Blake closed his eyes for the few moments it took him to reach a decision.

"Cease fire and activate the lightspeed catapult," he said. "Our target is Old Earth."

"What about the injectors?" said Decker, scrambling around for her needle.

Blake fumbled for his own case of injectors and found it was empty.

"Use them if you've got them. Lieutenant Cruz, send warning to Lieutenant McKinney. Get that catapult working and get us the hell out of here."

"Why don't we use the normal fission engines, sir?" asked Hawkins.

Blake smiled grimly. "I want to get there first."

Decker tried to laugh. "We've come this far, haven't we? Let's try the catapult one more time. Warming up. Core power at seven percent."

Moments before the Lightspeed Catapult fired, the Aranol showed that it wasn't finished. The Vraxar planetship had one more trick to play.

"Shit, the Aranol is changing phase," said Lieutenant Decker.

"What does that mean?"

"They're reverting to what we would think of as a normal place in time, sir. Once it shifts phase, it might become immune to all this heat we've put into its hull."

"You mean it might survive?"

"I don't know, sir. There's no time to think about it - the power core is at three percent and the Lightspeed Catapult is ready to fire."

Blake gritted his teeth. "Get us out of here."

The Lightspeed Catapult spooled up and launched the *ES Cataclysm* towards Old Earth. The last thing Blake noticed was the remaining time before the Aranol reached its destination: twenty minutes. He had no idea what the hell he was going to do this time.

The transit didn't kill him, but it wasn't a positive experience. The battlefield adrenaline coursing through his veins kept him alive and conscious.

This is what it's like to face a god, he thought.

CHAPTER TWENTY-EIGHT

THE *ES CATACLYSM* emerged from its transit, two million kilometres from Old Earth. The planet was the home of humanity and it held a special place in the hearts of most of the Confederation's citizens. Its blues and greens were a radiant, beautiful reminder of a romantic vision of home.

"We're at zero percent on the Obsidiar-Teronium core," said Lieutenant Decker. "It isn't showing any signs of recharge."

The power core would have to wait.

"Can you get in touch with anyone on Old Earth?" asked Blake.

"We're getting nothing from the comms," said Pointer. "And we're sensor blind."

Blake hit his clenched fist against the arm of his chair. "We're still out of phase."

"The Aranol is due in sixteen minutes," said Quinn.

"And there's nothing we can do to hurt it now," Blake replied, fighting the urge to swear repeatedly.

"We should do something to get a message to the Space Corps," said Hawkins.

"You're right. We can't leave the bridge in case the Aranol changes phase again and we get another shot at it. I'll send Lieutenant McKinney out in a shuttle. He can pass on the message for us."

"Lieutenant McKinney is in the troops' quarters along with the others, sir," said Cruz.

"Tell him what's required, please."

Lieutenant Cruz spoke briefly to McKinney. "He's on his way, sir. It'll take him a few minutes to get there."

"Fine."

With that, Blake sat back to wait.

———

IT TOOK MCKINNEY FIVE MINUTES' hard run to reach the transport and, on the way, he cursed his decision to take the squad into their quarters, rather than sitting it out in the *ES Cataclysm's* shuttle.

"What's going on?" asked Sergeant Li, keeping up with ease. "Did we kill the Aranol?"

"I'm not sure. Lieutenant Cruz told me there wasn't time to explain."

The two of them sprinted through the shuttle's open door, with Huey Roldan a few paces behind. This was a one-man mission, but McKinney didn't mind the company. He entered the cockpit and dropped into the seat.

"The bay doors are already open," said Roldan.

"And the shuttle is warmed up." McKinney pressed a button and the gravity clamps detached with a hollow boom. He used the control stick to guide the vessel away from the side wall of the bay. Once the craft was at a safe distance, McKinney pushed the stick forward. With a muted sound from its engines, the shuttle sped out of the bay.

"Five thousand klicks and we can get our message out?" asked Li.

"I've been told nothing's changed from last time. We've got some priority codes which should get noticed by the Space Corps high command. We do the job and then we come back."

"What's the message?"

"I don't know. Lieutenant Cruz has entered it into the shuttle's comms system for us to send."

"What if the bigwigs want to ask our opinion? Maybe even the fleet admiral himself?"

"Yeah, right," said Roldan.

"Look, here's the transmission packet," said Li, peering at the single comms screen.

"You shouldn't be poking around in that, Sergeant."

It was too late.

"Aw, shit. The Aranol is coming and it's going to kill everyone."

"Then we lost?" asked Roldan. "All that crap we went through and it wasn't enough?"

It was a struggle for McKinney to keep his expression neutral. "Sounds like it. Doesn't mean it's over, though."

"Of course it does, Lieutenant. We threw everything at that bastard."

"I'm not giving up, soldier."

"I didn't think you would, Lieutenant. You're like a machine. Me? I find it hard to keep going sometimes."

"You know what keeps me going, soldier? I tell myself the future hasn't happened until it happens. We aren't dead yet and Old Earth is still here."

"Coming up to the five thousand klick perimeter, after which we'll enter the same phase as everyone else in the Confederation," said Li. "This comms panel should light up at any moment."

The shuttle crossed the boundary and immediately, the *ES Cataclysm* vanished from sensor sight. McKinney took the vessel a further few hundred kilometres, just in case.

"Send the message, Sergeant."

"I've sent it," said Li. "How long are we expected to wait for a response?"

McKinney shrugged. "The Aranol is due any minute, so it may be that everyone's too busy to answer. Is there much hardware waiting for the enemy?"

"I thought we left it all at Rangel-3," said Roldan.

"There might be a few stragglers that didn't make it to the Alliance Fleet."

Li checked the sensors. "There's only one Space Corps ship in the sky, Lieutenant. It's not even a fighter – looks like a cargo vessel of some kind, maybe a cross between a lifter and a freighter. It's a million klicks ahead and coming our way at high speed."

"What the hell would that be doing up here?"

"Dunno, sir. I reckon it's going flat out."

"Why don't you ask them what's happening? The ground stations aren't responding."

Li tried to contact the freighter. "I'm getting an automated response, sir."

"Rude bastards," said Roldan.

"Maybe it's unmanned," said McKinney.

"What would an unmanned cargo vessel be doing out here in the middle of nowhere when the largest spaceship anyone's ever seen is due to arrive in...how long until it's here?" asked Roldan.

Sergeant Li wasn't a man to show his emotions, but on this occasion his jaw dropped open. "It's here," he said.

The Aranol appeared on the front sensor feed. The shuttle's array was crude but it provided enough image enhancement for the men to see that the enemy ship was badly damaged. Where it had once been a perfect sphere, now it was misshapen. Rivers of Obsidiar had coursed over its surface before hardening once again, leaving valleys and mountains. The heat from the over-charge repeater was gone, and the Aranol was as cold as the vacuum around it.

"Looks like a real moon now," said Roldan.

McKinney wasn't too concerned with the Aranol's physical appearance. He was more concerned with the zoom level on the sensor feed, which confirmed the enemy spacecraft was less than ten thousand kilometres away.

"We're not sticking around for a response from Old Earth," he said. "Let's get the hell out of here."

He pulled hard on the joystick, bringing the craft around. At that precise moment, he guessed why there might be an unmanned cargo vessel out here all on its own.

"A bomb," he said, suddenly wishing he'd kept right on the edge of the *ES Cataclysm*'s phase perimeter. "We have to get back."

At that moment, the comms came to life and a woman from one of the Old Earth command stations spoke, her tones clipped and laden with stress.

"We got your message. We are about to detonate an Obsidiar bomb. Can you go to lightspeed?"

"Of course we can't go to lightspeed," said Sergeant Li. "We're in a damned shuttle!"

McKinney clenched his jaw and pushed harder on the joystick, willing the shuttle's engines to give them some extra speed. The vessel crossed the perimeter and into the *ES Cataclysm*'s phase.

A fraction of a second later, the Benediction bomb onboard the cargo ship *ML Butterfly* went off. As with many which had gone before it, the bomb significantly exceeded expectations and its blast enveloped the Aranol. Without its energy shield to protect it, and now that it existed in the same phase as the bomb, the planetship was disassembled and thrown into the void – a god defeated and broken.

On Old Earth and elsewhere, the Space Corps personnel who knew what was coming cheered when the explosive sphere of the Benediction bomb left the planet untouched. It was a close-run thing.

THE BAR

Charlie Blake remembered this place well. The wooden floors, the appalling decoration and the bad smell which came into the room every time someone opened the toilet door. There was music playing tonight – music he remembered from his childhood which he'd hated at the time, but which now made him nostalgic. The bar was crowded and lively, in stark contrast to the previous visit.

"Is this where you spend all your time off-duty?" asked Caz Pointer with a smile. She was dressed in civilian clothes tonight and her blonde hair fell down her back, glittering in the light whenever she turned her head. She took his breath away.

"This is only the second time I've been here," said Blake. "I think it's one of Garcia's watering holes."

"And you thought it would be a good place to come on our first date?" She arched one eyebrow.

"I don't know what I thought," he said. "It just seemed appropriate somehow."

"Maybe you didn't want us to be seen together, so you brought me to the biggest dump on Prime?" She was teasing.

"It's a connection, that's all. A memory of times past and I thought maybe we should be here together for it."

Pointer took a sip of her drink and wrinkled her nose. "This smells like cow's piss."

"That's how I remember it." He grinned.

"Why didn't you tell me?"

"I thought it would be good to have a second opinion. Do you want something else?"

She took another sip. "It tastes better than it smells."

A draught of warm evening air wafted through the room and Blake caught sight of two people coming through the entrance.

"Hey, look at that!" said Pointer. "It's Eric and Maria! He looks different when he's not dressed in a spacesuit and carrying a rifle. He's holding the door for her as well, like a proper gentleman."

"I held the door..." He caught sight of her smile and he closed his mouth.

Caz Pointer wasn't shy. She stood up and waved vigorously. "Hey!" she shouted.

Cruz waved back happily and McKinney gave a self-conscious half-wave.

"I do believe I saw the good Lieutenant McKinney turn pink," said Pointer.

"I'm sure it was a trick of the light."

"Should we go over and see them? Would it be rude if we didn't?"

"This is their night. Let them have it and we'll have ours."

Caz Pointer was excellent company and Blake tried to forget that he'd once held a much lower opinion of her than he did now. The past was gone and the future was ahead. Blake caught himself thinking of the Vraxar and the Aranol. He wasn't going become one of those people who couldn't escape the memories of what they'd done, so he cut off the thoughts – for now at least.

"Are you okay?" asked Pointer, catching his expression.

"I've never been better."

He meant it.

END

John Nathan Duggan rose to leave his office for the final time. He spared a moment to take it all in and told himself he wouldn't miss any of it.

"It's time to move on," he said, sighing in spite of everything. The hardest person to lie to was always himself. A promise was a promise and his family deserved the father and the grandfather he'd tried so hard to be. There were never enough hours in the day and he hoped they recognized there was no choice for him. Duty above all.

No longer, he thought. *My duty is done and it's time to discover the man I could be once the chains are gone.*

He strode across the room and the door opened for him.

"Goodbye, Fleet Admiral," said Cerys. "It was a pleasure working with you."

Duggan felt his throat tighten and he hurried from the room. It was getting late, though many personnel remained at their desks in the open plan area outside. He'd delivered his leaving speech hours before and now the people kept their heads down, as if acknowledging his presence would be the wrong thing to do.

His wife waited for him, leaning against one of the empty desks. She came across and linked her arm through his.

"Is everything okay?"

"It will be."

Lucy Duggan understood perfectly.

Duggan's pace quickened and they left the administrative building. He breathed in the still-warm air and cast his gaze around the hulking grey buildings of the Raksol base. "I wish I'd knocked them all down and started again."

"It's not your concern."

He laughed. "It's my legacy."

She squeezed his arm. "No, it isn't. Your legacy is a lot more than square edged concrete and steel. Let's take a car and go see what's been happening out there – in the places away from fear and death."

"I can't wait."

They got into a gravity car and Lucy gave it directions. Duggan sat back in the foam seat and smiled.

———

Follow Anthony James on Facebook at
facebook.com/AnthonyJamesAuthor

ALSO BY ANTHONY JAMES

Printed in Great Britain
by Amazon

43932515R00170